"I want yo

"What? No!" Noelle exclaimed.

"Noelle, I want you far away from this case for your own safety," Eli insisted. "And we have to make sure anyone who knows you were working on the case says nothing about it. I don't want Scott coming after you to get to me."

"He already knows."

"Huh? How?"

"That morning I came by ABI, you told him you were including me on the investigation as a consultant."

Eli's gut swooped. "I did?"

"You did. What's more, someone has already come after me. Someone cut my brake line, remember?"

"Well, then, here's the new plan. I want you to stay close to me until we find him. I can protect you better if I'm with you than if I'm not."

"You really think I—"

"Or... Maybe you should go back to Seattle."

"Go home? Is that really what you want?"

"No. But I want you safe, and you'll be safer far away from Shelby."

"I'm not a quitter, Eli."

He jerked a sharp look her way and clenched his jaw. "Well, you were...once."

Dear Reader,

Things in Shelby, Alaska, are getting colder as winter approaches and fear of the Fiancée Killer spreads through the town. For Eli Colton, lead investigator on the case for the Alaska Bureau of Investigation, frustration is mounting at the lack of progress bringing the murderer in. When he learns one of the victims is the sister of his college sweetheart, the case takes a grim personal twist. Noelle Harris broke his heart years ago, but in order to catch a killer, can he set aside his feelings and accept her unique skills and perspective to break the manhunt wide open?

Colton continuities are always a fun challenge for me. This series, set in the rugged beauty of Alaska, was no different. I'm certainly pining for a vacation there in the coming months—minus the serial killer, of course! So sit back, brew a hot cup of your favorite beverage, tuck in under a cozy blanket and get ready to head north for the penultimate book in The Coltons of Alaska series!

Happy reading,

Beth

COLTON'S SECOND CHANCE

BETH CORNELISON

ROMANTIC SUSPENSE

If you purchased this book without a cover you should be aware that this book is stolen property. It was reported as "unsold and destroyed" to the publisher, and neither the author nor the publisher has received any payment for this "stripped book."

Special thanks and acknowledgment are given to Beth Cornelison for her contribution to The Coltons of Alaska miniseries.

ISBN-13: 978-1-335-47167-3

Colton's Second Chance

Copyright © 2025 by Harlequin Enterprises ULC

All rights reserved. No part of this book may be used or reproduced in any manner whatsoever without written permission.

Without limiting the author's and publisher's exclusive rights, any unauthorized use of this publication to train generative artificial intelligence (AI) technologies is expressly prohibited.

This is a work of fiction. Names, characters, places and incidents are either the product of the author's imagination or are used fictitiously. Any resemblance to actual persons, living or dead, businesses, companies, events or locales is entirely coincidental.

For questions and comments about the quality of this book, please contact us at CustomerService@Harlequin.com.

TM and ® are trademarks of Harlequin Enterprises ULC.

Harlequin Enterprises ULC
22 Adelaide St. West, 41st Floor
Toronto, Ontario M5H 4E3, Canada
www.Harlequin.com

Printed in Lithuania

Beth Cornelison began working in public relations before pursuing her love of writing romance. She has won numerous honors for her work, including a nomination for the RWA RITA® Award for *The Christmas Stranger*. She enjoys featuring her cats (or friends' pets) in her stories and always has another book in the pipeline! She currently lives in Louisiana with her husband, one son and three spoiled cats. Contact her via her website, bethcornelison.com.

Books by Beth Cornelison

Harlequin Romantic Suspense

The Coltons of Alaska

Colton's Second Chance

Cameron Glen

Mountain Retreat Murder
Kidnapping in Cameron Glen
Cameron Mountain Rescue
Protecting His Cameron Baby
Cameron Mountain Refuge
Her Cameron Defender

The Coltons of New York

Colton's Undercover Seduction

The Coltons of Owl Creek

Targeted with a Colton

Visit the Author Profile page at Harlequin.com for more titles.

For Paul, since college and always.

Prologue

Thirty years ago

San Diego, California

Will Colton stood on his parents' front porch watching his five-year-old son restlessly shift his weight from foot to foot. "Why didn't you go potty before we left the house?"

Eli glanced up, his nose wrinkling as he answered, "I didn't have to go then." The boy frowned and stared at the door as if he could will it open. "What's takin' them so long to let us in?"

"I don't know. I told them last night we were coming over this morning. Someone should be up." In deference to his son's emergency, Will knocked again, calling, "Mom? Dad? It's us."

Still no answer. Before Eli had an accident, Will twisted the knob of his childhood home and pushed the door open. A niggle of alarm crawled through him that they'd not locked the front door. They may not take the threats of the guy bothering Caroline seriously, but that didn't mean they should be lax in general home security.

Even a safe neighborhood held the potential for crime. "Hello? We're here."

Eli pushed past him and sprinted inside, making a beeline for the bathroom.

Will chuckled and turned to close the door and hang up his jacket. "Caroline? Mom? Where is everybody?"

The house was still dark, and no scent of brewing coffee welcomed him, which was odd, considering his mother considered coffee first thing in the morning an unbendable rule of life.

"It's for your own good," she'd tease. "You don't want to deal with me uncaffeinated."

So maybe the family had overslept? Will ducked his head in the kitchen, confirming no one was there before heading down the hall toward his parents' bedroom. He was just about to call out again, when Eli barreled out of the hall bathroom, zipping his jeans and crashing into Will. "Whoa, partner! No running in the house. Remember?"

"Sorry," Eli muttered, though, due to his recently lost front tooth, it came out more like *thorry.*

"I don't think Grandma and Grandpa are out of bed yet. Why don't you go wait in the kitchen, and I'll check on them. Okay?" Will turned Eli with a firm hand on his shoulder and nudged him down the hall.

With a shrug, Eli complied. "When are we eating breakfast? I'm hungry."

"Soon. Be patient."

As he headed down the hall to the last bedroom on the right, Will glanced in his younger sister Caroline's bedroom. Her bed was made, and the room appeared to be vacant. Again, this seemed odd. At seventeen, his sister typically slept until noon on Saturdays. For her to be up and gone early on a weekend morning was unusual. Had Caroline been given a last-minute modeling job? When they made plans last night to have breakfast together this morning, his mother had not mentioned anything on their calendar or Caroline's.

His parents' bedroom door was closed, and for a moment, he wondered if they might be taking advantage of Caroline's absence for a bit of morning—

Will shuddered, and with a wry snort, he shook his head. *Nope.* His brain refused to go there. His parents didn't have sex. He, Ryan and Caroline were brought by the stork. End of story.

Just the same, he knocked and waited for a reply before opening the door. When he got no response, he cracked the door open a sliver and called in, "Yo! Everybody decent in there?"

No answer. A pulse of growing confusion and, okay, *concern* pulsed through him. What was going on? Where was everyone?

He pushed the door wider. "Mom? Dad?" He peeked around the door. "Eli says he's hungry, and—"

Ice slithered through him. Horror froze him for a beat as he stared in disbelief at his parents lying in bed... blood soaking their sheets. The number of stab wounds, the pale color of their skin and the fixed stare of their eyes left no doubt they were dead.

Will opened his mouth to wail in grief and shock, but the sound that rang in his ears was not his voice but Eli's.

His son was screaming in terror.

Jolted from his own trauma by the fear in Eli's cries, Will stumbled backward from the bedroom and raced down the hall toward the kitchen. "Eli!"

But his boy's screams were coming from the family

room. Choking on the bile that rose in his throat, Will rushed to find Eli.

He found his son standing in the center of the room, shaking and crying, his wide blue eyes fixed on two figures on the sofa. Dread pooled in Will's gut as he rounded the end of the couch and took in the macabre scene.

Caroline was sitting on the couch, wearing a skimpy black dress. She had scarlet smears and bruises around her neck and was propped by decorative pillows to lean against a man. The man, whom Will recognized from police reports as Jason Stevens, Caroline's stalker, had blood all over his clothes and face and hands.

The bloody butcher knife that had likely been used to kill Will's parents was on the coffee table. A red-smudged syringe lay discarded on the couch beside Stevens. He and Caroline were both clearly dead.

Eli's continued screams shook Will from this fresh wave of disbelief and deep sadness. He wrapped Eli in a firm hug, trying to shield his eyes from the gory and disturbing tableau. When he could muster his nerve, he peeked at his sister again. She'd obviously been posed, her right arm draped around Stevens's shoulders, her left hand resting on her chest over her heart. Blinking away tears, he squinted when he noticed something on his sister's hand, winking in the early morning sunlight that peeked through the curtains.

A diamond engagement ring.

But... Caroline wasn't engaged to anyone, so where—

The answer came to him, and nausea roiled in his gut. The sicko Stevens had put the ring there, part of his delusion that he and Caroline were an item.

A roar of fury that his parents hadn't taken Jason Stevens's threat more seriously erupted from him.

Eli stiffened, then sobbed harder. "Daddy, I'm scared! Did that man hurt Aunt Caroline?"

Will lifted his son into his arms and carried him out of the house. "I'm afraid so, son. We… I have to call the police now, and…your mother to come get you."

"But I thought we were having breakfast with Grandma and Grandpa."

His son's innocence, his inability to grasp the magnitude of what had happened broke Will's heart. Because someday, Eli would realize what he'd seen. Someday the horror would reveal itself. And because he and Eli would never have breakfast with his parents or Caroline ever again.

Chapter 1

Twenty-eight years later
Seattle, Washington

Noelle Harris jolted when her phone rang. She'd been so deeply involved with the data on her computer screen, so enthralled by the analysis of her client's intricate web of finances that she'd shut out everything else. Until the melodic jingle of her ring tone had sliced into her concentration.

With an irritated huff, she glanced at the screen. Her caller ID identified the origin of the call as Shelby, Alaska, and her pulse bumped for the second time.

She aimed her finger at the red disconnect button, fully intending to reject the call. She had no interest in talking to anyone in Alaska. As a Korean-American, she'd always felt like an outsider growing up in Anchorage. Especially within her own white adoptive family. When she'd left for college, she'd put Alaska and all of its bad memories and heartache behind her, thank you very much.

But some odd niggle, a spike of pure curiosity made her shift her finger to the answer icon instead. Her muscles tensed as if bracing for a blow as she reluctantly raised the phone to her ear. "Hello?"

The caller took a beat before saying, "Noelle?"

"Yes." A tingle of premonition, a familiarity she couldn't quite place chased down her back in the few seconds it took before the caller continued.

"It's Eli." He cleared his throat and added, "Eli Colton," as if she wouldn't instantly know who Eli was, wouldn't know the voice she'd longed—or maybe dreaded—hearing from again.

Her fingers tightened around her phone, and her heartbeat reverberated so loudly in her ears, she could barely hear herself reply, "Eli. What…what in the world do you want?"

Yeah, her tone was a tad steely. But she had to project a coolness to mask the deep ripple of emotion his call triggered. She couldn't cave to the well of heartache she'd taken years to quash. As she'd asked twelve—no, thirteen years ago—she and Eli had maintained complete radio silence. But now he'd called her? What the actual heck?

Her gut coiled, and her already tight muscles knotted even more. She should just hang up on him. She didn't want to revive all those bittersweet, painful memories or—

"I'm afraid I'm calling with bad news, Noelle."

Noelle sat back in her desk chair, startled by his announcement. "Bad news? What do you mean?" Her doorbell chimed at that moment, and she groaned. Talk about bad timing. Ignoring the door, she said, "What kind of bad news?"

"Did I hear your doorbell?"

"Yeah, but I don't—"

"You need to answer it." Something about his tone sent a chill through her.

"Why? How would you know who—"

"Just…please let them in."

Her mind spinning and heart thumping, she made her

way from her home office to the front door. Two uniformed Seattle police officers were on her front stoop.

Bad news. Police officers. Noelle gripped the doorknob and silently waved the officers in.

They both introduced themselves in grim tones, and with legs trembling, she showed them into her living room and took a seat on the couch. "All right, Eli. The policemen are here. What's happened?"

He cleared his throat again, and she heard him take a deep breath. "There's no easy way to tell you this, but... your sister, Allison, has been killed."

Noelle replayed the words in her head, once...twice. Eli must have thought her silence meant she'd not heard or had hung up, because he repeated the stunning news.

"I heard you. I just... How? When? And why the hell are you calling to tell me instead of letting these officers you obviously sent deliver the news?"

"I'm with the Major Crimes Division of the Alaska Bureau of Investigation, and her murder is part of a bigger serial killer case I'm investigating. I thought I should be the one to break the news to you instead of a stranger, because of our history. But protocol calls for officers to be present in person, so..." He let his words trail off.

She angled a glance at the two Seattle officers who wore awkward expressions, as if expecting her to melt down any moment.

Except her brain felt numb. Overwhelmed. Eli... Allison... "I—d-does Aunt Jean know? I mean, she probably wouldn't call me even if she did, but—"

"No. I haven't informed your Aunt Jean yet. You are Allison's next of kin and—"

"Next of kin?" She barked a humorless laugh. "What a joke."

"I assure you this is no joke," Eli said. "Surely you don't think I'd do something that—"

"No. That's not what I meant. It's—" Noelle plowed one hand through her inky black hair, trying to process all the truth bombs Eli was dropping on her. Allison was dead. *Murdered*. He was an ABI agent. He was working a *serial killer* case.

She shoved off her sofa to pace. The explosion of adrenaline dumped into her system made her too restless to sit still. She felt the gazes of the officers following her. "Hang on. Back up. Allison was murdered by a *serial killer*?"

"I know. It's a lot to take in." Eli's voice was calm and soothing. Kind. Warm. Damn it, she remembered his dulcet baritone voice all too well and how whispered intimacies could make her burn for him.

She pinched the bridge of her nose. That was not where her thoughts needed to go at the moment. *Focus!*

"And you're in charge of the case to find the bastard who killed her?" She goggled as the pieces of the picture finally slotted into place.

"Me and my partner, Asher Rafferty, primarily. Although we have a large support team." He hesitated. "Why?"

She scoffed. "Well, because…you know. Of all the gin joints in all the world…"

He grunted. "Yeah. That was kinda what I thought when the victim's ID came across my desk."

"The victim?" An eerie chill sank into her bones as the reality of what Eli was telling her sharpened into focus. Her sister had been murdered by a serial killer. *Oh, Allison!* She and her sister hadn't been close for years, but no one deserved to be brutally killed—

"I'm sorry. I shouldn't be so clinical. Family notification

isn't usually my job, but I wanted… I thought you should hear it from me first. I thought I owed you that much."

Her gut roiled. He hadn't said how her sister had been killed. Had it been quick? Had she been tortured? Acid climbed her throat as the questions mounted and the horrific possibilities spun out.

"Noelle? Are you still there?"

One of the officers stood and crossed to her. "Are you all right, ma'am? Would you like to sit down?" He touched her arm gently, but she shook her head and paced away.

"How did it happen?" she asked Eli, hearing her voice shake. "Wh-what did he do to her? Has her killer been caught?"

"No. He's still at large, and we're still working on the details surrounding the manner of death. Her autopsy results are pending."

"Eli, don't play games with me. I want the truth! I can take it. Did she suffer?"

"I'm being honest with you. I don't have definitive answers yet, and I don't want to speculate. In truth, I can't reveal details of the investigation even if I had them. I only called because you are next of kin, and the medical examiner should be able to release the body for burial next week." His sigh filtered through the connection. "So you can make funeral arrangements…"

"Funeral arrangements," she whispered numbly. The shock of talking to Eli, the weight of this tragic news and the ramifications of her sister's murder all hit her anew. Her knees buckled, and she slumped down on the closest chair.

One of the officers moved to sit close by, a look of compassion creasing his forehead.

"Noelle, I'm so sorry. You'll need to come to Shelby to

sign paperwork at the ME's office. If you need anything while you're here for the funeral…if I can help in any way…"

While she was *there* for the funeral?

Her chest squeezed. Oh hell! She had to go back to Alaska to make the arrangements for her sister's funeral. Back to the state she'd avoided for half her life. To the town where Eli, the man who'd broken her heart, lived.

Her lungs seized, and she could only take small, shallow breaths.

Would she have to see Eli, deal with him at the ABI in order to claim her sister's body? She prayed not.

"Ma'am?" the officer nearest her said, leaning closer as she sucked in rapid pants.

"No." She lifted a hand to the officer and shook her head, answering both Eli and the Seattle uniform at the same time.

Get a grip! Fighting for calm, she mustered a firmer tone along with some semblance of composure. "No, Eli. I don't need anything from you. I don't *want* anything from you. It's too late for that."

Eli scoffed. "Right. I got *that* message a long time ago."

She bristled at his angry tone. "What does that mean?"

"Never mind. I didn't call to rehash our history. Again, I'm sorry for your loss. I'll text you the details about claiming Allison's remains. The Seattle officers can take it from here. Goodbye, Noelle."

She was still swallowing the harsh grittiness of the term *remains* and all it implied when he hung up. Before she could say any more. Before she could ask any more questions. Before they could poke any more old wounds.

Probably for the best. Her past with Eli was better off left in the past.

Lowering her phone from her ear, she stared at the floor blankly while the conversation rewound in her mind.

Allison. Murdered. Serial killer.

"Ms. Harris?"

She jerked her head up, having almost forgotten the two policemen in her living room. "I—I'm fine."

"Would you like a glass of water?"

She shook her head and rose unsteadily. "I'd just like to be alone right now."

The two officers exchanged dubious looks.

"Really. I'll be fine. Thank you for coming, but... I just need time to process it all." She crossed to her front door, signaling her readiness for the men to leave.

Finally with stiff nods and expressions of their sympathy, the two officers left.

Noelle leaned back against the closed door and choked on the sob that rose in her throat.

Despite the years of silence, the teenage disagreements, the favoritism her parents showed Allison, Noelle loved her sister. Allison had been her only family since their parents' deaths—if you didn't count her cold and cruel Aunt Jean and Uncle Clyde, whom Noelle didn't. Her mother's sister and brother-in-law had never accepted Noelle's adoption, never considered her real family. Especially after Allison, a daughter by birth, had come along. Noelle, being Korean-American, had been ostracized by her mother's family, not just because of her race, but because they felt Noelle's parents had been too hasty in adopting, too eager to have a child and had settled for Noelle too easily.

Settled. Damn that word still stung. *Settled* reeked of second best, of last resort and not good enough.

Noelle wiped the silent tears that rolled down her face.

She'd lived with the stigma of being the lesser daughter, her parents' bad decision, from the day Allison was born. From age ten until she'd left Alaska in her rearview mirror to attend college, Noelle had felt like an outsider in her own family. Or, as she'd overheard her parents call her one night when she was fourteen, *the mistake*.

So why was she going back to Alaska? Back to the hostile environment where she'd always felt so unwelcome and unwanted?

Noelle dragged herself back to the couch and flopped down on it. She leaned her head back and groaned. She was going back because it wasn't Allison's fault she'd been born. Allison might have been spoiled and held in higher esteem by the family, but she'd been an okay sister. Though Allison was not close in age or much of a friend, Noelle had loved her just the same.

And Noelle was going back to Alaska because it wasn't Allison's fault she'd been murdered. Allison deserved to have a proper burial and to have her only sister there to grieve her death.

More important, Allison deserved to have her killer caught and punished. Rising from the couch, Noelle firmed her resolve. Before she left Alaska again, she intended to see that Allison had justice.

Shelby, Alaska

After disconnecting the call with Noelle, Eli sat in his ABI office, fingers steepled and tapping his chin. He replayed the call, the sound of her voice and what wasn't said but plainly heard in the silences. Her flat refusal of his offer to help, saying she didn't need him, had cut him deeply and salted old sores. But he shouldn't have lost his cool, shouldn't have snarled at her the way he had.

I got that message a long time ago.

Eli winced at the memory of his harsh tone. Not the professional presentation he'd intended when he started the call. Maybe if she'd had even a morsel of warmth in her voice, sounded even a little bit happy to hear from him—

Happy? When he was giving her tragic news about her sister? *Come on, Colton. Get real.* The message was as clear now as it had been thirteen years ago. He'd always cared more for her than she had for him. How else could she have walked away from their relationship and cut off contact without a backward glance? He'd never understood her reasons for the breakup, but he had been left without any recourse. When Noelle left him, she was just…gone. She never took his calls again, never replied to texts, never explained herself.

And he'd never gotten over her. His love had been deep and true, and her departure wounded him, heart and soul.

"What's with you?" His partner, Asher Rafferty, strolled into their shared office. Rafferty brought both the clinging chill of the November day on his clothes and a cup of steaming coffee in his hand. "You look like you just lost your best friend."

Eli straightened in his chair and lowered his hands to his desktop. "Close."

Asher did a double take. "Dang. I was kidding, but… what's going on?"

"I just talked to Allison Harris's sister. I let her know we identified Allison as one of the Fiancée Killer's victims." He picked up a pen and tapped it on the file open on his desk.

"You made the next of kin notification by phone?"

"I made sure someone from Seattle PD was there with her. But I needed to be the one to break the news to her."

"Why? You didn't do the notification for any of the other victims' families."

"Because I know her. I was...involved with her in college. I wanted to be the one... If she found out I'm working the case and hadn't... I thought I owed her..."

"Because it was an excuse to talk to her again?" Asher asked, proving he was too perceptive to be convinced otherwise.

Eli rubbed the back of his neck and arched a dark brown eyebrow. "Maybe so. But isn't it better she knows I'm working the case before she gets here? Can you imagine if we meet by chance in the hall at the coroner's office or she reads my name in a newspaper article regarding the case? I don't want her to think I'm avoiding her."

"So she's coming up here?"

Eli nodded. "To claim the body and make the funeral arrangements."

"And you plan to see her? Even seek her out?" Asher asked, propping his feet on his desk.

"I, uh, guess I'll leave that up to fate. I don't plan to avoid her. If we run into each other..." Eli waved a hand, not knowing how to finish that sentence. What would he do if he saw Noelle while she was in town? His heart squeezed at the prospect.

"Yeah?" Asher prompted.

Eli bent over the file in front of him and flipped through the pages of notes. "Well, I'll cross that bridge when I get to it."

Two days later, when Eli stepped into the lobby of the medical examiner's office from the parking lot, he reached that bridge.

Chapter 2

Noelle stood with her arms crossed over her chest, clearly embroiled in a disagreement with an older couple whose backs were to him.

"My adoption made me her family. The law recognizes me as her sister, and that makes *me* next of kin!" Noelle said, her shoulders squared and her jaw rigid.

"Well, *I* don't recognize you as anything but trouble," the gray-haired woman retorted. "You're not our blood, and you shouldn't have a say in anything regarding *my niece.*"

His hackles raised on Noelle's behalf, Eli moved closer, blatantly eavesdropping. His approach caught Noelle's attention, and she visibly shuddered when she spotted him. Her distraction lasted only seconds before she raised her chin a notch, and fire blazed from her dark brown eyes.

Her hair was shorter than it had been in college, he noted. Her thick black hair hung in a straight curtain to her shoulders, parted on the side and tucked behind her ears.

The older woman had aimed a finger at Noelle and was still railing at her in caustic tones. "If you think you're going to get your grubby paws on my sister's inheritance or anything else that belongs to my family, you can think again!"

"Is there a problem here, ladies?" Eli said as he stepped into the ring Noelle and the older couple made.

The gray-haired woman pursed her mouth. "It's personal business and none of yours."

Eli reached in the inner pocket of his heavy winter coat and pulled out the bifold wallet where he kept his badge. He flashed it at the older couple. "It's my business if I feel you're disturbing the peace with your shouting. Besides, I'm a friend of Noelle's, and I don't like to see her being publicly berated."

The woman narrowed her gaze on him and flicked a glance to the badge. "Colton? You're the one in charge of the case. You're the ABI agent investigating Allison's murder."

"I am. The same," he answered, even though it hadn't been phrased as a question.

Noelle gave him a hard look. "I'm fine, Eli. I don't need you to defend me."

"Agent Colton, you can help us!" the woman said, angling her body to face him.

"And you are?" he asked, although he already had a hunch.

The older man finally spoke, extending his hand for Eli to shake. "Clyde and Jean Gates. Jean is Allison Harris's maternal aunt. We've come in from Anchorage to claim the body from the medical examiner."

When Eli dropped the man's hand, he stuck it in his coat pocket and divided a glance among the three parties. "I see. From what I overheard as I came in just now, you have some issue with Noelle's claim as next of kin. Is that right?"

"Eli," Noelle said in a dark tone under her breath. "I said I don't need your—"

"Darn right!" Jean interrupted. "She should have *no say* in what happens with Allison or my family's estate! We're Allison's blood relatives. She was just...*adopted*!" The bitter woman spit the word out with a timbre to her voice that said she considered Noelle no better than trash.

Noelle's mouth tightened, and she turned her head away. But not before Eli saw the sparkle of tears that puddled in her eyes.

His heart wrenched in sympathy for her while, in his pockets, his hands fisted in outrage for how her aunt was denigrating her.

"I understand that Allison's death is upsetting for you," he said with more composure than he felt. Years of serving the public and dealing with all manner of human emotion and irrationality served him well in that moment. "However, the law is clearly on Noelle's side. Because of her legal adoption, she *is* Allison's sister, and therefore her next of kin."

Jean Gates took a staggering step back as if pushed. She knitted her gray eyebrows in consternation. "What? You can't be serious! Blood always comes first!"

Eli shook his head. "No, ma'am. Noelle is legally—"

"Now see here, young man!" Clyde puffed out his chest as he faced off with Eli. "My wife is entitled to the money and heirlooms her family has collected over the years, and we're prepared to take the matter to court!"

Noelle pushed in between Clyde and Eli. She scowled at Eli first. "I said, I don't need your help!" Then facing her uncle, she growled, "I don't want any money or any of the family's dusty old furniture and ugly tchotchkes. But I will see that my sister receives a decent burial and not some gaudy display meant only to earn you sympathy and attention from your stuffy old friends."

"Gaudy?" Jean said, her lips pursed in offense. "And I suppose you intend to just throw her in a pine box and be done with it? You couldn't be bothered with the family for the last seventeen years, and suddenly you know what's best for Allison?"

"And how many times since I left for college has anyone in the family other than Allison bothered to reach out to me? I had maybe three calls and one letter in seventeen years. That's it! That's all the communication from my family I had. That's all anyone cared about *me*." Noelle's voice broke, and she slammed her eyes shut before drawing a deep breath and cutting an embarrassed glance at Eli.

Eli's gut twisted. He could remember how little Noelle had mentioned her family when they'd dated, but he was seeing a new side of the situation now. Had she been rejected by her parents? Clearly there was no love lost with her aunt and uncle. This vulnerable side of Noelle, whom he'd always known to be a pillar of strength, courage and capability, shook him.

Jean gave a haughty sniff. "Why should we be in touch? You're the one who left, and I say good riddance. You were nothing but trouble for your mother and father as a teenager."

Noelle raised a trembling hand. "Stop. I have no desire to rehash ancient history with you. I'm only in town to claim Allison's body and see her properly buried in the family plot outside town. You may come to the funeral, but beyond that I don't want to hear from you or see you again." She turned to walk away, but Jean Gates pursued and snatched at Noelle's arm.

"Just a minute, you! Allison is coming with *us* to be buried with my parents and the babies my sister lost before Allison was born. She should be with her *real* siblings for eternity!"

Noelle's back stiffened, hurt blazing in her eyes.

Eli had had enough. Noelle wouldn't thank him for interfering, but the argument was becoming a sideshow in the medical examiner's public lobby. He wedged himself between Noelle and her aunt and took the older woman by the arm. "That's enough. You need to leave now. You're disturbing the peace and blocking traffic in a public facility."

Jean shook his hand off her elbow. "Unhand me! I have business here. I'm not leaving without claiming my niece for burial!"

"I'm afraid not," Eli said, his tone brooking no resistance. "Noelle will be given custody of the body, but only when the medical examiner and police investigators are finished gathering needed evidence. Which will not be today. Now please leave the premises before I arrest you for harassment and disturbing the peace."

"What?" Jean shrieked, her voice a full octave higher. "Arrest me?"

Clyde Gates, clearly not wanting to press the issue, shuffled up to his wife and placed a hand on her shoulder. "Let's go, Jean. We'll let the lawyers handle it."

"No! I—" Jean met the uncompromising glare from her husband and snapped her mouth shut. With a disgruntled huff, she shot Noelle a narrow look. "This matter is not closed." Turning on her heel, the woman tromped outside into the icy November day.

After the door swished closed behind the older couple, Eli faced Noelle. "Are you all right?"

She rolled her eyes at him. "I'm fine. But maybe you should get your hearing checked. I said I didn't want your help."

"I heard you." He took a step closer to her, wanting to draw her into his arms and hug her, hold her, kiss her again after so many years apart. Instead, he curled his fingers into his palms, squelching the desire to reach for her. Her body language—arms folded over her chest, her jaw clamped tight, her eyebrows lowered—said she wanted no part of this reunion. He sighed. *As if her ghosting you for the past thirteen years hasn't sent that message already.* "Maybe I didn't like the way they were treating you, not listening to the legal facts."

She grunted. "Nothing I haven't dealt with most of my life." She blinked rapidly and angled her head away, but not before he saw the bloom of her tears.

Compassion and longing shoved aside restraint, and he laid a hand near her shoulder. "I'm sorry, Noelle. I never knew you—"

"Of course you didn't know. I never told you. On purpose."

"If you want to go somewhere more private, maybe get lunch, we could talk about it. You could vent to me."

She started toward the coroner's office, effectively removing his hand from her upper back. "I never said anything to you because I wanted to leave it behind. So why would I talk about it now?" With one final glance at Eli, she strode briskly toward the inner sanctum of the medical examiner's office.

"Because you're upset, and sometimes it helps to let off steam?" he said, keeping pace with her. "Can we not be friends, even if you don't want a deeper relationship?"

"Can I help you?" the receptionist in the medical examiner's office asked as Noelle stepped up to her desk.

"Yes. I'm Noelle Harris. I'm Allison Harris's sister, and I'm here to—" Noelle fell silent.

Eli angled his head toward her, and his chest squeezed, seeing her face crumple and tears break free from her eyelashes. He edged closer to her, his voice low and sympathetic. "Noelle…"

She raised a hand, holding him off as she sniffed. "I'm here to c-claim her body."

The receptionist yanked a facial tissue from the box on her desk and handed it to Noelle. "Of course, dear. Let me gather the paperwork. I'll need to see two forms of identification, please." The woman turned to Eli. "Are you here with Ms. Harris, Agent Colton, or was there something I can do for you?"

"I, uh, originally came to speak to Scott Montgomery about the Fiancée Killer case, but I ran into Noelle—Ms. Harris—in the lobby. Is Scott around?"

Noelle blew her nose on the tissue and wiped her cheeks with her sleeve. "Fiancée Killer? Is that what you're calling the case? Is that who killed Allison?"

Eli took another tissue from the receptionist's box and handed it to her. "Well, that's what we're calling the case now. The local media coined the term, because all the victims so far are wearing a diamond ring. Or a fake diamond anyway, clearly meant to look like an engagement solitaire."

Something in Noelle's expression shifted. "Even Allison? She was wearing one of these rings?"

Eli hesitated. He could understand why Noelle had questions. Having been living in Seattle, she'd have only recently heard of the serial killer he and the rest of local law enforcement had been tracking. She'd have not been privy to the media coverage as each body had been found and the links in the case pieced together.

As Eli debated what and how much to tell Noelle, the receptionist said, "Let me just go get the forms for Ms. Harris, and I'll see if the ME is available to speak to you, Agent Colton."

Eli nodded his thanks to the woman then pivoted back to Noelle. "I can't go into many of the details, but...yes. Allison was wearing a ring. That and..." he cleared his throat "...the way her body was posed when the searchers found her are why we consider her one of the Fiancée Killer's victims."

Noelle pressed a hand to her mouth, shaking her head. "Geez, that's...sick. Does that mean she...had a relationship with this creep? That she dated him or—" Her nose crinkled as if she couldn't stand to voice the other possibilities.

"We really don't know that yet. And even as a family member, you're not allowed to—" Eli stopped short, seeing the shift in her expression.

"Not allowed? Are you saying you won't tell me what's happening in the investigation to find *my sister's murderer*?"

"I'm sorry, Noelle. But there are rules and restrictions about how much information we can reveal to the public, including family members. Policies regarding how an investigation is handled are put in place to ensure the case isn't tainted or suspects tipped off or evidence jeopardized."

She opened her mouth as if to argue the point, but the receptionist returned at that moment. "Here we are. I'll need you to fill out all of these forms, sign and date them. May I see your two forms of ID now?"

Noelle dug in her purse and produced her driver's license and some other small card Eli couldn't read from where he stood. The receptionist glanced to Eli then. "Mr. Montgomery is in the middle of an autopsy at the moment, but if you'd like to schedule an appointment to meet with him tomorrow, I can see what time is available."

Eli sighed. He hated delays, especially now that the Fiancée Killer case was finally beginning to develop. "All right."

While Noelle carried a clipboard with forms to a chair in a corner of the reception area, Eli left a message for the forensic expert, Scott Montgomery, to come up to his office as soon as he was available.

His business finished, he had no real reason to hang around the medical examiner's office. But neither was he ready to leave when he had this chance to talk to Noelle. She was still dabbing at her eyes and blowing her nose with the crumpled tissue as she completed the documentation for the release of Allison's body.

She could deny it all she wanted, but she needed support today and an opportunity to blow off steam. Knowing Noelle was not from Shelby and hadn't been back to Anchorage in years, he doubted she still knew anyone in Alaska, other than her aunt and uncle. They obviously would not be a source of comfort and strength during Noelle's time of shock and grief.

Squaring his shoulders, Eli decided he'd wait in the lobby for Noelle. Whether she wanted his help or not, he would stand by her and give her all the support and friendship she would need for the coming days—because he knew burying her sister and hearing details about how Allison died would take its toll on Noelle.

Chapter 3

Noelle was emotionally drained after the confrontation with her aunt and uncle, signing the paperwork to claim Allison's body...and running into Eli. She had to have the worst luck imaginable to have timed her trip to the ME's office such that she ran into *both* her hateful relatives *and* the man she'd most wished to avoid while in Alaska.

Before leaving the medical examiner's office, she donned her knit hat and zipped her coat, bundling up before heading out in the cold Alaskan autumn. She had her head down, pulling on her gloves when she heard someone call her name.

Her heart lurched as she snapped her head up and spotted Eli crossing the lobby. Of course he'd waited for her. She'd been foolish to think he'd give up so quickly and leave her alone for the duration of her stay, now that the initial contact had been made.

She grabbed for her composure with both hands, squaring her shoulders and lifting her chin.

"Hi," he said as he approached, his head tipped to one side as he studied her expression. "I'm glad I caught you before you left."

"Isn't that why you're out here? You were waiting for me." She turned and stalked outside toward her rented car.

He didn't deny it. Instead, he bobbed a nod and caught her arm. "Wouldn't you rather talk inside, out of the cold?"

Noelle shook her head. "Just tell me what you want. Why did you wait for me?"

"Because we haven't talked in years. I'm interested in what you've been doing, *how* you've been doing. And... well, after that scene in the lobby with your aunt and uncle, I really thought you might want to vent to someone. Blow off steam. I can't drink on duty, but I know a place we can get lunch, and you can get a glass of wine or a Moscow mule if you want."

Her pulse thumped. *Moscow mule* was far too specific to be random. He'd remembered her favorite cocktail all these years. She didn't want to be impressed or, worse, *touched* that he remembered that detail about her. Yet the tug in her core was undeniable. For him to have held on to that tidbit meant he either had a great memory for details or she'd mattered enough to him that he'd tried to remember such things about her. She hoped it was the former. As a cop—or rather an agent with the Major Crimes Division of the Alaska Bureau of Investigation—he would need an eye and memory for detail. She'd go with that.

She opened her mouth to refuse his invitation, when a new thought occurred to her. *He's in charge of the murder investigation.* The serial killer investigation. If she was going to get details about what happened to Allison, who better to question than Eli? She could lean on their former relationship to beg the favor of inside information. Surely he wouldn't deny her the truth about her sister's case?

"Fine. We can get lunch. But I'll take my rental car and meet you." She aimed her thumb toward the small sedan she'd picked up at the airport after she'd landed last night.

Eli shrugged. "All right." He gave her the name and address of the sports bar and grill he had in mind, and once in her car, she plugged the information into the rental's GPS.

Ten minutes later, she and Eli were tucked in an intimate corner booth ordering drinks—coffee for him and a local beer for her. She'd have liked a Moscow mule, but she didn't want him to know how on the nose he'd been.

After the waiter left, Eli smiled broadly and exhaled. "I can't tell you how good it is to see you, Noelle." His brow dipped, and his expression sobered. "And also how sorry I am for the circumstances. When the report with the identification came through—" He dragged a hand over his mouth. "Well, it was a real shock for me, too. I can only imagine how hard this must be for you."

"Difficult, yes. But… Allison and I haven't been close in a long time. She's my sister and I love her, but—" Noelle heard what she'd said and hesitated. "She *was* my sister." She leaned back against the booth cushions with a sigh. "Dang. The reality is still settling in. It's so…unreal." Flattening both hands on the tabletop, she pinned a probing stare on Eli. "So…a serial killer? Seriously?"

"Looks that way."

He reached out, covering one of her hands with his. The warmth of his palm against her cold skin felt delicious. Reckless.

She slid her hand out from under his, scowling her disapproval at him. "Eli, this isn't—" She waved a hand between them, searching for the right word. A date? She didn't want to plant that idea if she had read him wrong. "We're not—I don't want—"

A weary look filled his eyes. "Yeah, I get that. But

for old times' sake, can't we be civil? Maybe even be friends?"

She'd sound like a real witch if she denied him that much after all these years. Besides, if she wanted him to share information with her, it didn't serve her cause to be adversarial with him. Puffing her cheeks out, she exhaled her concession. "Okay. *Friends*."

She made sure the word carried weight, so that he got the message that was all she could be. All her heart could take. Telling him goodbye once had been the hardest thing she'd ever done. To foster false hope of a reunion and break with him again would destroy her.

The waiter brought their drinks, and Noelle took a few large gulps of her beer before lifting her gaze to Eli again. "Tell me about the case. For starters, why was Allison brought here to Shelby? Last I heard, she lived in Anchorage, and I'm guessing the ABI office there is bigger, better equipped."

He arched a dark brown eyebrow. "Our office is smaller, yes, but we have access to all the same resources. And our people are top-notch. As far as why she was brought to the ME here in Shelby..." he paused and laced his fingers as he rested his hands on the table "...because Asher and I are the ones working the case. We're based here. And she and the first body were found closer to Shelby than any of the other satellite offices."

Noelle's stomach flip-flopped. Between the penetrating and memory-evoking blue of his eyes and the unsettling facts she was grappling with, she wasn't sure how she would eat anything. "How...how many other victims have you found?"

Eli seemed to measure his response, taking a beat before saying, "Allison was the second victim found. We've found five bodies with similar traits linking them to the same killer so far."

"And what is the unifying link between victims? Do you have any leads on who the killer is yet? Where were the bodies found? Were they together, like in a mass grave? Is there reason to think Allison knew any of the other victims? Why would the killer have singled out Allison?" She rattled off one question after another. While she had him talking, she intended to get as much information as she could. "You mentioned a fake diamond ring earlier. Is that what ties the victims to each other?"

Eli frowned and glanced away. "Like I said before, I'm not allowed to divulge detailed information—"

She held up a hand to cut him off, her mouth firming in frustration. "Eli, I understand the police have their policies, but some information has already been reported in the press. And while I read what I could find online on my trip up from Seattle, I know there's got to be more. I'm just asking you to fill in a few gaps, give me a better understanding of the big picture."

Eli shook his head. "I understand why you have questions, but I really can't divulge much. It could jeopardize the case. You wouldn't want that, would you?"

Noelle twisted her mouth, keying in on one word. "Much? Then you can tell me something. Right?"

He glanced away, and she gripped his hand to drag his attention back to her. "Come on, Eli. You know I won't tell anyone. I mean, I want this guy caught as much as anyone. I won't do anything to hurt the case."

"Noelle..." he said, his tone skeptical.

"You can trust me to keep everything you say confidential." The look she gave him pleaded for his cooperation, for his trust.

Eli pinched the bridge of his nose. Finally, with a sigh, he said, "Here's what I can say. Based on forensics, the first victim was killed about three years ago, indicating this guy has been operating for a while."

"Three years? That long?" She goggled at him. "H-how long ago was Allison killed?"

He leaned forward, angling his head as he narrowed his gaze on her. "Actually, you can help us with that question. When's the last time you heard from her? Did she mention anyone new in her life, romantically or otherwise? Maybe someone who was stalking or harassing her?"

Noelle dropped her gaze to the tabletop and chortled. "I rarely talked to anyone in my family after I left when I was eighteen. Don't you remember that I stayed on campus for holidays and worked internships during the summer?"

He nodded. "I remember everything about you and our time together. Including the fact you rarely talked about your family and changed the subject when I asked questions. But things could have changed since college. And you mentioned earlier you'd had some limited contact with Allison."

For her sanity's sake, she ignored his comment about their time together and focused on the investigation, on Allison. "I only had a handful of phone calls from Allison. One on my nineteenth birthday, another when I graduated from UW, and one when Mom and Dad were killed in the plane crash three years ago."

His expression shifted, and something akin to sorrow crossed his face. "Your parents were killed in a plane crash? I'm so sorry. I knew they were deceased because of our search for Allison's next of kin, but not..." He cleared his throat. "I'm sorry. That's terrible."

She pursed her mouth and gave a dismissive shrug. "Yeah, well, it was harder on Allison than me. I'd already grieved the loss of my parents for all practical purposes long before their plane went down in the mountains."

"What do you mean, you'd already grieved their loss? What happened?"

She waved off his question. "Not important now. All you need to know is that the call three years ago about our parents was the last time I talked to Allison. So, no, I know nothing about her love life or friends or new people."

Eli grunted. "Another dead end. Damn." His gaze flicked up, embarrassment flushing his cheeks. "Sorry. Poor word choice."

"Whatever." She wasn't concerned with semantics or tiptoeing around each other based on false sensibilities. Gathering her thoughts, she tried a new line of inquiry. "You keep saying 'he.' You're sure the killer is a man?"

He sipped his coffee, then nodded slowly. "Based on what little DNA we've found on the victims, yes. He's careful, though, and leaves little trace evidence behind. Unfortunately, his DNA is not in CODIS, which is the US database, or in Canada's system, either, so we haven't got an ID on him yet."

Their waiter appeared at the table again and asked if they were ready to order. When Noelle hesitated and scrabbled for the menu, Eli ordered his "regular."

"Grilled salmon sandwich with fries," the waiter said, not bothering to write it down.

Even though she could get all the fresh salmon she wanted in Seattle, Noelle told the waiter, "I'll have the same."

The waiter left, and Noelle nibbled her bottom lip as she processed what she'd learned. "So…he's not in the system. Meaning he's never been arrested before?"

"Not every person arrested is swabbed for DNA, but he likely hasn't been arrested for a sex crime, violent crime or a number of other significant felonies."

She frowned and lifted her beer for a sip, ruminating. "So what leads do you have? What ties the cases together? The news reports dubbed this guy the Fiancée Killer because of the diamond ring the victims wore, right?"

He nodded. "That's right."

"And I read that they were all found wearing a black dress. Right?"

He only stared at her with those heart-stopping blue eyes.

She took another swig of beer and steeled her nerve to ask a harder question. "How did Allison die? Did she suffer?"

He gave her a dubious look. "Noelle, do you really want to know the gritty details? Don't torture yourself with that kind of information."

Her grip tightened on her beer mug. "I know it's not pleasant. And I don't want to dwell on it, but... I need to know."

"Why? What good does it do?" His voice was gentle, compassionate. His expression said he didn't want to see her hurt.

Something in her core longed to reach out to him, to curl in the comfort his arms could provide...and sob. But her brain shut that foolish impulse down. She'd done what she had to in college in order to protect herself from that sort of vulnerability. When she'd felt herself growing dependent on him, falling in love with him, putting her heart at risk for him, she'd broken things off, shut him out. She wouldn't unravel the years of work she'd put in, knitting together a protective cocoon, constructing a new life for herself that put him in the past.

She squared her shoulders, hoping to present herself as more determined and courageous than she felt. "Because I need closure."

His blue eyes filled with sympathy and understanding. He nodded and appeared ready to tell her what she wanted to know, when she blew it by adding, "And because I want to work with you on the case. I want to help you catch the man who killed my sister."

Eli sloshed the coffee he'd lifted toward his mouth, so stunned by Noelle's pronouncement that he'd flinched. "What!"

"Before you get defensive—" she started, holding up her index finger.

He scoffed an incredulous laugh. "Not defensive. Just practical. And, well, following the *law*. You cannot be involved in this case. Period."

"Not even if I can be helpful? I can offer my services at no charge to the ABI, and I won't—"

"Your services?" His coffee splashed again as he thunked the ceramic mug onto the table harder than he intended. "Are you saying you're in law enforcement?"

She shifted her weight restlessly on the padded booth seat. "Uh, no. But—"

"Well, then that's an end to it. Case closed."

"Would you listen? I can be valuable to the investigation."

He lifted an eyebrow. "How so?"

Her jaw firmed, and she drilled him with a level, all-business stare. Despite the seriousness of her gaze, his belly jolted as he met her beautiful dark eyes, remembering...

"Analytics."

He frowned. "What?"

"Computer analytics. Statistics. Data mining. It's a way of looking at large amounts of information in new ways, looking for patterns and contrasts. Of maximizing data to reveal truths not readily apparent otherwise."

"I know what analytics means. I've heard of sports teams using computer statistics and so forth to find the best players and the best game strategies. How would you use analytics on the Fiancée Killer investigation?"

"I'd input everything you know about the—"

"Nope, nope, never mind." He waved both hands. "I shouldn't have asked. You can't be involved."

Her brow furrowed over her dark brown eyes, and her mouth pinched. "Not even if I can be useful? Are you so stuck on your blessed rules that you'd shut out an offer to make a difference in the case? To get a better perspective on the big picture? I might be able to help you get a clearer idea of the sort of person the killer is."

"That's what our profiler does. We're already compiling an outline of the killer's likely personality and physical traits."

The waiter arrived with their meals, and Eli hoped it would be enough to derail the conversation. But he should have known better.

"What has your profiler determined?" she asked, choosing a french fry from the stack on her plate.

He rolled his eyes. Noelle had always been stubborn. When she fixed her mind on an idea or plan of action, she could rarely be persuaded otherwise.

The most painful example of this was her notion that

because of their differences—a term she never defined—they couldn't have a future together. After an intense and passionate two years together in college, she'd abruptly broken things off. He'd tried to convince her he cared far more about the ways they were the same and that his love was strong enough to overcome any challenges. But she'd been certain their differences would someday come back to bite them. She'd said only that experience had taught her that even the people you loved and trusted most could change their mind about you and push you aside.

"Like you're doing now to me?" he'd retorted hotly.

Her guilty expression had said his comment had hit its mark. "Well, I learned from the best." She'd turned then and walked away, never to answer another call or text from him. Until two days ago, when he'd notified her of Allison's death.

Rather than answer her question, Eli picked up his salmon sandwich and took a big bite. Two could play this game. And he had the policies of the ABI backing his stance not to involve her in the investigation.

When it became clear to her that he didn't intend to answer, she groaned her frustration. "Okay then. I'll guess." She fixed a keen gaze on him, ignoring her food. He swore he could see the gears in her sharp brain turning. Calculating, even without her spreadsheets or analytics software.

"If he's been operating for three years and killed five women that you know of without getting caught..." she propped her chin on her hand, her elbow on the table "...he's patient. And if he hasn't left any significant, useful evidence behind, then he's intelligent. Smart enough to think things through and be careful. So, he's a planner. Organized."

Eli took another bite of his sandwich and chewed, trying to keep his face impassive despite being impressed with her logic. And accuracy.

She tilted her head to one side. "Am I right so far?"

He reached for the ketchup and squirted a puddle onto his plate.

"I am, aren't I? Your silence says yes, even if you don't."

He scowled at her. "That makes no sense. Silence is just silence. I'm not committing to anything one way or another."

When she continued to stare intently at him, clearly reading his expression, trying to catch him out, he dropped his gaze to his plate. He dipped a fry into the ketchup and grumbled when the sauce dripped on his shirt on the way to his mouth.

Noelle chuckled. "I am right. You would always get peevish and evasive when you knew you'd been outflanked. At chess or poker or in life."

That she'd remembered that detail about him, that she'd used it against him, only irritated him more. He huffed and pushed his plate away. "Fine. You're right about the killer's profile, but you haven't deducted anything our department hadn't figured out within the first few hours of gathering evidence from the first body."

She sat back with a smug smile on her face and lifted her beer for another long drink.

"But," he added before she tried to wheedle any more information from him, "I still can't tell you anything else about the case."

Her grin morphed to a disgruntled pout.

"Besides, I brought you here so you could release some

steam regarding your aunt's nasty behavior." He waved a hand. "So vent away."

Noelle rolled her eyes. "What's the point? It's nothing I'm not used to."

Eli cocked his head to the side. "What do you mean?"

She gave him a withering look. "I mean not every family is as happy and loving as the Coltons are. You may have grown up with familial harmony and support, but not everyone's so lucky."

"So your aunt's always been like that?" he asked, a pang of sympathy spearing him. He had been lucky in most family matters. He and his siblings were as close to his cousins as to each other. Holidays were joyful, celebratory events, and support was woven into the family motto, *Believe*.

Noelle lifted her sandwich rather than answering him. "Mmm. That's good fish. But isn't salmon fishing over this late in the year? It can't be wild caught, could it?"

"Depends on the weather. Some years, RTA takes groups out salmon fishing as late as October or early November. Mostly Coho this late in the season, though, if I remember right, but you'd have to ask my cousin, Spence. I don't get too involved in RTA business."

"RTA?" she asked.

"Rough Terrain Adventures."

She nodded. "Oh right. Your family's outdoor adventure tours company. I remember now."

He arched an eyebrow. "Now who's being evasive and stealthily changing the subject?"

She set down her sandwich and plucked up another fry. "We can go back to talking about the investigation if you like."

When she batted her eyelashes in feigned innocence, Eli laughed. "Oh, Noelle. I have missed you."

When her cheeks blanched and her eyes widened, he realized how his offhand remark had sounded. But he wouldn't take it back. Because he had missed Noelle. Terribly.

And now, with her back in town for a few days, he had his chance to repair the gulf between them. He had the chance to right whatever had gone wrong all those years ago.

Chapter 4

At her rented hotel room that night, Noelle stewed over Eli's dogged insistence not to share case information with her. She knew she had skills that could prove useful to the investigation if she could just convince Eli.

She meditated on what her next steps should be. She'd come all this way to Alaska and didn't want to waste her time here. She couldn't schedule the funeral for Allison until the medical examiner and forensic specialists had finished gathering all the information they could and released her remains. She'd cleared her work schedule before leaving Seattle, so she had a few days, maybe even as much as a couple weeks to devote her time to another project. She wanted that project to be finding Allison's killer.

She knew she wasn't magically going to come up with an answer that Eli and all the law enforcement professionals, with their training, databases and specialized equipment, hadn't found. But deep in her bones, she believed she could offer a fresh perspective on the information they'd gathered that might be of use to the investigators. Or...she hoped.

The killer had to be caught. Not just to save the lives of any potential new victims, but to give his previous victims justice.

Noelle punched her flat pillow in the too-soft bed and tried to get some sleep. The snippets she knew about the case taunted her. Fake engagement rings. Three years of killing. An intelligent and patient killer.

Intelligent and patient. Those words could be used to describe Eli. She'd admired his sharp mind when they were students together at the University of Washington. And when she'd seen the writing on the wall, when she'd begun to pull away from him, he'd been infinitely patient with her mercurial moods. Her swings between the deep passion she felt for him and the indifference she had to muster in order to leave him behind would have driven most men away. But Eli's devotion to her and patience with her hadn't faltered.

Noelle's heart, which she'd believed healed, stung. Seeing him today had been a blessing and a curse. While she'd been happy to see him doing so well, in a lead position in his chosen field, the intimate lunch had opened old wounds. Looking into his beautiful blue eyes, hearing the mellow baritone of his voice, feeling the warmth from his smile... Dang it. She'd had to fight not to tumble right back into his arms. She'd have to do a better job of steeling herself if she were to survive the next several days. She knew her quest to learn more about Allison's death and the investigation meant she'd run into Eli. Repeatedly.

The next morning, after a strong cup of coffee and thirty minutes of yoga to prepare herself, Noelle went to the ABI office and asked to speak to the forensic specialist in charge of the Fiancée Killer case. She was somewhat used to the winter darkness clinging to the night in Seattle, but here in Shelby, even at 8:15 in the morning, the sun had yet to rise. The lingering night added to her sense of disorientation and surrealism.

Allison was dead. Having not seen or spoken to her sister for so long, the loss was difficult to wrap her head around. Her absence wouldn't be significantly felt, yet the tragic nature of her death was unsettling.

When Noelle finally muddled her way into the state troopers' offices, the woman working the front desk seemed prepared to deny her request to meet with the forensic specialist or, at a minimum, grill her about her purpose for being there. But, as luck would have it, a tall, blond man was filling a mug at the coffeepot in the lobby and heard her request.

Grinning broadly, his green eyes bright, the handsome man strode over to Noelle and extended his hand. "I'm the ME on the Fiancée Killer case. Scott Montgomery at your service. How can I help, Ms.—?" He let the title draw out, asking her to fill in the blank with a lift of his brow.

She took his hand and gave it a firm shake. "Harris. Noelle Harris. And I'm interested in learning more about the case."

His expression grew skeptical, the way Eli's had yesterday, and her stomach sank. She braced herself for being turned away, mentally calculating the best argument to be allowed access.

"Are you a journalist, Ms. Harris?" Montgomery asked.

"No. I'm a family member of one of the victims. I'm just trying to get a better idea of what happened to my sister and where the case stands."

"Of course. I can understand that." Montgomery paused a moment, his expression belatedly shifting to one of sympathy. "And my condolences on your loss."

She smiled politely. "Thank you."

He offered her coffee, which she declined. "What exactly is it you wish to know about your sister?"

"Anything and everything you can tell me. Reports in the media have been—"

"Noelle?"

Her words died on her lips as she pivoted to find Eli and another woman standing just inside the front door.

The woman's gaze flicked to Scott, and a smile lit her face. "Good morning, Scott. Stealing the visitors' coffee again, I see."

The forensic specialist's face glowed as he greeted the woman. "Kansas! Hi." He lifted his mug to her in a sort of salute. "You have to admit, it's far better than the witch's brew back in the office."

Eli stepped forward, his attention fully focused on Noelle. "What's going on here?"

"This is Noelle Harris," Scott said, brandishing another handsome smile. "She's—"

"I know who she is," Eli said, not unkindly. His mouth twitched in a lopsided grin.

The woman Scott had called Kansas gasped. "You're Noelle? *The* Noelle?"

Noelle blinked and divided a look between Kansas and Eli. "I'm *a* Noelle. I'm not sure if that makes me *the* Noelle."

Eli cleared his throat and glanced at Kansas. "Yes, she's *the* Noelle." He sighed, adding, "And unfortunately, Allison Harris, the second body found, was her sister." He turned to Noelle. "What brings you by this morning?"

"She wanted to talk to me about the case, get some details," Montgomery said before Noelle could answer. "What do you mean, *the* Noelle? I'm missing something."

Eli shook his head and flicked a brief glance at his colleague. "Never mind. I'll explain later. Suffice to say, I've told her everything we can divulge on the case already. So…" He spread his hands. "Your trip this morning was in vain."

Kansas scoffed. "Eli, don't be rude! It's not in vain as far as I'm concerned, because it meant I got to meet you—finally! I'm Eli's cousin, Kansas Colton. I've heard so much about you."

Noelle gave Eli a querying look. "You have? Recently?"

"Well, not so much recently, but we all knew about you, heard all the stories, back when you were dating." Kansas shot her cousin a side glance as if realizing how awkward this meeting, years later, must be for Eli. "Um…" She hitched a thumb over her shoulder. "I better get going. I'm with the search and rescue team, and I'm just checking up on a few things before…the task force meeting. And I have to…report…" She let her excuse trail off, her cheeks flushing. "Well, it was nice to meet you, despite the sad circumstances."

Scott's eyes followed Kansas as she disappeared down the corridor, his expression clearly saying he wished he could escape the awkwardness himself but knew Noelle's wish to speak to him pinned him down.

Shifting her attention back to Eli, Noelle angled her head in query. "You told your family about me?"

Her question seemed to startle him. "Of course, I did. We were—" His gaze flicked to Scott before returning to her. After the briefest hesitation where he seemed to be choosing his words, he said, "Dating. Didn't you tell your family about me?"

Noelle, unwilling to get into their personal history or her family dynamic, especially with Scott listening, dodged the subject with a shrug. "Well, I don't want to keep you. I came to see Mr. Montgomery."

Eli squared his shoulders and divided a look between the two. "And I, as the lead on the Fiancée Killer case, am saying Scott is not at liberty to share any details I haven't already given you."

Noelle sputtered. "Wha—you haven't told me jack-diddly!"

"Exactly. Because we don't want anything to jeopardize the case." Eli directed a loaded look to Scott. "Isn't that right, Scott?"

The forensic expert raised both hands. "I'm sorry. My hands are tied."

Noelle gritted her teeth. She'd been sure Scott was ready to spill more details to her if Eli hadn't shown up. "Thank you anyway, Mr. Montgomery."

"Scott, please. Any friend of Eli's need not stand on ceremony with me."

She gave him a half smile as he retreated into the office. Facing Eli, she propped her hands on her hips, her gaze clashing with his. "I can't believe you're being so stubborn about this! I'm not a threat to the investigation. I can add value! I have software that can give you a deeper analysis of your data. I have a vested interest in seeing the case solved. I am trustworthy and honest and—"

"All right! All right!" Eli raised a palm, signaling defeat. He took her by the arm and led her to a corner of the lobby, out of the path of pedestrian traffic and away from the listening ears of the receptionist. "I have a meeting with the task force in a little while and interviews set up for this afternoon, but I can meet with you this evening. Where are you staying while you're in town?"

Noelle hesitated. Did she want him coming to her room at the hostel? That felt too…intimate. Nothing romantic would happen between them, of course, private setting or not, because she wouldn't let it. Sending him away had hurt too much in college to ever go through that pain again. But why tempt fate? The low hum of attraction still vibrated in her core when she was around him, and his piercing blue eyes could still stir heat in her blood. She needed a more public venue where societal decorum would ensure a chaste atmosphere.

"Why don't we meet at a restaurant instead and get dinner? My treat," she said.

He rubbed his chin as he studied her. "Okay. Yes to the restaurant, but no to you paying. I can't accept anything that even smells like a bribe."

She had to smile. "You always were honorable to a fault."

"The same place as yesterday?" he asked.

"That place was good, but I enjoy a bit of variety."

"Okay, then...the Cove is a nice place by the water. I can pick you up around six?"

His picking her up made the dinner feel like a date. Which it wasn't. Just the idea of a date with Eli made her chest squeeze with longing. She shook her head resolutely. "I have Google Maps. I'll meet you there. Six then?"

He frowned and opened his mouth as if to object. But after a beat, he sighed and bobbed his head in agreement.

That evening at 5:55, when she arrived, Eli was already at the restaurant. He'd gotten them a table by the window with a view of the marina, lit with twinkling lights strung along the pier. She'd had a tedious day of making funeral arrangements for Allison with a local mortuary and speaking to a lawyer about the probate of Allison's estate, and she was more than ready for dinner and a glass of wine to unwind.

He stood and pulled out her chair, greeting her with a

warm smile that made her stomach swoop. Mentally she checked herself. *This is only a business dinner. Nothing more.*

"You look beautiful," he said, his compliment catching her off guard.

Heat stung her cheeks, and she flashed a grin of appreciation. "Um, thank you. I wasn't sure these slacks were classy enough for this place, but since the only other dressy clothes I brought was a black dress for the funeral, I didn't have much choice."

He gave her an odd look, then a forced smile before returning to his chair.

"What?" she asked.

"*What* what?" he returned, lifting an eyebrow.

"That funny look you just gave me. Something I said bothered you. What and why?"

He sighed. "Your comment about bringing a black dress. It just..." He made a weary buzzing sound with his lips. "I've been immersed in crime scene photos this afternoon and—"

She gasped. "Oh, that's right! You said the victims were all dressed in black dresses."

His brow creased. "Did I tell you that?"

She put her napkin in her lap. "Didn't you? Or did I read that in a write-up online?" She seized the opening. "I know the coroner's report I received said Allison was in a black dress. But the other victims were wearing similar dresses, too, weren't they? Isn't that one of the details that links the victims?" She gave him a level stare. "Am I right?"

His hand was resting on the table, and he tapped an index finger, a clear indication of his agitation. Which meant she was right. She sat back in her chair and tried not to look self-satisfied that she had been correct.

"Yes," he said, his tone flat. "You're right."

"It seemed a logical assumption. If the killer went to the trouble of dressing Allison in a little black dress, and the press reported he's putting fake engagement rings on all of them, it wasn't a stretch to guess they'd be dressed similarly."

Eli only grunted in acknowledgment of her assertion.

The waiter arrived, delivering glasses of water and a basket of rolls, then asked for their drink order. Once the waiter left, Eli inquired about Noelle's day.

"It was depressing. But don't change the subject. We're supposed to be talking about the progress of investigation."

"Now, wait a minute. You can't tell me your day was depressing and expect me to brush over that. What happened?"

She rolled her eyes. "Funeral arrangements. Probate issues. My aunt and uncle have already filed a lawsuit to prevent me from inheriting anything, and I'm anticipating further interference with custody of her remains. So, nothing I want to talk about any further, because it will spoil my appetite."

"And discussing the details of a serial killer's modus operandi and forensic evidence won't?"

"Well, discussing the case over a meal wasn't my first choice." Noelle gave him a pointed look. "I wanted to talk in your office or Scott Montgomery's. Dinner was my backup plan."

"I'll give you that one." Eli's attention was fully focused on her, and he gave her a half smile. "You haven't changed a bit since college. You're just as beautiful, just as dogged, just as decisive as I remember."

Noelle blinked and gave an awkward chuckle. "If not for the beautiful part, I'm not sure I'd take that as a compliment."

"Definitely meant as a compliment. You knew your mind and were fiercely independent and self-assured, and I see no evidence that's changed. I remember you taking on the administration regarding the distribution of leftovers from the dining hall to food banks and the homeless. You didn't give up until changes were made. I was so proud of you fighting for a cause you believed in."

She shrugged. "If you give up easily, is it really a core belief or just a passing fancy?"

"You're right. And I remember how glad I was that the administration finally listened to your concerns, because I did not want to see you chain yourself to the dining hall doors and risk arrest. How would it have looked for me, pursuing a career in law enforcement, to have been dating someone arrested for trespassing and disturbing the peace?"

She frowned. "Would that have mattered to you? Was I supposed to abandon my cause to keep from embarrassing you?"

He shook his head, his smile fading. "Not at all. I was teasing. I never wanted you to change anything about yourself for me." His expression grew more serious. "Which is why I never understood why you ended things with me. All you ever said was that you could never be what I needed or wanted. That we were too different. But I never asked you to be anyone but yourself."

Noelle's heart tripped, and her palms grew clammy.

"Please, let's not rehash our breakup. That's hardly pleasant dinner conversation, either."

"Don't I deserve to understand why you cut me out of your life? We had something good. No, something *great*. And then it was just…gone in an instant."

Noelle took a moment, staring down at the starched white tablecloth. "You do deserve to understand. So I will try to explain it before I leave town."

"Good."

"But not now, not tonight. I just can't…" Her voice broke, and she had to catch her breath and shove her runaway emotions back in a box before she could meet his gaze again. "I'm sorry."

Eli saw the sparkle of tears filling Noelle's eyes, and pain cleaved his chest. He reached for her hand and pressed it between his. "Not now, then. We'll find something happier to discuss."

She pulled her hand from his and used her napkin to dab at her eyes. "I'm sorry. I think my emotions are just raw tonight because of the unpleasantness of my day. And I didn't sleep well."

"Don't apologize. You've been dealt a number of emotional blows lately." *Not the least of which being me showing up in your life again.* He let the obvious go unstated. "You're allowed to be on edge." He paused as their drinks arrived, and he searched for a topic he knew would comfort her. "I saw a cat in a bookstore window the other day that reminded me of your old neighbor Mrs. Hooper's cranky old cat. What was its name? Whiffles or something."

Noelle's expression brightened, and her nose wrinkled as she thought. "It started with a P. Puffy… Puffles—"

"Puffin!"

She snapped her fingers and pointed at him. "Yes. Puffin. It was black and white, and Mrs. Hooper thought it looked like a puffin when she found it on the shoreline." She chuckled. "And it wasn't cranky toward me. I think she just didn't like men."

"Who? Mrs. Hooper or her cat?" he teased. "Because Mrs. Hooper always gave me the stink eye when I came home with you, too."

"She was just protective of me. She didn't want some Lothario taking advantage of me."

Eli barked a laugh. "She didn't know you well, then. You were way too confident and smart for anyone to take advantage of you."

"I appreciated her concern, just the same." She dropped her gaze, and her voice softened. "It's nice for someone to care."

He detected an odd note of despondency in her tone, but rather than quiz her about it, he lifted his glass. "To Mrs. Hooper and Puffin."

Noelle joined him in the toast, clinking her wineglass to his. "Where is this bookstore? I wasn't sure how long I'd be in town or how much free time I'd have. I may want to pick up some reading material if the ME delays the funeral much longer."

"I'll be sure to point it out on the way home. It's near your hostel."

After a short, awkward lull in the conversation, Eli asked Noelle about her life. Did she live near the UW campus? No. She lived in Bellevue now. Was she still in touch with any of her old professors or friends? A few. She still met her mentor, Professor Norris, for coffee from time to time.

"Do you remember Kathleen Block and her boyfriend Tim Allscert?" Noelle asked.

"Sure. We went to the Lady Gaga concert with them. Had weekend barbeques and very competitive volleyball games. Why?"

"I've stayed friends with them. They married and had two kids. I went to their daughter's baptism last month. They…asked about you."

"Oh." He smiled and nodded. "What did you say?"

"That we'd lost touch. They'll be interested to hear we ran into each other this way and caught up."

He selected a roll from the basket. "I liked them. Tim had a great sense of humor."

"He still does."

"That Gaga concert was something else, wasn't it?"

Noelle smiled and nodded. "The woman has some pipes on her, huh?"

"I particularly liked what we did after the concert." He peered at her over his glass as he sipped water, wondering if she'd recall that part of the date.

She paused in the middle of buttering a roll, angled her gaze to his. "The first night I slept with you."

"Mmm-hmm."

An endearing flush rose in her cheeks, and a sultry smile tugged her mouth. "That part was nice."

He cocked his head, feigning insult. "Just nice?"

Noelle rolled her eyes. "Very nice. Superb. Best I've ever had." She grew somber then and whispered, "Our lovemaking was never the problem between us."

His chest clenched at the abrupt shift in the conversation back to the raw topic. "I thought you said we weren't going to talk about our breakup."

Noelle turned to stare out the window at the marina lights. "I know. I—"

"But if we don't talk now, when will we talk about it? You're leaving town again in a few days. When am I going to have another chance to see you, get answers?"

She stiffened. "Was that why you agreed to dinner, if you didn't plan to answer my questions about the investigation? So you could corner me into talking about our breakup?"

He sighed. "No. I agreed to come because I've missed you. I wanted to be with you. Maybe I even hoped we could...reconnect."

Noelle's dark brown eyes widened, bright with what he could only call alarm. She shook her head vehemently. "I can't go down that path again. It was hard enough getting over you the first time. If I let myself feel anything for you again—"

Eli fisted his hands in his lap. "It just...makes no sense to me, Noelle. If it was hard to get over me, if we had passion and shared interests and great sex, why would you throw that away? Why did you push me out? Was it something I did?"

She was silent for so long, her eyes misted with tears, he'd almost decided she was not going to answer. But finally, after several heartbreaking moments, she bit her bottom lip and raised her gaze to his. "No. You did nothing to deserve the pain I caused you. It was my family that did everything wrong."

Chapter 5

Eli opened his mouth and closed it again, clearly swallowing the burning questions that had to be bubbling inside him like magma, ready to erupt. Noelle respected his willpower, his ability to shove down the queries. But he was a man of integrity. He'd promised to let the topic rest during their dinner, and he would honor his promise.

"How about this?" she asked, reaching across the table to lay her hand on his. "Tomorrow or the next day, we can make a trade. You have questions about our breakup, and I have questions about my sister's murder. We'll meet somewhere quiet and swap information."

His brow dipped in consternation. "You're going to hold personal information about our relationship hostage if I don't give you classified intelligence on an active investigation? That's apples and oranges, Noelle. Not an even trade."

A pulse of heat spiked in her core. "When you put it that way, it sounds bad. I only meant we both want information…"

"I can't barter case information, Noelle."

She nodded, guilt plucking at her. "Of course not. Forget I asked."

"But..." His cheek dented, telling her he was biting the inside of his mouth.

She remembered from college this habit of his that told her he was deep in thought. Images of him from those earlier days flashed in her brain. Her chest knotted with bittersweet agony, and she sucked in a sharp breath.

"You mentioned before that you think your work in analytics could help us get a better overview of the case." Eli took a slow sip of his water. "How would that work?"

Noelle straightened in her chair, the first whispers of encouragement stirring in her since she'd arrived in Alaska. "It's really not as complicated as it sounds." She filled her tone with the enthusiasm for her job and the hope that she could offer something to the investigation. "I'll feed case data into the programs, at which point I can then break the information down statistically or create databases to search for commonalities or use for cross-reference. Tell me what would be most helpful, and I'll do my best to get the program to run that analysis for you."

He snorted and gave her a wry grin. "Any chance it can look at the case as a whole and spit out the name and address of the perpetrator? 'Cause that's what I need it to do."

Returning an enigmatic smile, she lifted her chin. "You never know until you try."

After finishing their meal, Eli had asked for a demonstration of Noelle's analytic programs. "I'm not promising anything regarding the Fiancée Killer case, but I am intrigued to see what you do for a living."

Noelle vacillated briefly. While she still wanted to avoid an overly intimate setting, she couldn't miss this opportunity to prove the value she could add to the investigation.

In the end, she had him follow her back to the hostel. As she set up her laptop, she tried not to think about the bed just feet away and how she'd tossed and turned the night before, her body aching for Eli and her mind replaying sensual encounters from their past. Summertime skinny-dipping. All-nighter studying that eventually evolved into sex at dawn. Dinners that turned into frisky food fights and creative uses for vanilla pudding and sugar sprinkles.

When the software was up and running, she cast a sly side glance at him. "The best way to show you the program's usefulness to you would be to input information from the case and let it run a simple algorithm."

He arched a dark eyebrow and gave a soft laugh. "You're right, of course." Turning up his palms, he stalked back toward the front door. "Fine. You've worn me down. I'll call you a hired consultant on the case, which means you're sworn to protect the information I share with you and keep the details confidential."

She lifted her chin, relieved to finally be getting what she wanted but also a tad hurt he'd felt the need to couch the access as he had. "You don't need to call me a consultant before you confide in me with the case information. Do you really not have any more faith in me than that?"

He sighed heavily, dipping his head as he stared at the floor. "Of course I trust you, but this satisfies the department's protocols."

"So why didn't you call me a consultant the first time I asked?"

His head came up, and the muscles in his jaw flexed and bunched. "Because your potential contribution to the case wasn't evident then. I can't grant every family member and inquisitive citizen special status on a whim." He flipped up his palm in query. "Why are you being prickly about this? You got what you wanted."

Why, indeed? She needed to rein in her turbulent emotions. She was already walking a thin line between professionalism and heartbreak with Eli. The only way she would survive this trip with her soul intact was to detach her emotions from her business. She only had to keep it together a few days, a couple weeks, and she could find closure with both Allison and Eli.

She exhaled a cleansing breath, sobered by the promise of putting the past firmly behind her at last. "You're right. I'm sorry. You're doing me a favor, and I'm being difficult. Forgive me."

He took a step nearer her and brushed a wisp of her hair back from her face. The tips of his fingers skimmed her cheek, and her pulse skittered. "Forgiven."

He lingered a moment too long. His gaze, the same startling blue of an Alaskan glacier, held hers, making her heart thump and a hum of longing stir deep inside her.

"Let me get my case files from the Jeep," he said at last. His timbre held a husky rasp that fanned the heat in her belly. "Be right back."

"So much for emotional distance," she muttered to herself as she returned to her laptop and opened the software. But then her body had a mind of its own, it seemed, when it came to Eli. How did she quash an attraction so strong that a simple touch or lingering look could turn her on so powerfully?

"Why couldn't the lead on the case have been some wrinkled, smelly, old man? Or a brash, icy woman?"

"What's that?" Eli asked, returning from his vehicle.

She chuckled awkwardly. "Just talking to myself. So what do you have?" She gestured to an empty spot where he could set his files as she slid her chair over to make room for him to pull another up beside her.

They huddled over the laptop, choosing bits of information that could be processed and organized in ways that might reveal patterns. The ages and physical description of the victims. Their level of education. Line of work. Home address. Frequently visited restaurants, stores, offices. Hobbies.

Noelle studied the data her program spit out, hoping some telling pattern or salient characteristic stood out.

"Hmm." Though thoughtful instead of sexual, Eli's low hum vibrated in her like a plucked guitar string.

Swallowing hard, she glanced at him and studied the furrow in his brow. "Do you see something new?"

"Not exactly, but it's interesting to look at things from a different angle, so to speak."

She found herself staring at the cut of his jaw and savoring the light scent of his aftershave. *Focus, Noelle. You're supposed to be helping. Show him the value you can offer the investigation.*

Turning back to the computer, she tapped a few keys. "We can analyze the raw data for a number of factors, even though our sample size is small." She hit Enter on the keyboard, and after a moment, the program displayed a number of graphs and charts. "Voilà!"

He nodded. "Impressive."

She studied the displayed information and pointed to the screen. "That's curious."

He leaned closer, squinting at the laptop. "Huh. All of the victims had dark brown hair and blue eyes."

"That's not a common combination." She pointed to the

statistic the program had produced. "Most dark brunettes have brown or green eyes, statistically speaking. I don't remember the exact percentage, but my parents used to comment on how special Allison's blue eyes made her." She forcefully quelled the spike of envy that reared its head. "Here..." She clicked the mouse and called up new data. "We can cross-reference and get the exact—wow. According to this, fewer than ten percent of people with black hair have blue eyes."

Eli gave a wry grunt. "Guess that makes my family the exception to the rule. Most of us have dark brown or black hair and blue eyes."

A tingle raced through her as she met the blue eyes in question. "Really? The whole family? That's exceptionally rare."

"That's genetics," he said with a grin. "My parents both have blue eyes. And my uncle Ryan."

"So does this mean anything to you?" She waved a hand at the laptop screen, indicating the new statistical data.

"Well... I don't believe in coincidence. Clearly this connects the victims in a new way we hadn't recognized. I'll take this to the team in the morning, but in the meantime..." He pivoted on his chair to fully face her. "You've made your point. Your analytics could prove very useful in breaking the case. Well done."

Pleasure poured through Noelle, disproportionate to the small admission from Eli. Having his approval, knowing she had something to add to the case, seeing the light that came into his eyes, directed at her, soothed an ancient ache. The hurt predated Eli by many years but had contributed to their breakup and a different sort of pain in the years since college.

She'd found ways to compensate for her childhood wounds, had built a life and a career and a self-confidence to match the one she projected to the world, but...

Returning to Alaska, seeing Eli and dealing with her aunt had all contributed to unearthing the vulnerabilities of her past. Raw places she'd thought healed were scraped and bleeding again.

"Noelle? Are you okay?"

She shook herself from her morose tangent and forced a smile. "Just thinking about the case."

Eli looked unconvinced but clapped both hands on his thighs as he pushed his chair back and rose. "So, I'm going to provide you a copy of my whole case file and see what your magic little computer comes up with."

She cast him a side glance as she shut down the computer program. "It's not magic. It's math. Science. Facts rearranged and viewed in new light."

He took her hand and pulled her to her feet. In the close quarters of the chairs and desk, she ended up pressed against his body. "Call it what you will, but I want more."

She inhaled his pine scent and savored the hard planes and sculpted sinew of his body. The warmth he radiated both from his skin and his smile. *I want more, too.*

"Can you stop by the ABI office in the morning to pick up the files? Give me until at least ten. There's a lot of copying to do, even if that's just sending it all to a jump drive for you."

"Sure. That gives me time to do my yoga and go by that bookstore before I come in."

He drew back slightly and lifted an eyebrow. "You practice yoga?"

"Yeah. Have for some years. I love it."

"My brother Mitchell is dating a—what would you call

her—a yogini?" He flapped a dismissive hand. "Anyway, Dove has a yoga studio in town. I'll give you the address if you want to take a class with her."

She shrugged. "Why not?"

Because the last thing you need is to become more entangled with Eli and his family before you leave town. Connecting with his family will only serve to remind you what you never had, with the chance that died with Allison.

Noelle curled her fingers into her palms. She really needed to find that pesky naysaying voice in her head a hobby. Maybe it could take up crochet?

"All righty then," Eli said, stretching his back and angling his chair to face her. "I did as I promised. Now it's your turn."

Noelle's pulse jumped. "What do you mean?"

"You promised you'd tell me what happened in college that changed your feelings about me."

Eli drilled Noelle with an even stare, determined to get answers from her. He'd lived with questions and an aching heart for all these years, and he wasn't going to let this chance to find the truth get away.

Noelle dropped her gaze to her hands. "I told you, you were never the problem."

"Then what *was* the problem? You never gave me an answer better than you couldn't be with me." He tried, and likely failed, to keep his hurt and residual frustration out of his tone. "You said that we were too different, and it was better to end things as friends than drag out the inevitable bad ending."

She chewed her bottom lip and continued to avoid his eyes. "I know I was vague, but… I couldn't verbalize my reasons well. It was a gut feeling, a growing sense of doom."

"Doom? Isn't that a bit melodramatic? What differences did you think spelled disaster for us? I thought we were great together. We had a lot in common."

"Not the right things, though."

Eli sat again and folded his arms over his chest with a grunt. "We had the same tastes in music, books, food, movies. We shared the same politics and aspirations, the same quirky sense of humor, the same love of animals. I enjoyed being in nature and taking risks more than you did because of my family's business, but I never forced you to go paragliding or snowmobiling or fishing—"

"I know!" Her chest rose and fell in quick short breaths, a sure indicator of her distress. "I guess I thought you were too good to be true. The love you gave me was so new to me, so unexpected. I didn't know whether I could trust it. Whether I could depend on it."

"And what did I ever do to make you think you couldn't trust me or my feelings for you?"

The jangling notes of an incoming call on Eli's cell phone interrupted. Reluctantly, he checked the caller ID. Asher. Which meant it could be important. He sighed. "Sorry, I need to take this. Asher, what's up?"

"Potential new victim of the Fiancée Killer. Uniform on his regular beat found the body of a woman around the same age as our victims in an alley. I'm headed out now. Can you meet me there?"

Eli took down the address and promised he was on his way. As he shoved his phone back into his pocket, he looked over to Noelle. "I have to go, but…we're not through with this conversation."

She opened her mouth as if to argue, then closed it again. "I'm still coming to your office in the morning?"

"Yeah. I'll have the files ready." He headed to the front

door but paused before crossing the floor back to her and capturing her face between his hands. He dropped a lingering kiss on her lips before backing away. "I enjoyed dinner, Noelle. And for the record, I'm glad you're here. I'm sorry about Allison, but this reunion is many years overdue."

Noelle's heart was in her eyes as he backed toward the door. Longing, sorrow, and some undefined pain that he was determined to get to the root of before she left. Whatever ghosts haunted Noelle, he would find a way to vanquish them, if only to save her from the pain that clearly plagued her life.

Chapter 6

The next morning, Noelle found Dove St. James's yoga studio and joined a class. Dove, a tall woman with long auburn hair, welcomed her warmly. A prick of something Noelle refused to call jealousy needled her as she prepared for the class and watched Dove greet the other participants. Eli's brother had found a lovely girlfriend—the sort of woman the Colton family likely wanted Eli to find.

"You're from out of town, you said?" Dove asked, returning to her after finishing with the other ladies. "How did you find the studio?"

"My hostel is just down the way a bit." Noelle chose not to mention her connection to Eli. She didn't want to answer the inevitable questions.

We're not through with this conversation.

Noelle shoved aside the unfinished business with Eli and tried to clear her mind as she worked through a few warm-up stretches. She had to admit, the soothing scent of diffused essential oils and tranquil music Dove played during the class helped her relax more than if she'd gone through the motions by herself at the hostel.

She thanked Dove at the end of the class, promised she'd be back, then went into the dressing room to change before heading to the ABI offices.

When she arrived at the ABI building an hour later, something big clearly had the staff busy and buzzing. The receptionist was on a phone call and held up a finger asking Noelle to wait. After a few minutes, Noelle called Eli directly from her cell phone.

"I'll be down in a moment. I'm wrapping up a meeting," he said.

She wandered across the lobby to the coffee pot, remembering that Scott Montgomery had claimed the lobby coffee was better than what was brewed in the offices. She'd just finished doctoring her java with creamer and sugar when Eli arrived from the stairs.

"Sorry for the wait. A patrol officer found a woman in an alley last night, and my team needed to look at the evidence in case she was a new victim of the Fiancée Killer."

Noelle gripped her coffee tighter, her stomach swirling. "And was she a new victim?"

Eli rubbed the back of his neck. "Probably not, it turns out, but we have to go over all the evidence." He hitched his head toward the stairs. "Come on. I have everything you need upstairs."

She followed him, casting her gaze around the office, knowing this space, these rooms, these people were a huge part of Eli's world now. She drank it in, wanting to fill in as many blanks about his life as she could. "How do you know this woman's not a new victim?"

He seemed ready to answer, then held up a finger. "Let's get in my office before we talk."

He led her through a door at the end of a long corridor and closed the door behind them. A man with light brown hair, beard and mustache glanced up from the desk across from Eli's. With a wag of his finger, Eli introduced Noelle to his partner, Asher Rafferty, and vice versa.

Asher rocked his swivel chair back and linked his hands behind his head. "I hear you're joining the investigation. You must have really dazzled Eli with your analytics skills."

"I'm not sure *dazzled* is the word," Eli said, "but I saw the merit of a fresh set of eyes and applying the unbiased perspective of latest technology to the case."

"I just want to help any way I can," Noelle said. Turning to Eli again, she said, "You were going to tell me about the woman found last night."

Eli motioned to the chair beside his desk, and she sat. "Right. Her age was what caught the patrol officer's attention. She was young and pretty like the other victims, but we think she died of a drug overdose. No sign of strangulation."

"No little black dress, no pose with her hand up, no diamond ring," Asher added.

The office door opened, and a familiar handsome face appeared. "I'm headed down to the morgue now to start the postmortem on—" Scott Montgomery spotted Noelle and stopped midsentence. "Oh sorry. I didn't know you had a visitor."

Eli waved the forensic specialist in. "It's okay. We're reading her in on the investigation as a consultant."

A curious wrinkle in his brow, Scott stepped into the office and closed the door behind him. "What kind of consultant?"

"Analytics," Noelle volunteered. "I use specialized computer software and statistics to look at data from any number of angles."

Scott sat on the corner of Asher's desk and folded his arms as he focused on her. "Interesting. What sort of things can your program tell us?"

Asher coughed in his hand. "Geek."

Noelle cast Eli's partner a glance. "What?"

Scott waved a dismissive hand. "Ignore him. He's just ragging on me because I love all kinds of science. Biology, computers, forensics… It all fascinates me. So you were saying about your program…?"

"Don't you have a body waiting in the morgue?" Eli cut in. "If Noelle's program comes up with anything relevant to your area of the investigation, we'll let you know."

"Yeah, vamoose!" Asher waved a file folder, swatting at the hip Scott had propped on Asher's desk. "City desk is waiting on your report on last night's Jane Doe."

Scott snorted and slid off the desk. "Spoilsports. It was just getting interesting in here." He nodded to Noelle. "Nice to see you again. Maybe we can get coffee and discuss your program some other time?"

She gave him a stiff smile. "Maybe."

Once Scott was gone, she turned back to Eli, who was frowning. "What?"

"He was flirting with you."

She wrinkled her nose. "No, he wasn't."

Asher scoffed. "He flirts all the time with Kansas, too. Drives me nuts."

"Why would that bother you?" Eli asked.

His partner shrugged. "No reason. Forget I said anything." Lifting a notepad, he deftly changed the subject. "We were talking about our latest Jane Doe."

Noelle sat taller, her interest engaged. "You were saying she doesn't fit the profile of the Fiancée Killer's other victims."

"Right. So just focus on what's here—" Eli unplugged a flash drive from his desktop and handed it to her "—and here." After rummaging through a stack of papers, he extracted a thick file. "Everything we've compiled on the case is in your hands now. Protect it. It's confidential for a reason."

She bobbed a nod. "Understood."

"How long do you think it will take your program to analyze all that material?" Asher asked.

"Not long, once I get it all fed in. It's transferring the data that will take a while." She stood. "Well, I'll let you get back to work." She hefted the massive paper file. "I have a full day ahead of myself, it seems."

Eli rose from his desk and escorted her back to the lobby. "Don't wait until you've gone through everything to report back. If you spot anything irregular or telling, call me immediately. Last night's Jane Doe may not have been one of the Fiancée Killer's victims, but he's still out there, and there's no telling when he might kill again."

Back at her hostel, Noelle set up a workstation on the tiny café table in the kitchenette. After brewing herself a cup of tea, she got to work, entering and double-checking the information in the files.

Though the input of data was tedious, she knew a sense of purpose. She was finally doing something useful while she waited for Allison's remains to be released. The notion that she could even help narrow the scope of the investigation and bring the killer to justice fueled her when her muscles grew achy from sitting in the hard chair. After hours of staring at the laptop screen, her sight blurred.

Deciding she needed a break and a meal, Noelle ventured out from her hostel around four that afternoon. Darkness was already gathering as she strolled the sidewalk down the quaint town street. Before long, she found the bookshop Eli must have been referring to at their dinner earlier in the week.

When she stepped inside, a tiny bell tinkled over the door, and a voice called from the back of the shop. "Hello! Please have a look around. I'll be right with you."

Noelle headed for the fiction shelves, admiring the stationery display and greeting cards as she passed them. Stopping at the end of the first shelf of novels, she was engrossed in the selection of books when she felt something brush her leg. Startled, she gasped as she glanced down to find a cat rubbing against her shin. "Well, hello, kitty."

She squatted to pat the feline, remembering that the cat was how the subject of the bookstore came up at dinner.

"Is Igor bothering you? I can put him in the backroom."

She stood, shaking loose fur from her fingers, to greet the woman who approached from the back of the shop. "Not at all. I love cats, but my current landlord doesn't allow pets. Igor was just convincing me it was time I moved to a more pet-friendly building."

"Well then, good job, Igor." The shop clerk smiled. "Can I help you find anything?"

"No, thanks. Just browsing."

The bell jangled again, and both the clerk and Noelle glanced toward the door. If Noelle hadn't already recognized the attractive brunette woman who breezed in, the store clerk's greeting confirmed the new arrival's identity.

"Hi there, Kansas! How can I help you? Are you ready for the next book in the *Outlander* series now?"

"Soon. I haven't had a lot of time to read lately, but I have some time coming around Christmas to curl up by the fire and dive in. I'm actually here for a birthday card. The family is having a big dinner this weekend for Aunt Sasha's birthday, and I need a card to go with the scarf I got her." Kansas spotted Noelle, and her expression brightened. "Oh hi! Noelle, isn't it?"

Noelle returned a smile. "That's right. Good memory."

Kansas turned her attention to the card rack but said, "I hear you and Eli have been spending a good bit of time together since you got to town. In fact, a little bird at the ABI office says you're consulting on the investigation. Is that true?"

Noelle hesitated. How much did she want to divulge? Of course, Kansas was at least tangentially involved in the case as a member of the search and rescue team that had recovered the victims' bodies. "I'm running some data analysis for Eli, yes."

Kansas inhaled sharply, her expression saying she'd just had an inspiring thought. "Has Eli mentioned the family dinner this Sunday? It's Aunt Sasha's birthday, and the whole family is getting together. You should come! We'd love for you to join us as Eli's plus-one."

"Oh, uh…" Noelle squatted to pat the cat again as a means to stall. "He hasn't said anything, and I probably shouldn't impose—"

"Nonsense! When you have a hoard as big as the Coltons, what's one more? Come as my plus-one if not Eli's. It will be a great chance to meet the whole family at last!"

Noelle's heart stuck in her throat, and her voice fled. Her whole life, she'd wanted to be part of a big, happy, loving family like the Coltons, but she had no right to horn in on this gathering. She and Eli weren't an item, and she wasn't staying in Shelby more than a few days. She didn't want to give Kansas or any of the Coltons the wrong idea about her relationship with Eli. Especially not Eli.

When she didn't answer, Kansas flapped a hand toward

her. "Don't worry. I'll talk to Eli about it and let Uncle Will know to count on one more. It'll be fine." She pulled a card from the rack, read it and walked to the counter to pay. "I'll take this one."

Noelle sighed and whispered to Igor the cat, "What have I gotten myself into?"

Chapter 7

"I saw Noelle yesterday at Tattered Pages," Kansas said the next morning.

Eli looked up from his computer monitor to find his cousin leaning against the doorframe to his and Asher's office. "You did?"

"Mmm-hmm. I invited her to Aunt Sasha's party on Sunday. Honestly, I'm surprised you hadn't already." Though she didn't verbalize the question, the *why not?* hung in her tone and lifted eyebrow.

"Don't meddle," he said. "I know you're trying to play matchmaker and get us back together, but our history is... complicated. Even I don't understand all the factors that went into our breakup, and if you push her, you might scare her off."

Kansas frowned. "Okay. I hear you. But...how can you not know what happened in your own relationship? She had to have given you a reason for dumping you."

"You'd think, but what little she said doesn't hold water. I'm hoping to get to the truth while she's in town, but I won't if she starts feeling pressured and withdraws."

"But she's working on the case with you," Kansas said. "Doesn't that count for anything?"

"Who's doing what with who?" Scott Montgomery said, appearing behind Kansas in the corridor.

"The analytics lady you met earlier," Asher volunteered from his desk, his mouth pressed into a scowl. "You need something, Montgomery?"

"I was just bringing Kansas a cup of coffee," Scott returned tartly, then softening his tone, he handed Kansas the paper cup. "Just the way you like it."

"I think Kansas can get her own coffee if she wants it," Asher said with a growl in his tone.

"And I think I can speak for myself, Asher." Kansas turned from Asher and smiled awkwardly. "Oh, uh, thanks, Scott, but I've already had all I plan to drink this morning. Any more, and I'll be too jittery."

Scott tightened his jaw, clearly disappointed in Kansas's response, but he gave her a small smile as he turned to leave.

Eli followed the exchange, conscious that there was a growing tension in the office involving the trio. But just as he'd asked Kansas not to meddle in his affairs, he'd stay out of her work relationships. If the strain between his coworkers and Kansas interfered with the business of the office, he'd step in. But until that time, he'd let the three of them handle it their own way.

"Well, I better scoot. Things to do, you know?" Kansas said, giving Asher an odd lingering look as she left the office.

"Speaking of Noelle," Asher said.

"Were we?"

"Have you heard from her this morning? Wasn't she going to run her analysis yesterday?" Asher's chair squeaked as he turned the seat to face Eli.

"She started yesterday, yes. But she said it could take

some time to enter all the information and get all the different angles covered." Eli drummed his fingers on his desktop.

He was restless, eager to not only see what Noelle's analysis found but anticipating their next chance to see each other.

Kansas had poked a sore spot with him. He was frustrated by Noelle's dodging of his questions about their relationship, and he longed for the day when he could invite her to family events without any doubts or reservations of how she'd react.

"It's just that with the media coverage of the investigation, and the recent steady discovery of body after body, I'm concerned that our killer is going to either flee and move to another state to continue his killing..." Asher steepled his fingers and propped his elbows on the arms of his chair "...or he'll ramp up his spree, and we'll have more murdered women on our hands before we find this creep. It's been months. Why can't we break this case?"

"I'm as anxious to wrap this case up as you are, but we don't need to get sloppy in our haste."

"I hear you. I get it. And I know cases like this can take years to solve sometimes, but..." Asher sighed. "I just have this pit in my gut when I think about the women of the community who could be his next victims. I mean, how would you feel if your sister or Kansas were the guy's next victim?"

Eli's hand balled into a fist, and nausea sawed in his gut. "I'd want to eviscerate the guy, but that doesn't change the fact that we have to be methodical and precise in our investigation. We have to get every step right, so that when we catch him—*when*, not if—the court doesn't have any reason to throw the case out. We have to get things absolutely right."

* * *

Something was wrong.

Noelle stared at the spreadsheet on her screen and double-checked that she'd entered all the variables correctly. She'd spent hours with the case files and documentation of forensic evidence, and her program was churning out consistently different results than Eli and his team came up with in key aspects of the investigation. She had to be missing something. She must have forgotten some piece of data, not accounted for some element of the forensic process or overlooked some detail of investigative case handling that would account for the discrepancies.

She sighed and gritted her teeth. She'd wanted to give Eli her findings today, but her eyes were so tired, they were virtually crossing. Fatigue didn't lend itself to careful and accurate work. Maybe she could just take a short nap. She'd been up late last night inputting data, then was back at the laptop early. She didn't function well on three hours of sleep.

Rubbing the kinks in her neck, she strolled to her kitchenette and fixed herself another cup of tea. Spotting an unopened yogurt on the counter, she realized she'd gotten so distracted by the case files this morning, she'd never eaten breakfast, either. Tossing the probably-now-spoiled yogurt in the trash, she grabbed the last banana from the small fruit basket she'd stocked earlier in the week and made a mental note to go shopping again. When she'd gotten groceries before, she hadn't thought she'd still be in town this long. Now it seemed it could be several more days before Allison's funeral happened and Noelle's part in helping Eli with the case was resolved. She refused to return to Seattle before she had closure on both matters.

And what about her past with Eli? Would she be able

to find closure there? *All he wants is the truth. He deserves that.*

If only the truth weren't so painful, so…shameful. So humiliating.

Her cell phone rang, shaking her from her personal pity party, and she tensed. Expecting the call to be Eli, wanting an update, she checked the caller ID reluctantly. Instead, the funeral home's number glowed from her screen, and she answered, praying this meant the funeral could proceed.

"Ms. Harris, I just wanted to confirm the changes you've requested regarding the service for your sister." The man sounded rattled, distressed even.

Confused, Noelle rubbed her dry and tired eyes. "Changes? What changes?"

But it clicked, just as the funeral director began his explanation, "The change in burial site and memorial service location."

Anger flashed hot in her blood. "Were these changes, by any chance, requested by Clyde or Jean Gates?"

She heard the rustle of paper, a murmur of voices.

"Why, yes. Mrs. Jean Gates of Anchorage. She's here now, asking for these changes." The man's voice quavered with stress. Aunt Jean did that to people.

Noelle took a breath, striving for calm. "Please put all of my original plans back in force. Jean Gates is not authorized to make any alterations to the funeral. She's a disgruntled family member who has no legal authority in this matter."

"Oh I, uh…apologize. I wasn't aware." He cleared his throat. "Unfortunately, Mrs. Gates ripped up the contract you signed with us. In order to reinstate your funeral arrangements, we need you to come by the office and sign a new contract."

Despite her irritation with Aunt Jean, Noelle felt sorry for the funeral home owner. She could hear her aunt in the background, arguing vociferously.

"Can't you email me a link to sign electronically?" Noelle asked, realizing almost as soon as the words left her mouth what the answer would be. When she'd been at the family-run funeral home last week making the initial arrangements, the owner, an elderly gentleman, had handwritten everything in their meeting, and the only computer she remembered seeing was a clunky desktop with a huge monitor that looked like it had been on the office desk since the 1990s. She wondered if they even had an internet connection.

When the funeral director confirmed her suspicion that she would, in fact, have to drive out to the funeral home again, she saved the work she was doing on her laptop and promised to be there before he closed the office that afternoon. She grumbled to herself as she gathered her coat, purse and gloves and swapped her comfy slippers for boots.

The winter sun was already low in the sky as she climbed in her rental car and backed out of her hostel's parking spot. She set the car's GPS navigator with the funeral home's address, letting her thoughts drift as she drove.

While she'd known returning to Alaska would bring a harsh reminder of all she'd escaped when she left for college, she hated having to deal with Aunt Jean on top of the painful reunion with Eli. Going back to her lonely apartment in Seattle and her routine fact-crunching job was starting to sound pretty good—if not for the tiny detail of how much she'd miss Eli.

Eli.

When Noelle returned from her errand, she'd have to notify Eli of the perplexing inconsistencies she was finding with her analysis. How would he take the news that she'd found glaring problems with the case data?

She sighed as she pulled onto the two-lane highway that bypassed the busiest parts of Shelby and was far more scenic. She turned on her headlights as she entered a stretch of road that was shaded on both sides by tall pines. The road grew curvier as it passed through the foothills of the nearby mountain range, and she tapped her brakes to slow the car before navigating an especially tight turn.

The brake pedal felt mushy to her, giving little resistance, and the car didn't slow nearly as much as it should have. Her pulse spiked as the rental car took the curve too fast, and she drifted into the oncoming traffic lane. Trembling with the rush of adrenaline, Noelle stepped on the brakes again, heard a squealing sound from under the hood. She gasped as the pedal went all the way to the floor without the car slowing.

Noelle's breath came in short, shallow pants as she grasped the danger she was in, speeding around mountainous curves and down hills without any way to stop or slow the car. Her hands sweated inside her gloves as she squeezed the steering wheel tighter. She continued to stomp the brakes, despite the lack of response. The twin beams of her headlamps lit only a few dozen feet in front of her, giving her little warning of what turns or obstacles lay ahead.

Could she use her parking brake to slow the car? Grasping the stick lever of the emergency brake, she pulled it up slowly. Her efforts earned her a grinding noise and a hot smell, but the rental car did seem to be slowing. She'd just released a sigh of relief when an elk doe stepped into the road from the shadowy shoulder.

With a shriek of surprise and dread, Noelle cut the wheel hard to the right, and the rental car bumped off the road. In quick succession, the headlights illuminated dirty snow drifts, weeds and a thatch of seedlings before a large pine trunk loomed before her. Instinctively, she braced her arms against the steering wheel. The airbag exploded, dousing her with powder as it smacked her in the face and chest.

For several seconds, Noelle only sat in stunned silence. She took a slow and careful inventory of her physical condition, her unexpected situation and her isolated location. She coughed as her frantic breathing led her to choke on the fine dust from the airbag. In her ears, she heard the thumping of her heartbeat. Her nose ached, but when she felt the length of it, she didn't think it was broken. She'd bitten her tongue, though, she realized, tasting the metallic flavor of blood.

The rental car was going nowhere without a tow truck, and she gritted her teeth in anger for the rental company having loaned her a faulty vehicle. She added Aunt Jean to the list for her grievances. If Jean hadn't messed with her funeral plans, she wouldn't have been out on this dark road in the first place. While she was at it, she grumbled mentally over the Luddite funeral home that didn't have the means to sign paperwork electronically.

Then tears pricked her eyes, and she wallowed for a moment in pity. She felt so alone. Why had she bothered to come to Alaska at all? Did she really think that Allison would have gone to this much trouble had their situations been reversed? If Noelle had been murdered, Allison likely wouldn't have even attended her sister's funeral. The relationship had always been lopsided that way. Noelle had tried to love her sister, but only received lukewarm sentiment in return.

Only Eli had ever matched her depth of emotion...

A stinging pang slashed through her chest, and she quickly shut down that line of thought. Wiping her face with trembling hands, she reached for her purse, which had landed on the floor of the passenger side. She fumbled out her cell phone, praying she had reception here. And groaned when she found she didn't.

Fortunately, another car came along ten minutes later and picked her up. She rode with the middle-aged woman and her three children back into the business district of town where, after Noelle refused to go to the ER as a precaution, the woman dropped her off at the car rental office.

The car rental company was in the process of closing for the day, but when they learned what happened to Noelle, the manager stayed late to help her. He set her up with an upgraded replacement vehicle at no charge and dispatched a tow truck to recover the wrecked sedan, all while repeatedly apologizing and asking after her health. The rental manager was so obsequious, Noelle grew awkward with his fawning.

"I can't imagine how this happened," he said, handing her the paperwork for the new vehicle. "We are meticulous in inspecting every vehicle and staying up to date on all maintenance. Our mechanic checks all of the cars routinely. He's not sloppy. I just don't understand. I'm so sorry! Can I get you anything else? Some water or coffee?"

"Just the replacement car, please. I'm not injured. Only rattled, and I want to get home and soak in a hot bath."

Her muscles would be plenty stiff tomorrow she was sure, hot soak or not.

"Of course." He took the keys from a hook on the wall and handed them to her. "The white Chrysler out front."

Noelle accepted the keys and headed for the door, pausing when a thought came to her. "When your mechanic has the wrecked car back and has determined why the brakes failed, will you call me with his diagnosis?"

The manager hesitated a moment before nodding. "Yes, ma'am. I will."

Noelle sat in the front seat of the new vehicle, familiarizing herself with all the knobs, screens and switches to operate the car. She pulled out her phone to call the funeral home and tell the director she would not be able to make it tonight but would try again first thing in the morning.

She debated calling Eli to tell him what had happened but discarded the idea. He was already loaded with responsibilities and worries due to the serial killer case. Since she was, except for a sore nose and some muscle aches, no worse for the wear, she would spare him the news. As it was, she had to tell him about the strange inconsistencies she was uncovering in his case files. One bad news bomb was enough.

Once she'd driven back to the hostel, she filled her bathtub with the hottest water she could stand and climbed in to soak. She tried to relax, to regroup, but the terrifying moments before the car crashed left her edgy. The knowledge her aunt was undermining her with Allison's final arrangements and the disturbing results of her initial analysis of the Fiancée Killer files paraded through her brain, leaving her more tense and achy than before the bath.

She found much the same that night when, even after taking an over-the-counter pain medicine for her body aches, she lay awake and restless for hours. Finally, fed up with her insomnia, Noelle got up and crept back to the makeshift desk where she'd left her laptop. If she was awake, she might as well work. Maybe she'd figure out why her results were so skewed. Before she alerted Eli to the strange results she'd gotten in her first run of the data, she wanted to double-check her work, try new calculations and confirm everything.

If she was going to turn his investigation upside down, she darn well wanted to be sure of her facts.

Two days later, Eli was deep in the weeds of record-keeping and witness reports when his cell phone rang. He rubbed both eyes with the heel of his hands, attempting to ease the fatigue of tedium before he answered. His pulse jumped when he saw Noelle's number.

"Have you got something for me?" he asked without preamble.

After a beat of silence that felt heavy, Noelle said, "Do you think I could come by your house for a while?"

He detected a strange quality to her voice. Was this a booty call? His blood heated at the thought, and he had to consciously calm himself. "I can't right now, Noelle. I'm at work until at least five."

"I'm aware. But this is…important. *Very important.*"

The emphasis she put on the words rang alarm bells. He started saving files on his computer and closing up things at his desk for the day. "All right then. I'll meet you there as soon as I can."

He was already shoving back his desk chair by the time

he disconnected. "I'm going out," he called to Asher. "Not sure if I'll be back tonight."

"What's up? Should I come with you?" Asher asked.

Eli waved him off. "No. I don't think so, but I'll ring if it turns out I need backup."

"Backup?" Scott asked, strolling in with a cup of coffee in one hand and a file in his other. "What's happened? Another body?"

Eli brushed past the forensics specialist and shook his head. "No. Personal business."

As he pulled on his coat and hurried out of the office, he heard Scott ask, "What sort of personal business requires your backup?"

"I don't know," Asher said, "and mind your own."

A weak winter sun peeked through the clouds as Eli rushed to his Jeep. At 3:30 in the afternoon, the sun was already low in the sky, approaching sunset. The long nights and cold winds from the bay added a gloom to the season that wouldn't release its hold until spring.

Traffic was light, and he made his way home in record time. His mind taunted him with all manner of disaster as he drove—from plumbing backups at her hostel to a hostile visit from her aunt to the Fiancée Killer having detected her work on the case and tracked her down.

By the time he arrived at his house, she was already in his driveway. His heart drummed double time as he climbed out and rushed to her. Taking her by both arms, he drew her against his chest, thankful she seemed physically unharmed. She grunted as he hugged her, and he tried not to let her odd response to his embrace bug him. Was all physical contact between them off the table? He'd thought they were reconnecting at least as friends.

A large messenger bag slid from her shoulder, and she

backed away from him and grabbed the strap before the bag could hit the ground.

"Thanks for coming so quickly," she said, avoiding his eyes. She seemed unhurried, stiff as they moved inside.

"Of course I came. You said there was an emergency."

Noelle wrinkled her nose, and he noticed dark smudges like bruises under her eyes. "No, I didn't. I said it was important."

"But you sounded—" He rubbed his temple and tried again. "Just...tell me what's wrong."

"I'd rather show you." She crooked a finger and strolled to his kitchen table. She opened the messenger bag and pulled out her laptop and a few paper files. He offered her a drink while she set up her makeshift desk, but she declined. She woke her laptop and clicked through a series of screens with charts, maps, spreadsheets and graphs. "I've spent the last three days inputting all the information in the files you gave me on the Fiancée Killer crime scenes and the condition of the women's bodies."

"Okay. And?"

"And it doesn't add up."

He flashed a wry grin. "I could have told you that. If it added up, we'd have found our killer and arrested him by now."

She shook her head and angled a stern look at him. "What I mean is, the information in the files is...wrong."

Chapter 8

Irritation plucked at Eli as he absorbed Noelle's assessment. "Oh really? And you're basing this on all of your personal experience in criminal investigations."

She lifted a calming hand. "Don't get testy."

"Those files are based on expert witness testimony, missing person reports, the latest investigative technology and—"

"Eli! Listen to me." She scowled and grabbed his sleeve to quiet him. "I'm not questioning your expertise or skills as an investigator. But somewhere along the way, some data got…" She hesitated, clearly looking for a word that wouldn't set him off.

"Got what?"

She groaned. "Let me just show you." She opened a spreadsheet and pointed to the screen. "This is the file where I input all the data from your case files. You can double-check it, but I've gone over it three times to make sure I didn't input anything incorrectly." She closed that screen and opened another program. "In this file, I have all the data Scott Montgomery included. His report details information on the relevant parameters and contributing conditions that factored into his determination of how, where and when the victims were killed. His determinations were based on degree of decomposition, evidence of insect, bacteria and wildlife damage, temperature, environmental conditions such as sun or shade at the crime scene, soil or rock, moisture—"

"Yeah, I'm familiar with the things that go into his forensic analysis."

"Right. Well, so that is all here..." she pointed to the screen "...as well as dates and locations gathered through interviews with the victims' families about when they went missing, where they were last seen..." She glanced up at him, and his face must have reflected impatience, because she waved a hand, saying, "Et cetera."

Eli saw that her explanation could take a while, so he dragged a chair over to sit beside her. She scooted aside, so he had a better view of her screen. "I researched how forensic data is compiled and the rates of decomposition. There are calculators for that sort of thing available online and through professional journals. Did you know that?"

"Are you saying the average layman could do the job we're paying Scott Montgomery to do?" Eli asked wryly.

"No. I'm not. In fact, I called experts in Seattle, both at our alma mater and the Seattle medical examiner's office, for explanations of some of the process. I also asked them to look at the data and results I got to see if my conclusions were sound."

Eli shifted uneasily on the hard chair. "And what conclusions did you come to?"

She took a breath, nibbling her bottom lip nervously. "Well, I wanted to be absolutely sure I had the data that could be easily verified correct first."

Her extensive preamble told him she was building up to a bombshell and wanted to buoy the veracity of her findings. Eli could feel his body drawing tighter, coiling as if bracing for an attack.

"I used official weather bureau historical records regarding daily temperature, humidity and rainfall and compared it to what your guy used to make his calculations." She paused and gave him a disconcerted glance. "Eli, when I ran the numbers, Scott Montgomery's data was consistently off by more than ten percent."

"What?" Eli shot her a dubious look. "You're sure?"

"I'm sure. You understand that amount of variation will throw off calculations significantly, right?"

"I do. But Scott's usually so precise. I don't get it."

Her expression darkened further. "The experts I consulted also found discrepancies in other areas relevant to determining when the women were killed. I can show you the details of the science if you want, but when I input the new information from the forensic specialists in Seattle, my analysis program and the Seattle experts' both came up with far different results than Scott did. His estimations concerning the length of time since death for all of the bodies was off across the board."

"But that makes no sense. Scott knows what he's doing. He's never been wrong before." Eli leaned closer to stare at the jumble of data that could have been in German for all the sense the statistics and detailed charts made for him.

"And..."

Eli's gut clenched. "And? You mean there's more?"

She nodded. "The experts asked why critical information from the more recently killed victims didn't contain more detailed information about fingernail scrapings or inconsistent hairs or carpet fibers found on the victims, the sorts of things that can help identify the perpetrator were missing or incomplete."

Eli ran a hand over his mouth, dredging up conversations in task force meetings and how Scott had explained his findings. "When we asked him about that, Scott said he hadn't found any such evidence. We wrote it off as the killer knowing what he was doing and taking pains to leave a clean crime scene."

"Well, that may be true. But the experts found it suspicious." Noelle's returned frown echoed his concern. Fueled his suspicions. "Anyway, I knew this was big. That's why I had my contacts in Seattle double-check everything in my work, and they agreed. Scott's work is significantly flawed. But also *uniformly* flawed. The incorrect data was consistently off by a specific measure. Possibly to make the discrepancy harder to spot than a single outlier."

Eli flopped back in the wooden chair and scrubbed both hands on his face. "Were any of Scott's analyses *right*? Have we been on a complete goose chase? Did the experts you talked to—and I'm going to need their phone numbers, so I can interview them myself," he added, wiggling a finger in her direction, "did they agree with strangulation as the cause of death, for example?"

"Yes. Mechanical asphyxia is the term they used, but you can see here..." she pulled up a document and pointed to the laptop screen "...they mention strangulation when they refer to the damage to the hyoid bone."

"Well, that's something anyway." Eli shoved out of the chair and stalked the room like a caged tiger. "If we accuse Scott of negligence or, worse, malfeasance, every case he ever worked for us would suddenly be subject to review. It's a huge can of worms to be opening, Noelle."

"I get that. But there's another issue I don't think you've grasped yet."

Eli swung back to face her. "Go on."

"What I found wasn't one careless error. It was a systematic misrepresentation of easily verifiable data. The glaring omissions all fell under the same category. The pattern of errors indicates he did it on purpose. The question we should be asking is why?"

A chill ran through Eli. "You think he was intentionally throwing off the investigation?"

Noelle raised her hands, her expression regretful. "From my outside perspective, that's how it looks. Dr. Chou in Seattle suggested as much as well and threatened to call the FBI. I asked him to hold off until I spoke to you. I knew you weren't party to any fraud or malfeasance, so…" Noelle sighed heavily. "I asked him to give you and the ABI a chance to sort it out, for the sake of your ongoing investigation and the department's reputation."

Gratitude poured through him that she'd asked for a reprieve, for time for his office to sort this mess out. In the bigger picture of Scott's miscalculations, Eli didn't miss her statement of faith in his own integrity as a law enforcement officer. Was that belief in him enough to build a foundation for their future? He filed away the gift she'd given him, unwilling to let the ugliness of Scott's apparent errors—perhaps even corruption—defile the sweetness of her professed trust.

"I need to talk to Asher, but not at work. I need him to come here. I don't want to risk anyone overhearing this discussion at the office. We have to proceed carefully." The weight of her discovery settled on his shoulders and in his gut like sacks of sand.

Was it possible Montgomery had tampered with the investigation? To what end? Was he covering for someone? Could he have simply made a consistent error throughout his calculations? The notion of his colleague being so sloppy with his work was disheartening. But the idea that Scott misrepresented his work intentionally was... sickening. Infuriating.

Eli stumbled into his living room and dropped heavily onto the couch, growling his frustration.

Noelle crossed the room to sit next to him. "I'm sorry, Eli. I know this is upsetting to you, and that was the last thing I wanted when I offered to help. I wanted to ameliorate the stress you were under, not add to it. I thought my analysis would pinpoint answers or support evidence. Instead, I've all but torn the case apart."

"Don't apologize." He angled his body to face her, sliding a hand beneath her hair to cup her cheek. "If you're right—and I'm not questioning your work. I'm just saying I want to look into it more myself before we do anything drastic that we can't undo," he amended quickly when he felt her tense beneath his fingers, "then you've shined a light on a truth that needed to be exposed. Our priority is finding the truth, no matter where it leads, bringing the killer to justice and giving the victims' families closure."

"That's what I want, too. I just wish my efforts didn't hurt you in the process."

He stroked her jawline with his thumb. "Thanks for that. And for all your hard work. It sounds like you've spent hours on this."

She pulled a half grin. "I've spent a few late nights and missed a few lunches working on it. But I don't regret it. Not if it proves useful."

Focusing again on the dark smudges under her eyes,

Eli touched them lightly with one finger. "Are these... bruises?"

Her eyes closed as she winced. "Probably."

He sat up straighter. "What happened?"

"I...had an accident." She lifted a dismissive shrug. "Hit my nose. I'll be fine."

His phone rang before he could question her further about her injury, and he reluctantly leaned back from her to take the call. Seeing Asher's name on his screen, he answered with, "I was just about to call you. What's up?"

"Nothing really. But before I headed home and got in the shower, I wanted to make sure you don't need me. You mentioned backup before..."

"Right. Well, it turned out to be a different sort of emergency. Get your shower and a meal, then come by my place later to talk."

"It won't keep until morning at the office?" Asher asked.

"No. It won't. Let's say eight? I have a few other calls to make before we talk."

"You going to tell me what this mysterious heart-to-heart is about?"

Eli exhaled his frustration. "The investigation. But I'd rather not say more until we meet."

Once Eli disconnected the call, he turned back to Noelle. "You better give me a detailed rundown on your analysis." He checked the time. "But first I want to try to catch your experts in the office. You have their phone numbers handy?"

Chapter 9

Three hours later, after speaking to both forensic experts in Seattle and taking a deeper dive into the statistics and charts Noelle pulled up for him, Eli was convinced the pattern of incorrect information throughout Montgomery's work was no accident. He kneaded the tense muscles in his neck as he leaned back in his chair.

Noelle, who'd been milling about the kitchen, making them sandwiches for dinner and randomly tidying to keep busy while he perused her data, stepped up behind him and bumped his hands out of the way. She rubbed his shoulders and neck and applied direct pressure to spots that were especially knotted with tension.

The warmth of her hands and relaxing massage worked magic on him. He felt a catharsis and release of the stress he'd been harboring while at the same time growing keenly aroused by the erotic manipulation of her hands. Shoving the files aside, he turned in the kitchen chair and drew her into his lap.

Noelle gave a feeble protest which he quieted with a kiss.

"I made us a little dinner. Are you hungry?" she asked, her voice breathless enough that the question sounded like a sexy invitation.

"Not for food," he said, capturing the back of her head and kissing her again.

Noelle draped her arms around his neck, twisting her lips into a lusty grin. "I think I have what you need."

Eli groaned his pleasure as he rose from the chair with Noelle in his arms and carried her to the nearest flat surface. Laying her down on the couch, he covered her body with his own and plundered her mouth. His tongue dueled with hers, and his hands tugged at her clothes. Years of pent-up desire and longing were unleashed as they touched and nibbled and explored each other.

"I want to make love to you, Noelle. But not unless you're sure it's what you want, too." He levered up on one arm to peer directly into her soulful brown eyes. "I moved on with my life after college, but I never stopped wanting you."

Noelle's breath stuck in her lungs. Desire had her body humming and left her mind a muddle. She still clung to enough of her senses to realize Eli had said he'd wanted her, not that he'd loved her. For a moment, she knew the sting of disappointment. A too-familiar pain swelled in her chest.

Unloved. A complication. A burden.

A mistake.

The word she'd heard her mother use echoed hollowly inside her.

When Eli brushed his fingers through her hair and narrowed an inquiring look on her, she realized she'd never answered him. "Oh. I, uh…"

This works well for you, a part of her brain justified. *You can satisfy your hunger for him, perhaps even work him out of your system for good and leave town again without entanglements. If he doesn't love you, you won't break his heart again when you go.*

Noelle forcibly dismissed the whisper that argued, *And what about breaking your own heart?*

Fisting her fingers in his hair, she drew greedily on his mouth, then whispered, "I'm a big girl, Eli. I know what I want and can take care of myself."

A frown flickered across his face, but she didn't let herself think too hard about the reason behind it. After toeing off her shoes, she stroked her foot down his jean-clad leg, before encouraging him to continue by raising her hips to meet his.

His shirt came off, then hers. Hands stroked, lips searched and sampled, and the heat rose quickly in her blood.

Eli had just unhooked her bra when a loud knock sounded on his front door. They both froze like high school kids discovered necking in a parent's car.

"Are you expecting someone?" she whispered.

"No. I told Asher to come at eight. If that's him pushing things earlier, I swear I'll…" He didn't finish the threat as another knock pounded on his door.

Scrambling to right his clothes, Eli headed for the door, hesitating only long enough for her to restore her bra and shirt as well.

An attractive young couple, their arms around each other, waited on Eli's front porch when he opened the door.

"Took you long enough," the man with shaggy brown hair said, pushing past Eli without a verbal invitation to enter. His gaze took in Eli's rumpled hair and clothes as he ushered the blonde with him inside. "Were you asleep?"

"Um, no. Why—?"

The couple pulled up short when they spotted Noelle sitting on the couch, finger combing her hair. She knew her lips were swollen and that she'd missed a button when fastening her blouse. *Busted.*

"Oh hello." The blonde glanced from Noelle to Eli to her partner. "We didn't know you had company. I'm sorry."

Eli dismissed the woman's concerns with a flick of his hand. "You're not interrupting anything. I was just, uh, discussing the Fiancée Killer case with Noelle. Her sister was one of the victims, and she, um, wanted a briefing."

"A briefing? Is that what the kids are calling it these days?" The shaggy-haired man's eyes twinkled with mischief.

Eli rolled his eyes and punched the guy's arm lightly. "Don't be crude, man." Motioning with his hand, Eli introduced the couple, his younger brother Parker and Parker's girlfriend, Genna. "So, you had a reason for stopping by I assume?"

Instead of answering his brother's question, Parker sent Noelle a curious look, much like the one Kansas had given her when they met earlier in the week. Noelle braced herself for the connection and suppositions. For subsequent necessary explanations. For judgments.

When Parker remained silent for several seconds, Genna answered, "We're taking a quick trip up north to check conditions before a group from Boston arrives to go snowmobiling and cross-country skiing. We want to go now so we don't miss your mom's party this weekend." She divided a glance between Parker and Noelle, her brow creasing as she elbowed Parker. Returning her attention to Eli, Genna said, "Anyway, I left my snowshoes in Hetty's plane, and she's out on a trip at the moment, so I was hoping I could borrow yours?"

"Um, yeah. I'll go dig them out of my closet." Eli started to leave but noticed his brother still staring at Noelle. "Parker? If you have something to say, just say it."

Parker slanted a sly grin at his brother. "No. Nothing. But I am glad you took my advice."

"Advice?" Genna sent Parker a querying look.

"Likewise, brother," Eli said before turning to Genna. "A couple months back Parker and I had a conversation about…not missing opportunities."

Genna glanced at Noelle. "Do you have any idea what they're talking about?"

Noelle lifted her shoulders. "None."

Parker motioned for Eli to hurry. "You were getting the snowshoes? We have a few more errands to run and have to arrange a plane that can leave at first light tomorrow." He smirked. "And we want to let you get back to what you were doing."

Noelle felt the heat that stung her cheeks, and she self-consciously smoothed a hand over her misbuttoned blouse.

Eli sent his brother a withering look as he headed down the hall to his bedroom.

"So…your sister was one of the women killed by the creep Eli is looking for?" Parker asked, his tone sympathetic. "I'm so sorry. I hate that we're meeting under these circumstances, but I'm glad to finally make your acquaintance."

Genna blinked and glanced at Noelle. "What am I missing?"

"Noelle and Eli dated in college. They were pretty serious to hear Eli tell it. But the family never got the chance to meet her before they went their separate ways after graduation."

"Oh," Genna said, then, "Oh!" as if suddenly remembering who Noelle was. A pink flush rose in her cheeks as she flashed an embarrassed grin and schooled her reaction. "Yes, it's nice to meet you, Noelle. I hope we'll be seeing more of you in the future." Genna's tone put a period at the end of the sentence, but a lift of her eyebrows made it a question.

"I don't know. I only plan to be in town until my sister's funeral, but that's on hold until the medical examiner releases her body."

Parker and Genna exchanged a look Noelle couldn't interpret, and she fumbled for a way to change the topic.

"Has Eli asked you to our mom's party?" Parker asked.

"Um, no. Kansas has, but I don't think—"

Parker snorted. "What is wrong with my brother? Of course you're invited. I'll talk to him."

"You don't have to—I mean, I appreciate the invitation, but..." Desperate for a way to change the subject, Noelle started to ask why they weren't driving to their destination, then caught herself. Had she really been gone from Alaska that long? The sheer size of the state and vast wilderness without any roads meant getting to remote areas required small planes, often seaplanes that landed in lakes or on rivers. What few roads there were often required long roundabout trips around mountain ranges to get from point A to point B.

Fortunately, Eli returned a moment later, carrying his snowshoes with him. "Glad someone can get some use out of them. Until I wrap up this case, I don't see myself getting away anywhere for recreation."

"Except Sasha's party, you mean?" Genna asked.

"We've invited Noelle to come, so you two work out the details, okay?"

Parker leaned close to his brother and muttered something like "finishing what he started" under his breath, his grin wickedly teasing.

Eli sighed and opened the front door. "Don't you have to be going now?"

Parker laughed and gave his big brother a hug on the way out. Genna, too, stopped for an embrace and a cheek kiss. "Thank you, Eli. We'll bring them back in a couple days." Turning to Noelle, she waved and called, "Nice to meet you, Noelle."

Noelle returned a wave as the door closed behind the couple.

Eli faced her and groaned. "Sorry about that. I hope they didn't put you on the spot while I was out of the room."

"You mean any more than we already did looking like this?" She waved a hand to her buttons and ran her fingers through her hair.

Eli skewed his face with mortification. "I haven't heard the end of this. Parker will pull this out to embarrass me at family dinners for years to come."

Noelle noticed he didn't mention the upcoming party, and her chest squeezed. Was there a reason he hadn't invited her before now? And since the subject had come up with Parker and Genna, why wasn't he asking her now? Noelle had to battle down a swell of hurt. Was her relationship with Eli amusing to the family? She wanted to believe he meant the fact that Parker had interrupted their interlude, but old demons whispered that she might be the source of the awkwardness.

Did his family have a problem with Eli dating a woman

of Korean descent? Was there another reason Eli seemed reluctant to introduce her to the whole family?

She swung away from him, struggling to keep her composure. How many times had she fretted over these questions in college? Eli's family was so important to him, such a big part of his life. How could she ever fit in? Even if race weren't a part of the equation, she didn't have warm familial experiences as any sort of reference. She was terrified that once the Coltons met her, she'd prove a disappointment somehow. That she'd embarrass Eli or cause dissension in the family in some way, because that was all she knew of family life. Rejection. Regret. Isolation.

Eli moved up behind her and wrapped his arms around her, kissing the side of her neck. "Now where were we?"

She wiggled free and buttoned her blouse correctly, tucking the tail in her slacks. "Maybe it's a good thing Parker and Genna stopped by when he did. They saved us from making a mistake we'd regret."

"A mistake?" He sounded truly stunned by her assessment, and she pivoted to face him, frowning.

"Yes, a mistake. I'm only in town for a few days, and sex between us would be fraught with all kinds of emotional baggage. We'd be foolish to open old wounds like that."

He lowered himself slowly to the couch. "Emotional baggage," he mumbled and bit the inside of his cheek. Then glancing up at her, he firmed his jaw. "The night we went to the Cove for dinner, you agreed to answer my questions about why you shut me out after college if I shared case information with you."

Her gut swooped, and her mouth dried.

"I found a way to legitimately include you in the investigation. I've given you access to confidential files in the name of finding the killer. Now it's your turn to make good on our deal."

Noelle rubbed her hands on her slacks and moved across the room. If only the physical distance were enough to reestablish the emotional distance she'd once created.

Or had she? Seeing Eli again, the speed with which she'd fallen back under the spell of his blue eyes, his intoxicating kisses, his magnetism would say she'd never gotten over him the way she pretended. Maybe all she'd ever done was bury her feelings, hide from the truth, fool her heart into believing she could find happiness without him.

But had she been happy these past many years?

Content, maybe. But she'd had no interest in dating anyone else. She'd not wanted second best. She'd searched for ways to fill the hole in her life by reading romances, learning yoga, working overtime. All of her attempts helped, in their own way, yet the empty ache remained.

"Is it smart to start this conversation when Asher is due here in a little while? Maybe we should wait until—"

"Noelle." Eli's tone stopped her. "I deserve answers, and I want them. Now."

Chapter 10

Noelle took a deep breath as if fortifying herself for a giant task. Her unease with this conversation pooled anxiety in Eli's gut as well. Did he want the truth? Was there some dark story? Another man? A life-threatening illness?

He fisted his hands, bracing for what was coming, expecting a sucker punch and tensing his abs to receive the blow.

"You're right," she said, her chin bowed to her chest, her fingers tangling nervously. "Like I said before, it was never your fault. Truly. I just…" She turned to stare out his window at the November darkness. "I was scared."

"Of what?"

"More of what I already knew."

"What does that mean? Wasn't I good to you?"

"Not you. My family."

Eli huffed in frustration. "Noelle, come sit by me. I don't want to talk to your back."

She turned, and when he saw the glimmer of tears on her cheeks, his heartbeat stilled. Softening his tone, he patted the cushion next to him and murmured, "Please, sweetheart. Come here."

Her shoulders slumped, but she finally joined him on

the sofa. He placed a hand on her knee and nodded once. "Okay, go on."

"Geez, where to start?" She wiped her cheeks and lifted her gaze to his. "You saw how hostile my aunt was toward me. She doesn't want me to inherit, doesn't want me to have a say in Allison's burial, because she doesn't accept me as real family."

"Because you were adopted?" he ventured.

"Right. Thing is, my mother and father tried for years to have a child. When they couldn't, they adopted me. I was six years old, not the baby they wanted, but I was the first child that came available through the agency they were using."

"What happened to your biological parents? Where did you live before you were adopted?"

She lifted one shoulder and pulled a tissue from her pocket to blow her nose. "I never knew my real parents. I was told I lived with my biological grandmother for a couple years, but I was too much for her to handle apparently. She turned me over to the orphanage. My earliest memory is of crying and clinging to an older woman, who turned her back and walked away, leaving me with a stern lady at the children's home."

"Oh, Noelle. I'm sorry."

"So...anyway, my dad was eager to finish the adoption process, and he pushed Mom to accept me rather than wait for a baby. Apparently, my parents had a few strikes against them that made them less than sterling potential parents. Lower income, some minor reservations from the social worker... Nothing to stop the adoption, but Dad didn't want to risk being knocked off the list, I guess. Mom was never one hundred percent on board, but they took me in just the same so they would have the child they wanted."

Eli scowled. "How do you know all this? You were only six."

"Oh, they told me. More than once. It was held over my head when I acted out. 'Be grateful you have a home at all. You weren't our first choice.'"

Eli's jaw dropped, and he gaped at her. "Are you serious? That's awful!"

"I took it to heart, too. I did everything I could think of to earn their love and make them glad I was their child. I lived in fear of them sending me away if I didn't behave just right or proved unworthy in some way."

He continued to goggle at her, nausea churning inside him as he imagined the stress and emotional pain she grew up with. "That's a terrible thing for them to have put on you! Good grief, Noelle…"

She raised a hand. "There's more." She took a beat to gather her thoughts, and Eli edged closer, wrapping her hand in his. "I was the only Korean student in my school in Anchorage. We had a few Black students and a large Inuit population along with white people, but I was…the only Asian. I stuck out—or at least I felt like I stuck out. I had a friend or two, but kids are fickle, and they would abandon me for other friends when I got teased."

Eli's chest hurt. He could only imagine how Noelle had struggled and ached as a child. He wanted to scoop that young girl into his arms and hug her and tell her she was valued and loved. Instead, he drew grown-up Noelle into his arms and pressed her head to his shoulder. "I'm so sorry, sweetheart. That's horrible. I never knew."

"Because I didn't want you to know. I never wanted you to know anything about my family or my past. I wanted to leave my past behind me. I knew how golden your childhood was and how you treasured your big family, and I had nothing that remotely resembled that."

He opened his mouth to say something, anything to soothe her pain, but she must have anticipated what he intended, because she cut him off, adding, "And I especially didn't want your pity. I still don't. Back then, I wanted anything you felt for me to be genuine, to be mine because you really cared and not because you felt sorry for me."

"Can't I feel sorry for how you were treated and still care about you for who you are?" He stroked her hair and felt the tremble that raced through her. He tightened his hold on her, wanting to pour himself into her and chase out all the ugly memories, all the hurtful words and unfair shame her parents put on her.

"Maybe. I don't know. I didn't think so for a lot of years." She exhaled, and her warm breath on his neck stirred something tender deep in his core. "Allison was born when I was ten. Just like that, my parents had the baby, the biological child, they'd dreamed of. They pampered and coddled and spoiled her. She could do no wrong, whereas I was just in the way."

"And you're sure this wasn't just your youthful jealousy of the new baby talking? Couldn't some of your memories be skewed by immaturity? I know I had a hard time sharing my parents' attention when my brothers came along."

"You have to *have* your parents love and attention to be jealous of losing it." Her voice cracked, and she paused and cleared her throat. "No, I knew I was in the way, that they didn't want me around, because I overheard my mother tell my aunt—"

Her phone rang, interrupting her, and Eli grimaced.

He hated for her story, her explanation to be left hanging at such a crucial point.

"Don't answer it. Finish what you were saying."

But when she glanced at her phone, she held up a finger. "I should take this. It'll only be a minute."

He leaned back on the sofa cushions and watched as she carried her phone across the room to take the call.

"Yes? And what did he find?" Noelle's face creased with what appeared to be confusion. "Are you sure? But I didn't have a problem before—" Her face grew pale, her expression stark.

Eli sat forward, alarmed by Noelle's reaction to her call.

"I see. Yes, of course. Thank you for calling." She disconnected, then stood with the phone in her hand, staring blankly at the floor.

He shoved to his feet and crossed to her. "What was that about?"

Noelle jerked her head up as if startled to find him there. "I, um…" She shook her head, then took a deep breath. "Do you remember earlier I said I'd had an accident, hit my nose?"

He lifted a finger to the purple smudges still coloring her face. "Which gave you these souvenirs."

She nodded. "It was a car accident."

Eli stiffened. "What? When?"

"A few nights ago. I was driving over the mountain ridge to redo the paperwork on Allison's funeral—that's another story—and my rental car's brakes failed. I left the road and hit a tree. Airbag did this. Otherwise, I'm fine. Sore muscles, but fine."

"Okay," he said, his tone anything but okay. "So who was that call?"

"The rental company. Their mechanic examined the brakes to determine why they failed."

"And?" he asked, his gut tightening as if bracing for a blow.

"The brake fluid had drained out. It was fine the first several days I drove it, but...within a few hours of when I wrecked, the brake line had been cut."

"Cut?" Eli repeated, stunned. Chilled.

Noelle lifted a shaking hand to her mouth. "The mechanic said it was a clean slice, not a tear."

"Then it was intentional. Someone wanted you to wreck."

She raised wide frightened eyes to his. "It seems so."

Chapter 11

Asher arrived a few minutes later and strode into the living room, dividing an all-business look between Noelle and Eli. "All right, what's going on? Have you made a break in the case?"

After a perfunctory greeting, Noelle turned her back and found a tissue to blow her nose and wipe her face. Asher sent Eli a curious look that silently asked about Noelle's emotional state.

Eli debated telling his partner about Noelle's accident and the cause, but until he figured out if and how it fit in with the Fiancée Killer case, he wouldn't distract his partner with it. Eli would keep a close eye on Noelle himself, while Asher focused on the new twists to the murder investigation.

He led Asher to the kitchen table where Noelle's laptop and paperwork were still spread out, and he walked Asher through her findings. Eli covered what he'd learned after speaking to the experts in Seattle and the incriminating evidence that Scott's work was significantly skewed.

Throughout Eli's explanation to his partner, Noelle hovered close by, nodding her confirmation whenever Asher looked to her in stunned disbelief.

When Eli finished spelling everything out, Asher's expression reflected the same shock and righteous anger that had racked Eli since he'd learned the news. Asher huffed his exasperation and slapped a palm on the tabletop.

"That son of a—" Asher cut his eyes to Noelle and swallowed the rest of the epithet. Taking a moment, his jaw tight, Asher asked, "Have you confronted Montgomery yet?"

"No. I wanted you to be in the loop first. And we need to proceed carefully. This is volatile stuff. Until we get an explanation from him, we can't fly off the handle, or—"

"Or punch him in his geeky, coffee-guzzling face?"

Eli chuffed a humorless laugh. "I know how you feel, but before we blow this case up, we need to be sure we're reading this right and not making false assumptions. We should build our case before we confront him. This—" he waved his hand at the laptop "—may have a legitimate explanation."

Asher arched an eyebrow. "Really? I think there are only two possible explanations. He's covering for the killer, or he's incompetent in his job. Both are pretty damning for Montgomery."

Noelle moved from the counter where she'd been leaning, listening, and said quietly, "It could be worse than that."

Both men lifted their eyes to her.

She wet her lips. "I think you should consider the possibility that Scott *is* the Fiancée Killer."

Noelle watched the color drain from Eli's face, then, in the next moment, his blue eyes turned flinty. "You're right. All options have to be on the table."

Asher balled and flexed his fist on the tabletop, clearly struggling with a fresh wave of rage. "Right under our noses," he muttered before rising from the table to stalk the floor.

"So what is our next move?" Eli asked.

"Call him on it." Asher braced his hands on his hips, and his nostrils flared as he stared back at his partner. "We show up at his house tonight with a warrant to search his place for evidence."

"Is what we have here, the discrepancies in his work, enough for a judge to issue a warrant?" Noelle asked. "I offered the worst scenario only to keep all the possibilities open. But we can't dismiss the possibility he just made some uniform errors or something threw off his calculations or—" She raised her shoulders and shook her head.

"So we gather more evidence against him," Asher said flatly. "Where do we start?"

"Well," Noelle said, moving to her laptop and scrolling through the open files and charts. She bit her fingernail as she mulled over what they knew and turned it to look at different angles in her mind. "The thrust of the misinformation has to do with the time of death, the amount of time the bodies had been left to decompose. Why would he focus on that?"

Eli drew a slow breath as he scrubbed hands over his face. "Alibi."

Noelle cut a sharp look at him. "What?"

"The time of death helps us in several ways, but a key factor in regard to eliminating suspects is whether they can provide an alibi for the time the crime was committed."

She considered this, a niggling sense they were on the verge of breakthrough teasing her brain, dancing just out of reach. "But we don't have precise times for the women's deaths," Noelle said. "Just estimates, give or take *days*. Even *weeks* for the first victims."

Asher joined them at the small kitchen table again, his eyes bright with determination. "*Does* Montgomery have an alibi? Where was he for the days or weeks when we believe the women were killed, based on the adjusted estimates the Seattle experts derived?"

Eli shook his head slowly, his frown dark and troubled. "I don't know, but we need to figure that out."

"How?" Noelle asked. If her own gut was twisting in knots and adrenaline spiking her pulse, she couldn't imagine how Eli and Asher felt.

Frustrated? Edgy? Betrayed? Guilt pinched her for having dumped this seismic information on them. But if it was the break they needed, if it led them to catching Allison's killer, if it meant other women's lives were spared, she couldn't regret it.

Squaring her shoulders, she asked, "In order to get to the remote areas where the bodies were found and commit the murders without leaving any evidence that connected him to the crime, the killer would need more than a few hours. That takes planning and time for execution." She grimaced. "Sorry poor word choice. I mean, time to commit the murder without leaving key evidence behind."

The men exchanged a look, and Eli nodded. "She's right."

"So who at your office would have a record of when Scott took leaves of absence from work or called in sick? He'd have to have an excuse for being gone for several days at a time without raising questions. Wouldn't he?"

Eli's face brightened. "He would." He checked his phone. "It's pretty late. Do you think we can get Joetta from HR down to the office now to show us Scott's personnel file?"

"Not without a court order," Asher replied.

"Well, then, let's get busy. Wake a judge or two."

Three hours later, the groggy and disgruntled human resources manager handed Eli the file with Scott Montgomery's personnel information. "Can I ask what this is about?"

"You can ask, but I can't answer."

The HR manager rolled her eyes. "I don't see why it couldn't have waited until morning."

"Sorry to have disturbed your sleep, Joetta, but this is urgent," Asher said, looking over Eli's shoulder as Eli thumbed through the file. The men thanked her again and took the file upstairs to their office where Noelle was waiting.

"Well?" Noelle asked.

Eli waved the file and took a seat behind his desk to spread the pages out for examination. "Let's see. Vacation time requests... Here we go." Eli read out the dates of Scott's past vacation days while Asher cross-checked the times with the new information about the murders Noelle's work had derived. One after another, the dates synced with the newly adjusted timeline for the women's murders.

"So every time one of the Fiancée Killer victims was murdered, Scott was on leave from work." Noelle's expression hardened. "That sounds pretty incriminating to me."

Eli ground his back teeth. "Yeah, but it's also circumstantial. I'm just not ready yet to make such a drastic accusation without hard evidence tying him to the crimes." He glanced at Asher. "We need to talk to him, clear this up. I'll call him and ask for a meeting first thing tomorrow."

"What'd he say?" Asher asked the next morning, long before anyone else in the ABI had made it into the office.

Unable to sleep with this new information ping-ponging in his brain, Eli had come to work, only to find Asher already there.

"He was understandably curious and concerned why we wanted to talk to him, and when I told him it was a personal matter, he suggested we come to his house rather than discuss it at the office. I agreed."

"His house?" Asher grunted. "As long as we're going, should we get a search warrant for his house and car?"

Eli nodded. "Can't hurt. Let's send it to Matthews again since he just granted the one for Scott's personnel records and is familiar with the case."

"Right," Asher said, turning his chair to get started on the legal forms to request the search warrant.

Eli, meantime, called Noelle and updated her. "We're meeting with Montgomery at his house later this morning. Do me a favor and don't go anywhere alone until we figure out who cut your brakes and why."

She was silent for a moment but finally agreed. "Call me as soon as you get back from Scott's?"

"I will."

"And you be careful, too. I guess I don't have to tell you if he is the killer, and he realizes you've picked up his scent, he's likely to be dangerous."

"I'm trained for this stuff, Noelle. But...thank you for your concern." He gave a half grin she couldn't see, but he poured gentleness into his tone. "It's nice to know you care."

She was quiet again, then said softly, "Of course I care. That's never been the issue for us." He heard her sigh. "But we'll finish that talk later. Today you need to concentrate on handling Scott and solving this case. There'll be time for our personal problems later."

"I'm going to hold you to that."

Across the room, Asher stood and grabbed his coat. "We're on. Judge Matthews will see us in his chambers in fifteen minutes. Let's ride."

When Eli and Asher had the search warrant for Scott's home and car secured, they headed to the street address listed in his personnel file, using a GPS map application as a guide.

"You've never been to his house before, either?" Asher asked as Eli drove. "Do you not find that odd?"

"No. There are plenty of folks at the office whose homes I haven't been to. I got along with him well enough at the office or if he joined the group for a drink after hours, but I never considered him a close enough friend to drop by his house."

Asher scowled.

"Look, this should go without saying," Eli said, "but since I know you're both interested in Kansas—"

"What!"

Eli raised a hand to stave off argument. "Dude, I have eyes. I'm not stupid. You both stare at her like she hung the moon when she's not looking. All I was going to say is, keep an open mind. We have to keep our personal feelings about Montgomery and the possibility he's duped us all these years in check. Be professional."

Asher gave a nod and pressed his splayed hands on his thighs. "I know. I'm cool."

The voice on Eli's GPS directed him to turn, and as he did, he asked, "What's the house number again?"

"Two twenty. That'd be it," Asher said, bending forward for a better view through the front windshield. "I'm beginning to see why he never had us over for beers after work. That's one of the smallest houses I've ever seen."

"Don't judge. He's a bachelor, and a little house is all he needs. Besides, it may be bigger on the inside than it looks." Eli parked on the street in front of the small house.

"You're sure he's expecting us? The windows look dark." Asher opened the passenger door and climbed out.

"He picked the time, so he knew we were coming." Eli got out and joined Asher on the sidewalk to the front door. The lawn was winter-dead, and the deciduous trees appeared skeletal without their leaves, but Scott's yard was neat and trimmed, showing it had been cared for through the summer. "If he's not here, then we let ourselves in. We have the warrant, so we're covered."

Eli reached the door first and knocked firmly.

Asher tucked his hands in his pockets and scanned the yard. "This is a nice area. Not a lot of neighbors, but if you like privacy, that's a plus."

When Scott didn't answer the door after a minute or so, Asher knocked again louder, calling, "Scott? Are you there? Open up! It's Eli and Asher."

Eli moved his gaze over the doorframe, looking for a Ring or similar app-synced camera. No buzzer, but he did locate a small camera over the door. He looked right into the camera and waved. "Scott? You there? Can you let us in?"

Asher tested the doorknob, and when it turned, he pushed the door open. "Scott? Hey, Montgomery, are you here?"

They both stepped inside, and Eli led the way deeper into the house. Lights appeared to be off throughout the residence.

"I'll check the bedroom," Asher said as he moved down the short hall to the next room.

Eli swept the living room with an attentive gaze. The room was sparsely decorated and had only basic furniture—a couch, a side table with a lamp, a flat screen TV on the wall. The only wall art was a modern piece in dark tones and slashing lines that gave Eli a creepy sensation.

Turning from the disturbing art, he spotted a piece of paper taped to the bottom of the TV screen. His name had been printed on the folded sheet in block letters. He pulled the paper down and opened it. The note read simply, *Surprise!*

As he puzzled over the note, the blink of a green light caught his attention from the corner of his eye, and he turned to look for the source. What he found under the side table chilled him to the marrow. The wires, tubes and countdown timer attached to an initiator left no doubt.

Scott had rigged his house with a bomb. Eli and Asher had likely triggered the timer when they'd entered the house.

The timer screen read 00:12.

00:11

00:10

Eli's feet started running before his brain could fully form his next thought.

"Asher, run! Bomb!" he yelled as he fled the living room.

Chapter 12

Eli tore through the front door and down the sidewalk toward his Jeep. He dove behind his Renegade for protection. From behind his vehicle and with a mental clock counting *four, three, two,* he rose only enough to see if Asher was behind him.

Asher appeared in the front door just as Eli's mental clock hit one.

Ducking low again and raising his arms around his head, Eli braced, prayed.

The explosion shook the ground, thundered in his ears and echoed in his chest. Bits of building material rained down on him as the small house was blown to bits.

When his ears quit ringing, the sound that reached Eli first was a guttural cry of anguish.

Asher.

Pulse racing, Eli ran back toward the house and found his partner lying among the blasted debris and burning detritus of Scott's house. "Asher!"

He knelt beside his friend, who, while in one piece, had clearly caught a considerable amount of the building-supply shrapnel. Glass shards, splintered wood, bent metal and tattered roofing tiles lay in a mosaic of destruction, with Asher in the middle. Bleeding. Groaning. But alive.

"Where were you hit worst?" Eli asked, hearing the note of panic in his voice. *Stay calm. You can't freak out. Manage the situation.*

"Hard to say," Asher rasped, his face pinched in pain.

Eli did a quick survey of Asher's limbs, head and torso, checking for any critical injuries. He yanked off his coat and draped it over Asher, hoping to stave off shock. Next he stripped down to his undershirt, pulling the T-shirt off to soak up blood as he applied pressure to his partner's injured leg. "Can you hold this while I call for an ambulance and some uniforms to secure the scene?"

After pulling his top shirt back on, Eli called for help, his gaze taking in the rubble.

Clearly Scott had no intention of returning, was in full fugitive mode now. If there had been any evidence in the house to support or refute Scott's involvement in the Fiancée Killer case, it was now either burning or scattered, shredded and tossed to the four winds.

Eli gritted his teeth, frustration and adrenaline tap dancing along his nerves. He hated that Scott's duplicity had been right under his nose, and he'd missed it. He refused to let the bastard win. Whatever his part in the Fiancée Killer murders, whether perpetrator or accomplice, Eli swore that he would make Scott Montgomery pay.

Noelle read the data that her latest calculations had spit out and frowned. She'd spent the entire night and morning gathering information, statistics and expert opinions from both forensic specialists and data analysts to double- and triple-check her results.

But the more information she got, the more certain she was that Scott Montgomery was either the sloppiest scientist and most negligent medical examiner in history or one of the smartest to have so neatly altered the crime scene data and forensic data to yield the results that served him best. And gotten away with it. Until now.

She didn't want to believe Scott was guilty of anything nefarious, largely for Eli's sake. Being betrayed by someone he worked with and trusted had to be a painful blow. *Like the sucker punch you dealt him when you walked away.*

She shook her head and shoved the guilty thought aside. She could reexamine her past with Eli once the pressing issues related to this murder investigation were resolved.

She was scanning the table integrating meteorologic history, entomological findings, environmental conditions and decomposition studies with everything the investigation had yielded when her phone rang.

Her pulse skipped seeing Eli's number on her screen. "Hi, did you talk to Scott? What did you learn?"

"No and a lot. In a sense. I—" He sounded odd. His voice quavered a bit, which was highly unusual for the man with the courage and constitution to investigate gruesome serial murders and manage the roughest of criminals.

"Eli? What's wrong?"

"I'm at the hospital."

"What!" she cried, not caring how much her reaction gave away about her feelings for him.

"I'm fine. But Asher's pretty banged up." She heard him exhale heavily. Wearily. "We're both lucky to be alive. Montgomery had rigged his place with a bomb that was triggered when we entered his house. Clearly he had something to hide and wanted to both destroy the evidence and take out the people who were onto him. He accomplished one of the two goals."

Noelle sank onto a nearby chair. Her mind spun as she rattled off questions. "How bad are Asher's injuries? Is there anything I can do? Where is Scott?"

"Asher will live, but he's going to be in the hospital for a few days, recovering. He's in radiology now for CT scans, checking for internal injuries."

"But how—" She cut herself off. "Never mind. I'll get the whole story when I get there. Which hospital?"

"The only one in town." He forced a note of humor to his tone. "We're lucky we weren't farther out in the mountains. He was bleeding pretty heavily."

"And you promise you're all right?" she asked, a lump knotting her throat at the idea of anything happening to Eli.

"Minor cuts and scrapes. I'll be fine. You really don't have to come to the hospital."

"Of course I'm coming," she said, already gathering her purse and coat and keys to the replacement rental car. "Your partner was injured, and I want to be there for you."

And my findings are the reason you were at Scott's house to begin with. She clenched her jaw as guilt tripped through her.

Eli didn't reply, and for a moment she thought she'd lost her connection.

"Hello? Eli?"

"Thanks, Noelle," he said, his voice thick. "I'd appreciate the company. I'm in the ER waiting room at the moment, but they'll be moving Asher to a room soon."

She paused at the hostel door, glancing back at her laptop and the files spread out. On an impulse, she went back inside and packed her laptop into her messenger bag.

Noelle made it to the hospital in record time, but when she arrived, Asher was already settled in a private room.

Eli sat in a chair by the side of Asher's bed, but Noelle's focus was entirely on Eli, until she'd assured herself he was as whole and unharmed as he claimed. She gave him a fierce hug and clung to him for several long moments, betraying the depth of her concern and relief that he was safe. Her fingers combed through his hair, and he kissed the top of her head.

"What's this?" Asher said from the bed, his voice slurring slightly, likely because of pain medication. "Judging from…that steamy hug, she's more than…just a consultant." His lips twitched in a groggy grin.

They were spared from replying when the sound of quick footsteps preceded Kansas's appearance at the door. Her face was pale, her expression distressed, and her gaze flew to the bed immediately.

"Asher! Oh my God! What… Are you…?" Her boots clattered on the linoleum floor as she crossed to the side of Asher's bed and took in his battered and bandaged appearance. "Are you okay? Really?" When Kansas's gaze flew to Eli, a note of reproach hovered in her glare. "How did this happen?"

"Long story." Eli motioned for Noelle to take his seat, then returned a wry look to his cousin. "I'm fine, by the way. Thanks for asking."

His cousin's eyes widened. "You were there, too? At the explosion site?"

"I was. We both very nearly bought the farm. I only spotted the bomb with a few seconds to spare. Scott clearly wanted to take us out along with any evidence in his house."

Both of Kansas's hands flew up, palms toward Eli. "Hold on. Back up. Scott who? Not our Scott?"

"Our Scott," Asher said, though his eyes were closed, "isn't our Scott, after all."

"What?" Kansas said, dividing a stunned look between her cousin and Asher.

Eli moved to the corner of the room to drag another chair close to Asher's bedside. "Have a seat. I'll give you the lowdown after I get another chair from the hall."

Noelle gave Kansas a quick smile of greeting when the confused woman glanced at her.

"Noelle, hi." Kansas blinked as if surprised to see her there. "Were you with them, too?"

"No. I'm just here…for support."

Clearly Kansas heard the hesitation in her voice, since she gave Noelle a curious look.

"And why are *you* here?" Eli asked his cousin when he stepped back into the room with another chair. "You and Rafferty are always sniping at each other. I wouldn't have thought after you knew he survived that you'd be so worried about his sorry hide."

Kansas sat taller in the chair and cast an inscrutable look to Asher before glancing back at her oldest cousin. "Let's just say things aren't always what they seem."

Eli's brow snapped into a deep V. "What?"

Kansas ignored her cousin's confused frown. "Answer my question first. What did you mean about Scott? How is he connected to the explosion?"

"His house," Asher said.

Kansas gasped. "Was Scott hurt? Was he—"

"He wasn't there," Eli said quickly. "He's likely the one who set the bomb, with the intention of killing me and anyone who came with me to his house."

Kansas was clearly having a hard time taking in the truths Eli was laying out. Recognizing this, Noelle stepped in with more background.

"I volunteered to help Eli analyze the case with some data software I work with," she explained, "and it turned up inconsistencies with the forensic data. Based on the patterns of irregular information the program revealed, we think Scott Montgomery has been deliberately sabotaging the Fiancée Killer investigation."

Kansas glanced to her cousin, then to Asher for confirmation.

Eli nodded, and Noelle expounded on the information from the files she'd input, the resources she'd used as backup, the cross-references, the charts she'd double-checked and the patterns of misinformation her analysis had uncovered.

"I called Scott early this morning, after Noelle showed us what she'd found. He agreed to meet with me. He asked that we meet at his house for privacy." Eli took a beat, and his expression darkened. Noelle saw guilt in his eyes when he glanced at his injured partner. "I asked Asher to come with me as backup."

"Wasn't there. Rigged a bomb for us," Asher mumbled, clearly fuzzy from his painkiller.

"He left a note," Eli said, pulling a crumped sheet from his pocket. "Just says *surprise*. I'd say that's evidence the bomb was intentional."

"Surprise... I'd say so." Asher chuckled dryly, then groaned in pain.

Noelle frowned as she mulled the situation. "Are you saying he had time to rig a bomb and make his getaway in the couple of hours between your call this morning and when you arrived? That's hard to fathom."

Eli shot her a startled look. "I hadn't thought about that before now, but you're right. He had to have had the materials at his house already and known what he was doing to rig the explosive that quickly."

Asher grunted. "Or already made. In case we found out."

Noelle gasped. "So he could have been waiting for you to make the connection between him and the Fiancée Killer and set the trap days or weeks ago?"

"And only set the trigger at the door when he knew we were coming for him," Eli said in a dark tone of dawning understanding. "Damn it."

"But I don't..." Kansas began, her expression saying she was struggling to take in this turn of events. "You're saying you think Scott Montgomery is the Fiancée Killer? That's...crazy. I mean, Scott has always been so...nice." She furrowed her brow and slumped in her chair, her hurt and confusion plain in her expression. "A bit of a geek, yes. But he's never seemed like the sort who could kill anyone. Much less *five* women. Or his coworkers!"

"Serial killers are good at hiding their deviant tendencies," Eli said, then shook his head. "It burns me up that we missed what was right under our noses, though."

"The bastard..." Asher said, sounding even more groggy.

"Maybe we should relocate to the waiting room and let the patient have peace to sleep?" Noelle suggested.

"No," Asher muttered, "I'm fine." The word was barely out of his mouth before his breathing shifted to a deep, slumberous cadence.

Kansas leaned forward and gently touched his cheek, whispering, "Oh, Asher. I'm sorry I've been so awful to you. Please get better." When Kansas glanced up, her gaze narrowed on her cousin's puzzled look. "What? Can't I be worried about a colleague?"

"Did I say anything?" Eli asked, his grin teasing.

"So, Scott's on the run?" Noelle asked, in summary more than for information. "Now what happens with the investigation?"

Eli's blue eyes were icy with purpose when he faced her. "We find him."

The afternoon stretched out, with Asher's three visitors finding ways to pass the time and grapple in their own ways with the twist the investigation had taken. Neither Eli nor Kansas was willing to leave Asher's bedside for more than a few minutes to get coffee or use the restroom.

When the doctor checked on Asher, he said that CT scans showed Asher had a concussion. While the doctor was also concerned about possible infection in his numerous open wounds, antibiotics and a few days of rest would get him over the hump.

"When can he return to work?" Eli asked, knowing that he needed Asher's help to bring Scott in. The sooner, the better. Sure, he could read in ABI agents from other offices in the state, but Asher had been with the investigation from the beginning and shared the personal interest in bringing Montgomery to justice.

"Let's not rush things," the doctor said. "He'll need a couple days here before he's released, then a week or more bed rest at home. After he's released, someone will need to stay with him and monitor him for side effects. Seizures, trouble walking, signs of memory or sensory loss. Head trauma is serious business, and healing takes time. And he'll need clean bandages every day until the wounds are past the worst."

After the doctor left, Noelle could see Kansas's stress levels were off the charts. Clearly she was fretting over Asher's condition in light of the doctor's caution. Deciding she could help Kansas by distracting her from her worry, Noelle searched for a conversation topic they hadn't already covered that afternoon. "Tell me more about your role with the ABI, Kansas."

Eli's cousin smiled weakly at Noelle, though concern for Asher still filled her eyes. "I'm not specifically with the ABI. I'm with the state troopers in search and rescue."

"That's right." Noelle said, remembering that from when she'd been introduced to Kansas last week. "That's got to be difficult work. Stressful."

Kansas nodded distractedly. "But satisfying. Recently, I've helped with a few cases of missing persons that the ABI was involved with. In fact, we've had more cases than usual for such a small town recently, because—"

Eli's cousin stopped herself. Shivered. "I just can't get over the idea that Scott could be responsible for..." Her blue eyes found Eli's again. "I worked with Scott on the Whitlaw case a couple months ago, and he was so friendly toward me. He even apologized for not being more helpful with what his DNA tests revealed." Her nose wrinkled. "It makes my skin crawl, thinking he could be involved with the murders of those women!"

Eli nodded. "I know. We don't have more than circumstantial evidence against him now, but it certainly looks bad for him."

"I don't know how you two deal with so much tragedy and evil every day and not lose all faith in humanity," Noelle said, again trying to steer the conversation away from Scott, at least for a while. "My computers and numbers are dry and boring sometimes, but comfortably emotionless and drama-free."

"Oh, not all of my searches have sad outcomes." Kansas tugged up a corner of her mouth. "In fact, much of the time we're witnesses to happy endings."

"I love a happy ending," Noelle said.

"Don't we all?" Kansas grinned, then continued. "For example, a few months ago, we saved a couple of lost hikers at the Muskee Glacier Pass. They'd gotten dehydrated and confused and were wandering aimlessly until a bush pilot spotted them from the air. Then last summer, we found a runaway teenager from Shelby on the Two Bears River Trail north of town. His mother was so relieved to have her boy back safely, she hugged us as hard as she hugged him."

"I can imagine," Noelle said, though her heart stung, knowing her parents had never loved her that deeply.

"Probably the sweetest rescue was when we brought an elderly fisherman home after he got stranded. We reunited him with his wife on their forty-fifth wedding anniversary. She cried and said we'd given her the best anniversary present of all."

When Eli grunted, Noelle glanced his way, expecting to see him grinning over Kansas's stories. Instead, his frown was deeper than earlier. He stared at the floor, clearly lost in thought.

"Eli, what's wrong?" Noelle asked.

"Where was the fisherman found?" he asked, his dark gaze lifting to Kansas. "Was it Lake Chahoogee?"

Kansas tipped her head and blinked. "Um, no. He was on Byers Lake. But..." she wrinkled her brow in thought "...we did have a medical evac from Chahoogee a couple years ago. After a few years, you get calls from all over the state. Why do you ask?"

Eli dragged a hand down his face as he mumbled a curse under his breath.

"What is it, Eli?" Noelle asked, his behavior stirring a jittery feeling in her belly. Lake Chahoogee rang a discordant bell with her, as well, though she couldn't determine why. It unsettled her to think Eli had struck on something disconcerting as well.

He rose from his chair and split a look between Noelle and his cousin. "I don't want to say anything yet. It's probably nothing, but—" He flexed and balled his hands at his sides, and his mouth tightened. "I want to run an errand and check something. I'll be back soon."

Noelle stood as well. "I'll come with you."

His gaze shifted to his partner in the hospital bed. "I don't want to leave Asher—"

"Go," Kansas said. "Do what you need to. I'll stay with Asher."

Eli lifted one eyebrow. "If you're sure?"

"I am." Kansas waved him out of the room. "Both of you go. Do your thing. I'm fine."

Noelle followed Eli out of the room, having to take two steps for every one he took to keep up with his brisk strides. "Want to tell me what's going on?"

"Not yet. I don't want to alarm anyone if I'm wrong."

"Wrong about what?"

"Let's just say I don't believe in coincidence, and I've just realized something important about the Fiancée Killer investigation."

"Can I help?" Noelle asked. "Maybe run some new data through the algorithms? I have my laptop." She patted the messenger bag that hung from her shoulder.

"Not yet. First I want to talk to my father."

Not the answer she expected. Noelle ran a few steps to get ahead of Eli and stood in front of him to stop him. "Your father? What does he have to do with any of this?"

"Hopefully nothing." He took her hand and towed her forward with him as he plowed through the hospital door and into the parking lot. "But I'm afraid he can shed an important light on a disturbing angle of the Fiancée Killer investigation."

Chapter 13

Eli was largely silent and brooding on the drive to his parents' house. Noelle didn't pester him about his disturbing hunch and questions for his father. If he wanted her to know, he'd have told her what he suspected. Besides, she had her own preoccupying thoughts swirling in her brain.

Eli's parents. She was about to meet Eli's parents. Not in the way that a couple announced their serious intentions toward each other, of course, but she was nervous just the same. They were Eli's parents, after all.

Despite him asking many times in college for her to accompany him home, she'd always put him off. Healthy family dynamics were not her forte, and she'd feared that after meeting her, his family would disapprove of their relationship. If her own birth mother and adoptive family could all shun her, what other family could ever want her part of their ranks?

Eli parked at the side of his parents' house, a beautiful home outside town with views of the Chugach Mountains from their front porch and tall trees in the backyard.

Noelle took a deep breath of the pine-scented air as she climbed from the passenger seat. "You grew up here? In this house?"

"After about age six. We moved here from California,

and my father and uncle opened the outdoor adventures business the younger Coltons still operate." Eli hitched his head toward a building behind the main house. "Let's try back here first. Dad's probably hanging out with Mom while she works."

"While she works? Visitors don't distract her?" Noelle asked. She couldn't imagine having people around, talking and bothering her while she tried to concentrate.

"On the contrary, she claims people give her more creative energy. She loves having Dad's company."

"Creative energy? What does she do?"

"Come see." Eli took her hand and led her to the door of the building. He paused and stuck his head inside, calling, "Hello? Anybody home?"

Noelle heard joyful voices reply, "Eli! What a treat."

"Come in!"

Eli tugged her forward, and Noelle shuffled into the brightly lit space that was nothing she'd expected. Muddy-looking tables and shelves were filled with earthenware in varying states of completion. The works in progress cramped one end of the large room, while a pottery wheel and large kiln took up most of the far side of the room. The mingled scents of clay, paint and the herbal scent from an essential oil diffuser perfumed the air, while classic rock played from the speakers mounted on the walls.

A petite woman, with a face much younger than her silver hair would imply, rose from behind the pottery wheel, wiping her hands on a towel as she crossed the room. Her long hair was twisted into a messy bun, and her blue eyes were so like Eli's as to identify her as his mother even without context. She wrapped Eli in a tight embrace and kissed his cheek. "It's so good to see you, sweetheart!" The smile on his mother's face faltered as her eyes dropped to Eli's hip, where he wore his service weapon. "Oh, son. You know I don't like you wearing that thing when you're here."

"Sorry, Mom. But I'm on duty." With a wave of his hand, he gestured for Noelle to step forward. "Mom, Dad, this is Noelle Harris. She's a friend from my college days, and she's helping me with my current case." He motioned from Noelle to his mother, then to a man with salt-and-pepper hair, who moved out from behind a table in the corner of the room. "Noelle, my parents, Will and Sasha Colton."

Sasha's eyes glittered warmly as she drew close, smiling broadly. "Noelle! So nice to finally meet you!" Both of the older woman's hands stretched toward Noelle, but when Noelle raised her right hand to shake Sasha's, Eli's mother drew her into a firm hug instead. "We've heard so much about you!"

Noelle blinked. "You have?"

Sasha backed away to arm's length, still holding Noelle's shoulders and grinning. "Of course. You were the love of our oldest boy's life for years. He spoke of little else when he came home on holidays. I'm so glad you two have been able to renew your friendship."

"We, uh—"

Will tugged his wife's arm. "No hogging the guest, honey." He stuck his hand out, and Noelle took it in hers. Will pumped her hand heartily and offered his welcome.

Sasha faced her son then and gasped. "Eli, dear! What on earth happened to you?" His mother reached to touch the bandage on his forehead and scanned the other cuts on his face and hands.

"I was involved in an incident earlier today."

"An incident?" his father echoed, his tone saying he wasn't buying Eli's euphemism.

"I'm fine, but… Asher is in the hospital." Eli frowned, before continuing, "A house we were visiting as part of our investigation was rigged with a bomb. I saw it in time to warn Asher, and we both got out alive."

"How badly was Asher hurt?" Sasha asked, her face gone pale with worry.

"No broken bones, just a concussion. Mostly he's cut up and had a few bits of shrapnel removed from his legs and torso. He'll be fine with a few days of rest."

"Gracious!" Sasha put her hand to her chest and sank down on a nearby stool. "Days like this do not help me sleep at night, Eli. I worry enough about you taking on criminals without knowing you're nearly blown up by bombs!"

Eli stepped over to hug his mother again. "I know you worry, and I'm sorry. But I swear I'm as careful as I can be."

Noelle shifted her weight from one foot to the other. Sasha's maternal concern was touching but also foreign to Noelle. And it left her off-balance. She faltered, feeling both hollow for what she'd been deprived of as a child and a tad jealous of Eli's good fortune and strong bond with his mother.

Sasha shook her head and pasted on another smile. "Where are my manners? Noelle, can I get you something warm to drink? Coffee or hot tea?"

"No, thank you."

"Whiskey or gin?" Will asked with a wink. "It's five o'clock somewhere."

Noelle gave a polite chuckle. "I'm fine."

"How about you, son?" Will asked.

Eli refused a drink, as well. "On duty. I came because I need to talk to you about something important, Dad."

Will's gray-flecked eyebrows lifted. "Oh my. Well, sure. We can go in the house if you want privacy."

Eli nodded. "Noelle, do you mind chatting with Mom until I get back?"

Noelle's stomach flip-flopped. What if his mother drilled her about her past relationship with Eli? Or their current status? Or her family? Or—

Sasha hooked her arm with Noelle's and led her toward one of the cleaner tables and chairs. "You boys go on. Noelle and I will be getting to know each other."

Once the men exited, Sasha gave Noelle a warm but serious look. "Well, I feel like I already know you, thanks to everything Eli said about you when you were dating."

"That's what others have told me," Noelle said and flashed an awkward smile.

"What I don't know is what changed. Eli went from top of the world to a living hell. And forgive me for being blunt, dear, but I surely don't want to see him hurt again. If we can figure out what went wrong before, maybe we can put things right now." Sasha tipped her head as she invited Noelle to reply with a bob of her head.

"It's a long story. A complicated one for me to explain." Noelle chewed her bottom lip. How on earth did she give Eli's mother any kind of understanding or resolution when she was struggling for the strength and courage to give Eli the whole picture?

Sasha remained silent, patiently waiting for Noelle to say more, to find some words. Finally, Noelle swallowed hard and offered, "I guess it boils down to...fear. I loved him, but—"

"Stop." Sasha's blue eyes flashed hot as she pinned

a hard gaze on Noelle and raised a hand. "My dear, do not ever use *I love you* and *but* in the same sentence. Nor should you use *trust* and *but* together. Love and trust have to be unconditional. If you could not commit to Eli fully and unconditionally, then perhaps what you felt wasn't love at all."

Noelle flinched, the harsh assessment like a slap to her. Yet at the same time, Sasha's words seeped into the cracks and pits that had riddled Noelle since she broke up with Eli. She *had* let fear win. If she could do that, put fear over Eli, maybe she hadn't loved him enough.

She curled her fingers into fists and drew a restorative breath. "So how do I fix it? How do I get past the things that scare me so that I can love and trust Eli unconditionally?"

Sasha smiled broadly and pulled her into a firm hug. "Oh, Noelle, darling girl, you've just taken the first step. Wanting to change things is the first step."

"What's up?" Will asked as he took a seat in his favorite recliner. "And what are you leaving out about the bombed house you visited this morning?"

Eli settled on the couch across from his father and sighed. "I've said all I can for now. It's related to the serial murder case I'm working."

Will scowled, then bobbed a nod. "Then what is it you want to discuss?"

Eli drew a deep breath. "Caroline."

His father's chin jerked up. "What?"

"I know you don't like to talk about your sister, but I need to know a few details about her murder."

Will shook his head, a dark scowl drawing down the corners of his mouth. "Son, that case has been closed for decades. Our family has gone to great lengths to put that evil behind us."

Eli scooted to the edge of the cushion, leaning toward his father as he pressed on. "I know that. But I need to look at it again, and I only remember fragments of that day, the crime scene we stumbled upon. I need clarification. Confirmation. Details filled in that my child's mind may have warped or blocked."

His father dragged a hand down his face. "Eli, please don't go there. We moved to Shelby to put our loss, the media attention and notoriety behind us. Your mother and I made the decision long ago not to discuss her death with you any further after you finished the counseling sessions your doctor recommended. We felt it was better for you to put it behind you and build a new life, with happy memories here in Alaska. For *all of us* to make a fresh start."

"I understand your reasons and can appreciate what you did, but I need information."

His father sighed and tipped his head back against his chair. "All right. I don't like it, but if you say you need answers, I believe you."

Believe. His family's motto filtered through Eli's mind. As he had many times growing up, he appreciated his family's determination to have an open mind and trust each other. To support each other in all circumstances.

Eli studied the grim tension in his father's face. Revisiting his family's brutal murders, the disturbing crime scene he'd stumbled upon, had to be difficult for Will. "I'm sorry, Dad. I wouldn't dig this up if it weren't important."

His jaw tight and eyes bleak, Will raised one hand from his lap. "Ask your questions."

"I'm primarily interested in how Aunt Caroline's killer—"

"Jason Stevens." His father spat the name out in a low growl, like a foul word. "I don't like giving him the anonymity of a tag like *Caroline's killer*. He should bear the guilt and be recognized for the evil man he was."

"Stevens then." Eli paused to gather his thoughts. "I remember that Caroline and Stevens were both sitting on the couch in the living room when I found them. At first I thought they were asleep, but I realized soon after that that Aunt Caroline looked…odd. The color of her skin… Her eyes bulging—" He stopped short, knowing a more graphic description of his aunt's body was unneeded.

"Yes. You've told us this. The scene frightened you as a child, gave you nightmares for weeks until your counselor helped you manage your fears and memories."

"Maybe too well." Eli rubbed his hands on his jeans. "Some of the details are fuzzy. What was Aunt Caroline wearing? Her nightgown?"

"Wh—" His father blinked rapidly. "Why?"

"I hope it's nothing, but tell me. Please."

Will's hands fisted, and he swallowed hard. "Stevens had put her in a little black dress and stuck a diamond ring on her finger, playing out his fantasy that they were a couple."

Eli's gut clenched, and bile rose in his throat.

"After he drugged her and strangled her to death," his father continued, "he posed her with her left hand over her heart, so we didn't miss the ring, and her right arm around him as if they were cuddling." His father gave his head a small shake as if shuddering at the vile memory.

"Go on. What else did the investigators conclude?"

"Stevens had initially injected Caroline with a sedative.

Once he'd killed her and posed her, he injected himself with a lethal dose of the same sedative and died beside her. A far more peaceful demise than he deserved, the bastard."

Eli dropped his gaze to the floor, his brain processing this information with a growing unrest in his soul. Black dress. Diamond ring. Posed.

"Is that what you needed to know?" his father asked.

Scrubbing a hand over his chin, he sighed. "I'm afraid so."

"Can you tell me now why you needed to resurrect this dark period from our family history?"

Eli hesitated. Could he divulge what he suspected? It wasn't confirmed yet. His hunch was just that—a hunch. But what his father had shared was too similar to the current investigation to be coincidence. *I don't believe in coincidence*, he'd told Noelle earlier.

He cleared his throat and gave his father a grim stare. "When the victims of the Fiancée Killer were found, they were all wearing a diamond ring. Even the older more skeletal remains still had a ring on the left hand."

Will nodded. "So the news reports have said. That's how the case got that name, right?"

Eli gave a nod. "They're also wearing short black dresses, and the cause of death has been pinned as strangulation." For all that Montgomery had tainted the forensic records, at least that much could be confirmed.

"Like Caroline," his father said darkly.

"Very like Caroline. The victims we've found before scavengers got to the bodies have been posed with the ring hand up."

"Also like Caroline," his father rasped, his blue eyes

widening. "Are you saying the current killer is copying Caroline's murder?"

"Maybe. I need to run more checks and verify—"

"But why? Caroline was killed twenty-eight years ago! In southern California! What's the link?" His father stiffened. "Do you think that whoever is doing this could harm our family? Is he doing it to taunt us or—?"

Eli raised both hands. "I don't know anything for certain yet. I can't make assumptions without facts." He raked fingers through his hair and expelled a frustrated breath. He refused to believe that his assignment as the lead in this case and having been the first to find Aunt Caroline murdered was a coincidence. Was *he* the link? "Just in case, keep a close eye on Mom. Don't let her go anywhere alone."

His father's grim expression said he clearly read between the lines. "I'll tell her not to—"

"No." Eli lifted a hand in apology for his abruptness, then took a beat before adding, "You can't tell her or anyone else anything yet. This is confidential information related to my case. Besides, I don't want her frightened. Just…stay alert." Eli shoved to his feet. "I'll let you know what I learn after I look at this angle more closely."

His father stood, as well. "Eli, I—I'm sorry if we failed you back then, after Caroline and your grandparents' murders. That had to be a traumatizing thing for you to walk into."

Eli shrugged one shoulder. "You got me counseling."

"Some. But was it enough? Were we right to move you away from your friends and the only home you knew? To make such a drastic change when you were grappling with such horrible memories? Maybe it was a mistake for us to stop talking about it and shut it out like it never happened." His father raised a shaky hand to his mouth. "We thought we were doing what was best, but if we made it harder on you…"

Eli stepped over to his father and placed a hand on his shoulder. "I know you did your best with what you knew at the time."

"Were we wrong? Could you forget?"

"Clearly I shut out some of it," he said. "That's why I needed your help today. But… I did have nightmares of losing family. Finding my siblings and cousins dead or running from a monster who wanted to kill me. I still do on occasion."

Will's face reflected pain and sympathy. "Oh, son. I'm sorry. If we could do it over, your mother and I would do so many things differently."

Eli squeezed his father's shoulder. "Hey, don't dwell on it. We all do the best we can with the information and life experience we have at the time." He gave a soft, wry chuckle. "And I turned out all right, didn't I?"

His father's eyes grew moist, and he clamped both hands on Eli's upper arms. "You turned out better than all right. I am so very proud of you, Eli. Your work, your ethics, your support of our family… You're an inspiration, my boy." He drew Eli into a firm hug and pounded his back. "I just wish—well, never mind."

Eli backed out of the embrace and tilted his head. "No, say it. What do you wish?"

Will snorted and glanced away before drilling him with a look that was warm despite the ice blue of his father's eyes. The same eyes Eli saw every morning in the mirror. "Your mother and I have been so happy together. We fulfill each other and take strength from each other. She makes me so incredibly grateful."

Eli smiled. "It's obvious to anyone who knows you."

"I want that same happiness for you, dear boy. I wish you could find someone who brings you joy, someone you can settle down with and make a family. I don't want you to be alone, Eli. Not when marriage has been so good to me and your mother."

Eli's heart kicked. Images from a few nights earlier, the passionate kisses and whispered intimacies he'd shared with Noelle, flickered in his mind's eye. "I want that, too. I have for a long time, but…the woman I want to settle down with keeps pushing me away. I believe she loves me, but she's scared for some reason. She's been hurt before, and she hasn't trusted me enough yet to open up about what frightens her about our relationship."

"May I assume you're talking about the young lady out in the pottery studio with your mother right now?"

"Noelle. Yes."

"She's the one who broke your heart in college, isn't she?" his father asked.

"How do you know about that?" Eli asked. He thought he'd kept his personal affairs and heartache more private than that.

"To be honest, your mother picked up on it first. You went from talking about Noelle frequently when you were home on holiday to saying nothing at all after graduation. And you were far more subdued, even glum at times. Your mother put two and two together and shared her theory with me."

"Of course she did," Eli said and flashed a half grin. "She doesn't miss much. I never could get away with any shenanigans growing up."

His father chuckled. "That's as likely because you're

a terrible liar. You have more tells than a novice poker player."

Eli's eyebrows shot up. "I do? Like what?"

His father hitched his head toward the door, and Eli followed him out toward his mother's studio. "I'm not telling you. How would I ever beat you at poker again?"

Eli groaned. "I may never play poker again."

Giving him a clap on the back, Will sobered. "Just as long as you don't give up on Noelle. If you love her, fight for her. Be her safe place, and with patience and encouragement, she's bound to come around." Will's expression perked. "Say, why don't you bring her on Sunday to the family party?"

"It's been suggested, but she doesn't seem keen to meet the whole boisterous brood of us."

"Pssh." His father waved a dismissive hand. "I'll invite her and let her know we're nothing to fear. No vipers among us. No one bites. Teddy bears all."

Before Eli could mount a counterargument, his father headed out to the pottery shed.

Eli hurried to catch up to him. If his father came on too strong, would he scare Noelle away? He recalled what she'd said about her cold family, her isolation as a child and her discomfort with the dynamics of a large family.

When they reached his mother's studio, Noelle's expression was stark, her cheeks tearstained. His mother sat close beside her, an arm around Noelle's shoulders and clay-crusted fingers dabbing moisture from Noelle's face, leaving dirty smudges in her wake.

Eli's gut lurched. What the heck had happened? What had his mother said to Noelle?

He rushed to Noelle's side and crouched by her chair.

"Sweetheart, what's wrong?" He shot his mother a quick, scolding look.

Sasha lifted her chin. "Don't glare at me in that tone of voice. I did nothing wrong."

Eli grinned at his mother's familiar catachresis.

Noelle sucked in a deep breath and blew her nose on a questionable-looking rag from his mother's pottery cleanup supplies. "I'm all right. Really. And your mother has been nothing but kind."

Eli angled his head, trying to meet her eyes. "If you're sure…" Placing a hand on Noelle's knee, he asked, "Are you ready to go? I have what I need from my dad."

Noelle sniffled again and nodded. She led the way out of the pottery studio, clearly eager to leave.

Before following her, Eli hugged his mother and gave her a searching look. "What happened?" he mouthed.

"Talk to her," his mother whispered back.

Eli nodded. He planned to do exactly that.

Chapter 14

"You want to tell me what upset you when you were with my mother?" Eli asked when they were back in his Jeep headed to Shelby. "We have some time now to talk. Alone. No distractions."

"Yeah. Okay, but I want to know from you what this trip was about, too. You were very mysterious concerning what your father could contribute to the investigation."

"Sorry," he said, "I wasn't trying to be mysterious. I just didn't want to say anything until I was sure about my suspicion."

"And now you are sure?" she asked.

Eli cut a glance from the road to Noelle and nodded. "I am. I'm just not sure what to do with it."

"So spill. What did you learn?"

Eli drew a fortifying breath. "In college, did I ever tell you I had an aunt who was murdered when I was five years old?"

He heard her low gasp. "What!" Then a beat later, she said, "Wait. I think you did, just in passing. You didn't want to talk about it, so I let it drop. I mean, I had my touchy subjects that were taboo, so…" Noelle shifted on her seat. "What about your aunt?"

"The details of the murder scene, how she was killed,

how she was dressed and posed, even the engagement ring her killer put on her hand and made sure we saw are almost identical to the Fiancée Killer. My aunt's killer left her in my grandparents' living room, not out in the wilderness, and he killed himself beside her. But there are too many similarities to disregard."

Noelle said nothing for a moment, and when he glanced her way, her expression said she was deep in thought, digesting this new information in light of what they knew.

"Maybe it's just a coincidence?" she said, though her tone said she didn't believe that theory any more than he did.

"I've told you my belief about coincidence, especially in police work."

"But if Scott is behind all this, like we think, and he's recreating the scene of your aunt's murder—"

"Which I was the first to come across when it happened."

Noelle inhaled sharply. "Eli! You never told me that! At five, you saw your murdered aunt?"

He confirmed this with a bob of his head. "And here I am investigating the new murders."

"How can you sound so casual about this? He set a bomb to try to kill you when you sniffed out his guilt!" Noelle raised both hands to her face and groaned. "Eli, has this all been about some grudge Scott has against you? I mean, we determined earlier that the victims all have dark hair and blue eyes like the Coltons, like *you*! But when he started killing women, how could Scott have known you'd get the case instead of some other ABI agent? And what in the world did you do to set him off like this?"

Eli scrubbed a hand over his chin. "Hell if I know.

Scott's never really registered on my radar before now. He was just this geeky guy from forensics I saw around the office from time to time. I may have teased him at some point, but nothing vicious. Just the kind of good-natured ribbing all men do with each other."

"So, what does this mean? If this has something to do with a vendetta against you, where does it go now that Scott knows you're onto him and his first attempt to kill you failed?"

"Well, for one thing, I want you out."

"What? No!"

"Noelle, I want you far away from this case for your own safety. And we have to make sure anyone who knows you were working on the case with me says nothing about it. I don't want him coming after you to get to me."

She touched his arm, drawing his attention away from the road. Her face was grim. "He already knows."

"Huh? How?"

"That morning I came by ABI headquarters to get your files on the case, he stopped by. You told him you were including me on the investigation as a consultant."

Eli's gut swooped. "I did?"

"You did."

When the day in question replayed in his brain, Eli slapped the steering wheel and muttered a bad word.

"What's more, someone has already come after me. Someone cut my brake line, remember?"

The heat of anger rose in his blood and climbed to his cheeks. His temples pounded as he mulled the truth from a new perspective. Someone had targeted Noelle. Scott knew of her involvement helping with the case. Fresh resolve hardened inside him. "Well, then, here's the new plan. I want you to stay close to me until we figure out where he is and what he's planning. I know that puts you in the line of fire, so to speak, but I can protect you better if I'm with you than if I'm not."

"You really think I—"

"Or..." Eli squeezed the steering wheel as another option occurred to him. "Maybe you should go back to Seattle now. Handle your sister's funeral from there. I can see that your directions for her remains are handled the way you want."

"Go home?" Her voice was soft and flat. "Is that really what you want?"

"No. But I want you safe, and you'll be safer far away from Shelby."

"What if I'm willing to take the risk in order to see this case through? To see my responsibilities to Allison through? I'm not a quitter, Eli."

He jerked a sharp look her way and clenched his jaw. "Well, you were once."

Her despondent sigh reached him. "Oh. That. Right."

When he glanced at her, she was staring out the side window, her brow puckered.

"I guess it's my turn to spill." She angled her gaze to him again. "I was crying at your parents because your mom was so sweet to me, so interested in me and my life, so...caring..." She sniffed, then opened her purse to pull out a tissue and wipe her eyes, her nose. "It just drilled home to me all the more what I'd missed not having a mother who valued me."

Eli frowned his sympathy. "I hate that you felt unloved, Noelle. But are you sure you're not remembering it through a dark lens? Maybe the fact that they favored your sister means you were a little jealous and saw things in a dimmer light than reality. I mean, they adopted you. Parents who want a child enough to adopt don't—"

"I know what I lived, Eli." She huffed her frustration, and he was jabbed with self-recrimination. The Coltons had pledged to live by the credo *believe*, yet the first time Noelle presented him with truths about her life that he found hard to swallow, he'd doubted her. Was that why she'd broken up with him years ago? Had he unwittingly given her the perception he didn't believe her? Had he diminished her truths and discounted her reality without knowing? Guilt kicked him at the notion he could have broken the family's core value with the person he wanted to form his own family with.

"I'm sorry. You're right." He reached for her leg and gave it a quick squeeze of apology. "Only you can know what you experienced and how it shaped you. Please go on."

She blinked at him as if his confession caught her off guard. "Thank you for that. I—" She cleared her throat. "The thing is, after a point, I got what I asked for. I gave them reason not to want me, not to love me. I became belligerent and acted out. I pushed the limits and rebelled after I heard—"

When she fell abruptly silent, he cut a side glance to her. "Heard what?" Eli held his breath. He didn't want to know the awful thing she'd heard that had clearly caused a deep rift and a lasting pain.

"I heard my mother and aunt talking in the kitchen one day when I was about fourteen. After years of trying to be perfect for them and a model student and daughter, I heard my mother say it had been a *mistake* to adopt me. A mistake she regretted every day."

Eli muttered a curse and reached for her knee. "Lord, Noelle, I am so sorry. What a terrible thing for her to say!"

"Yeah. Well, that was the truth I lived with. Once I knew she didn't care about me, I saw no reason to behave or try to earn her love any more. I was angry and hurt, and I saw no reason not to be as difficult and unlovable as they seemed to believe I was. I couldn't leave home soon enough. The animosity grew between us throughout high school. After I left for college, I never went back to Anchorage. Never really even spoke to my parents and only talked to Allison occasionally."

Eli pulled the car to the side of the road. Once the Jeep was stopped, he turned on his emergency blinkers and the dome light. Facing Noelle, he cupped her cheek and held her gaze. She was telling him the deepest hurts of her life, and he owed her his undivided attention, his undiluted care and comfort. "Noelle, I—I wish I could do something..."

"You can't, though. Nothing can change the past." She squared her shoulders, then raised her chin. "I'm all right now. I've learned to move forward. I have my career, friends, and I've built a new life without my family."

"I hate to think of you not having the kind of family support I've had," he said. "I can't imagine how lonely you must have felt growing up. Why didn't you tell me all this in college?"

"I told you earlier. I didn't want your pity. We had something special, and I didn't want to tarnish it by dumping my miserable history on you. When I heard how you talked about your family and how important they were to you, I just couldn't tell you how terribly my own family didn't measure up to yours."

"We *did* have something special, Noelle." Eli framed

her face between his palms, his gaze probing hers, his heart breaking all over again. "And having heard all this about how heartless and cold your family was toward you, I have to wonder all the more why you would give up what we had."

"It's hard to explain. I'm not even sure I understand all the reasons. Fear can be complicat—"

Eli's phone rang, making Noelle start and fall abruptly quiet. "Ignore it," he said. "Finish what you were saying. This conversation is more important to me than whatever the person on the other end of that call has to say."

Noelle's expression softened, and her eyes reflected an appreciation and affection that made Eli's chest ache all the more. His precious Noelle had been deprived of love, undervalued for so many years. Yet knowing the strong, intelligent and capable woman she'd become despite her circumstances made him appreciate her even more.

The phone quit ringing, and he gave her an encouraging nod. "There. All gone. Now finish."

"I was only saying I'm still figuring out for myself what—"

Again his phone rang, and Eli growled his frustration.

"Answer it," Noelle said, pushing his hands from her face. "Your partner is in the hospital, and a colleague suspected of mass murder is on the run. Odds are it's *very* important."

A quiver chased to his core at the reminder of the chaos he'd left behind in Shelby for this side venture. "True enough."

He took the call, and without a greeting, Kansas said, "Thank goodness! I was starting to worry! How could you take off on some mysterious errand and not be in touch for hours when we know Scott tried to kill you this morning?"

"Sorry if I worried you. Noelle and I are headed back now."

"You missed Asher's neurologist, the one who'll be treating his concussion. He stressed the importance of Asher resting, no screens, no reading print, no activity for several days. His brain needs time to heal."

"Damn. Bad time for him to be out of commission, too," Eli grumbled. "This case just burst wide open, and our prime suspect is on the lam."

He heard Kansas grunt. "I'm sure he'd much rather be helping you hunt down that bastard than be lying in the hospital with a cracked head."

Eli pinched the bridge of his nose. "You're right. That was insensitive of me."

"No." Kansas groaned. "I'm sorry, Eli. I'm just edgy and out of sorts because of everything that's happened."

"We all are. Look, I'll check by the hospital when we get back in town, but then I have to go to the office and start putting these new puzzle pieces in place."

He disconnected with Kansas, and after putting his phone away, he faced Noelle again. "Okay. No more interruptions, I promise. Please…finish what you were saying. I want to hear everything."

"You have the gist of it, I think. What's important now is finding Scott, whether or not he turns out to be the Fiancée Killer."

"He's the key to solving the case, at a minimum." Eli nodded. "All right. Let's go home." After turning off the dome light, he pulled back onto the dark highway.

"We," Noelle said.

Head buzzing with too many thoughts, Eli blinked at her. "What?"

"You told Kansas *you* would be working on the new puzzle the case has presented. But I'm going to be working on it with you. You just said you're shorthanded since Asher is in the hospital. So *we* are going to figure this out together."

Warmth filled Eli's chest. He liked the sound of that. Sparing a glance from the road, he smiled at her and repeated, "We."

In order to have the space to spread out and the privacy to talk openly about their suspicions without someone in the ABI office overhearing, Eli and Noelle decided to work at his house.

"I'd like to stop by the hostel and pick up a few things if this is going to be an all-nighter, as I suspect—" Noelle caught the intrigued lift of Eli's eyebrow as he cut a lustful glance her way. She returned a dry look. "A *working* all-nighter, Colton. We're trying to catch a killer, remember."

He shrugged. "First we work, then we play."

Noelle snorted indelicately but gave no other reply. She turned her gaze out the passenger window, studying the lights of the town and harbor as they approached her hostel. Was *play* how he viewed any intimacies between them at this point? Noelle had never considered their lovemaking anything but the most private and intentional connection between them. Nothing about it had been casual. Playful at times, but never casual or intended as cheap thrills.

But if that was how Eli now thought of potential sex between them—an itch to be scratched, a fun distraction or stress reliever—perhaps it would do her well to rethink her position.

She angled her head back toward Eli, studying the masculine cut of his cheeks and jaw, made all the sharper and more defined in the dim glow from his Renegade's dashboard lights. His lips were pressed in a grim line at the moment, a sure indication his thoughts had reverted to his case. Scott's deception and vicious attack or some other stressor from a long litany clearly haunted him. She let her attention linger on his mouth, remembering all the sensations those lips had stirred in her in past years, all the private places on her body they'd grazed, tasted and wakened with tender manipulation.

A tingling flush raced over her skin, and she felt her breath hitch, as if Eli were kissing her now.

The crunch of gravel under tires roused her as Eli pulled onto the drive of her hostel and parked. She sobered quickly and retrieved her keys from the front pocket of her messenger bag. Seeing the empty place where her rental should be parked reminded her she'd left it in the hospital lot.

"We should probably pick up my car from the hospital parking lot on the way to your place," she said as she climbed out of his Jeep.

"Good idea," he said, waiting at his front bumper for her to precede him up the walkway to her door.

Hostel key in hand, Noelle approached the small concrete landing and aimed the key for the knob—and noticed the door stood ajar.

The wood around the latch plate was freshly scarred and splintered.

She gasped, and a chill washed through her.

Eli seized her arm. He tugged her backward, dragging her behind him with one hand while his other unsnapped the holster of his service weapon. "Stay here."

"But it's—"

His blue eyes glinted with steel. *"Stay here."*

Crossing her arms over her chest to ward off both the

cold of the Alaskan night and the foreboding of what could be inside, Noelle waited. Her breath clouded around her, the white puffs lit by the pinkish glow of the security lamp at the edge of the street. After a couple of minutes, she drew a breath, prepared to call to Eli for a progress report but stopped, the words in her throat. If someone was inside with Eli, she couldn't alert the prowler to Eli's presence.

Then she remembered what had happened the last time Eli had investigated suspicious circumstances at a house.

Rigged with a bomb...triggered when we entered...

His hoarse voice from earlier in the day echoed in her brain, and her blood flashed hot, then icy. "Eli, no! Get out! There could be another bomb!"

He appeared at the door, his face grim but calm. "It's all good. I checked for a trigger as I walked in, but when I saw the condition of the place, I realized a bomb wasn't the intruder's goal."

She frowned. "Condition of the place?"

He pulled the door open wider and waved a hand for her to enter.

Noelle looked past him, wary. "No bombs? You're sure?"

"I gave the place a pretty thorough search. No sign of anything remotely resembling an explosive device or components."

She hesitated another few seconds, working up her courage, until Eli sent her a look that asked, *Don't you trust me?*

She did trust Eli. With her life. But was she ready to trust him with her heart?

Another problem for another time.

He took her hand and led her inside the dark studio

apartment. He flipped the light switch by the door and lit the room.

Noelle squawked her shock at the upheaval that greeted her. The furniture had been upended, cushions flung about and ripped open. Her suitcase was dumped on the floor. Her possessions had been ransacked, broken, scattered. Loose paper was spread everywhere, and books unshelved. Drawers were open and carelessly emptied on the countertop. The scene was pure chaos. Pure destruction.

A sense of rage and vulnerability swamped her. The invasion of her privacy, the mistreatment of her belongings, the calculated disregard and intrusion...

She swayed on her feet, and Eli caught her elbow. Clinging to his coat sleeve, she wobbled to the kitchen chair that he righted for her.

"You should see if anything is missing and report the break-in to the landlord."

She nodded, numb and shaking. "Who would do this?" she muttered. "Why?"

Noelle covered her face with her hands and allowed a frustrated and rather frightened growl to roll from her throat. "I haven't even been here for two weeks! Hardly anyone even knows I'm here besides you, and my aunt and unc—" She snapped her head toward Eli, her hands balling in rage. "My aunt and uncle! I've already had to sign a second contract with the funeral home because of their meddling. Do you suppose...is their grudge against me, their disdain for me so great that they'd—" She stopped short.

Eli was shaking his head slowly, the anger and clarity in his gaze unnerving.

"Then who?" As soon as she spoke, an echo reverberated in her head. She'd asked the same question when she'd learned her brake line had been sabotaged.

"You're right that very few people know you're in town. But Scott is one of them, and he knows we had a relationship once, knows we've been spending time together since you arrived. If this is about me, as I'm starting to suspect, he could have lured you here to taunt me. He could have targeted Allison to get you here because of our past. The Fiancée Killer has already dug up my aunt's murder and copied it. Based on everything else we're learning, I'd say he's striking out at me through you."

If she hadn't already been sitting, Noelle might have slumped to the floor. As it was, her body shuddered, and her head spun. "You really think he killed Allison to lure me here? So that he could get at you... How? By hurting me?"

Or killing me. Ice rippled through her.

When Eli squatted beside her, she met his gentle eyes. "Noelle, think about it. Your brakes were cut. Intentionally." His voice was calm and soothing despite his frightening message. "I'd say Scott has already tried to hurt you. Or worse."

Scott...

Noelle sucked in a sharp breath as her gaze cut to the table where she'd been working. It was empty. A sensation like electricity raced through her veins. "Oh no," she rasped.

"What?" Eli whipped his head around to look across the room where she stared in horror.

"The paper files. All the sheets I'd printed off and the hard copies of information you gave me on the case." She swallowed hard, regret churning in her gut. "I—I had them on that table when I left."

Eli's eyes widened, and he mumbled a curse. Surging to his feet, he moved to look among the detritus scattered around the base of the empty table, then scanned the room slowly, as she did, for any evidence of the files. But they were gone.

"I'm sorry," she whispered, guilt filling her. "You trusted me with those files and—"

He touched a finger to her lips to silence her. "No. You've done nothing wrong. The files were locked in a room where you had every expectation they would be safe."

Her heart tripped, doubting she deserved the grace he offered her. She should have kept the paper case files as secure as she'd kept her computer. Scott—because she, too, felt in her bones the forensic specialist was behind the break-in—now knew the details of what they'd uncovered about his tampering with the case.

"So, now what happens?" She hated the tremor in her voice, but this turn of events, piled on top of so much other emotional upheaval in recent days left her off-balance.

"Well, I'll call the locals to come take pictures and dust for prints, but you can bet he was wearing gloves if it really was Scott."

"I meant now that he has your files."

Eli scratched his chin. "If Montgomery is the one who broke in here and took the files, then all he's really gained is confirmation we're onto him. He was already privy to most of the casework already."

She pressed a hand to her mouth and sighed. "And we know he's still close, somewhere in town. Or was here within the last few hours, anyway."

Eli nodded, stroking her cheek to brush her hair back. "Another thing I know is you're not staying here at the hostel any longer. When you notify the landlord about the break-in, tell him you're checking out."

She jolted, more surprised and hurt by his suggestion than she wanted to admit. "You're sending me back to Seattle?"

He blinked. Frowned. "No. I'm moving you to my house. I'm keeping you near me until—" His expression shifted, softened with sorrow and acceptance. "Although it's true. You might be safer in Seattle...if that's where you'd rather go."

Here was her chance to walk away if she chose. No one could blame her if she left before Allison's funeral. She'd already made the funeral arrangements and signed the paperwork at the coroner's office. Did she really want to stay for the service?

Someone had tried to kill her. Her lodgings had been ransacked. And the longer she stayed near Eli, the harder it would be to avoid breaking his heart and her own again when they parted. Staying would be foolish, wouldn't it?

Yet another part of her refused to leave before Allison's killer had been caught or before Scott Montgomery was brought in for attempting to kill Asher and Eli or before she'd done everything she could to help Eli resolve the Fiancée Killer case for the sake of the victims' families.

Drawing a deep breath, she found her resolve and squared her shoulders as she angled her body toward Eli. "No. I'm not going anywhere yet. We have work to do, and I won't leave until Allison and the others have justice."

Eli swallowed against the lump that swelled in his throat. He couldn't be sure whether the rise of emotion choking him was rooted in relief that Noelle was staying or pride in her conviction to see the case through. Either way, he leaned in to give her a quick kiss.

He cleared his throat as he rose to his feet and held a hand out to her. "All right, let's get the police out here to take a report. Once they take pictures and process the scene, you can pack a bag, and we'll get you settled at my house."

The local police worked for close to an hour before they allowed Noelle to organize and pack her possessions. While the police were processing the scene, Noelle and Eli stopped in the landlord's office to turn in her key and report the crime. Eli asked the hostel owner about security cameras for the property, both for his own knowledge and to speed the process for the local uniforms.

"Not inside the rental, but there's one that covers the front door and one for the backyard," the landlord said.

"I want a copy of the footage. Tonight." When the owner started shaking his head, Eli pulled out his badge and narrowed a hard look on the man. When the man sighed and jerked a nod, Eli added a tight, "Thank you."

He told the landlord that the local police were already on-site, collecting evidence, and to make an additional copy of the video for them. After handing the man his business card with the email to send the video footage, Eli escorted Noelle to his car.

When he took her to pick up her car in the hospital parking lot, they dropped in to check on Asher briefly. He was asleep, but a nurse informed them Asher was doing fine and not showing any adverse symptoms. Kansas, the nurse added, had left to get a meal and some rest only a few minutes before they'd arrived.

In the parking lot, Eli searched Noelle's rental car for sabotage before she got in to follow him to his house.

The idea that someone, probably Montgomery, had targeted Noelle, likely because of her association with him, sat like glacial ice in Eli's gut. Now that he was aware of the danger his coworker posed to her, Eli swore Scott would have to come through him to get near Noelle again.

Noelle set her bags in a corner of Eli's living room, and he, eager to get back to work on catching Scott Montgomery, cleared a spot on his kitchen table again to be their workspace. He booted up his home laptop to check his email and found the security video from the hostel had already arrived.

Noelle looked over his shoulder as he played the footage from the relevant hours of that day. They saw Noelle leaving, hurrying to the hospital following his call, a moose that wandered through the backyard, but nothing else.

"Damn. I was sure we'd have Scott dead to rights on camera." Eli groaned and laced his fingers behind his head as he leaned his chair up on the two back legs.

Noelle returned to her seat with a sigh. "He's no fool. He'd know to be wary of security cameras and not to be caught. He could have gone in a window at the side or out of frame at the back."

"True enough." Eli closed the lid of his laptop and faced her. "Where were we on your analysis?"

"I've run everything we had before this morning, but until we have more quantifiable evidence to add to the algorithm, I don't know how I can help with building your case against Scott."

Her phrasing hit him in the gut like a fist. Eli pressed his mouth in a hard line and held up a hand. "Hang on. Stop there. I know the evidence we've got now all points to Scott, but my job, the job of the ABI is not to build a case against anyone. That's the DA's job after he's arrested and formally charged. Our job is to collect evidence and follow the case wherever the evidence leads. I can't make the mistake of letting my personal bias or fears dictate a particular spin on the findings. When we have enough evidence to support an arrest, we make the arrest. But we can't fall in the trap of making assumptions about a person's guilt and risk getting tunnel vision, missing the bigger picture and wasting time going down the wrong path."

"But don't you have enough evidence against Scott to arrest him now?" Noelle asked, sounding as frustrated as he felt.

Eli twisted his mouth, skeptical. "Evidence he tried to kill me and Asher with the bomb at his house? Maybe. Indications that he tampered with the evidence and sabotaged our investigation? Yes. Proof that he's the Fiancée Killer? Not as much. We need physical evidence, eyewitnesses, a confession...something solid that connects him specifically with the women's deaths. Right now all we really have is a lot of incriminating circumstantial evidence. And we don't have any solid proof he's the one targeting you. Just hunches and gut feelings."

"So where should we focus tonight? I can help you look at the big picture."

Eli nodded. "Yeah. The big picture is likely where we'll find his motive, for trying to blow me and Asher up if nothing else. From there, we follow the evidence." He drilled his finger on the tabletop as he made his point. Scowling, he pulled out his cell phone. "Speaking of evidence, let me see what the forensic crew with the Shelby PD found in the rubble of Scott's house and if anything there helps our case."

While Eli talked to the Shelby PD, he watched Noelle doodle on a notepad, drawing boxes, connecting lines and sketching Venn diagrams. Her expression was one of intense concentration, a look he remembered well from college and studying together. His fingers itched to soothe the tiny line that creased her forehead between her eyebrows, and his lips tingled at the notion of kissing the taut line of her mouth.

He was so involved in her every move and subtle facial shift that he almost missed the Shelby police detective's comment when he finally came on the line.

"We're still combing through the debris and cataloging what's found. The fire department wouldn't let us get at it until they were sure there were no more explosive materials or smoldering embers that could reignite."

Smoldering... Yeah, Eli could use that word to describe Noelle as she nibbled her bottom lip and angled her head so that her long hair brushed her cheek.

Eli pressed the pads of his fingers into his closed eyes, trying to redirect his thoughts. "All right. Just...please be sure your officers know that there could be critical evidence related to a serial murder case at the site. Call me immediately if anything related to the Fiancée Killer victims, the crime scene locations...or my family comes up."

Noelle looked up, a degree of surprise lifting her eyebrows.

"Your family?" the police detective asked, echoing what was written on Noelle's face.

"Long story. And that link is both unconfirmed and confidential. Do you understand, Detective?" Eli thanked the local detective and disconnected. "Nothing useful from Scott's house yet. They're still processing it."

"You're pretty sure this is about you or your family

then? Is that the bigger picture we need to look at?" Noelle said, her pen tapping her notepad restlessly.

"Since a significant number of those lines—" he pointed to her sketches "—have me at the center, it's something we need to explore." Eli paused, then leaning toward Noelle, he shot her a quizzical look. "Right?"

She blinked. "You're asking me?"

He spread his hands and stated in a serious tone, "I just want to be sure I'm not being…egocentric or biased in some way. Those connections…" he tapped her pad again where she'd graphically linked him to Scott and the murders "…can't be coincidence, can they?"

"You don't believe in coincidence. Or so you keep telling me."

"But am I right?"

A tender expression lit Noelle's face. "You are an intelligent man and an excellent lawman. I've always known you to have good instincts. Trust them. If your gut's telling you to pursue this path, there's something there to be discovered. And for what it's worth, that's what my gut is telling me, too."

He smiled his appreciation for her reassurances and leaned in to give her a kiss. "Then let's get to work."

Chapter 15

Five hours later, Eli threw his pen down on his coffee table with a frustrated huff. "This is getting us nowhere. Meanwhile, Montgomery is who knows where, doing who knows what. Maybe the *why* isn't as important right now as just catching him and making sure he can't kill anyone else."

Sitting beside him on his living room couch, Noelle reached over to massage Eli's shoulder. Tension radiated from him like heat waves off pavement in summer. They'd been looking for an incident or other link between Eli and Scott Montgomery that would explain why Scott was targeting women who looked like Eli's murdered aunt, why he was copying the MO of Caroline's murder. Did Scott have a grudge against Eli or the family as a whole? Had Eli somehow cost Scott a promotion? Embarrassed him personally or professionally? Had Scott used the Colton family's adventure company and formed a grievance as a result?

But every avenue they pursued appeared to be a dead end, and their previous convictions about Montgomery's motives and Eli's links to the case wobbled.

Eli rolled his shoulders as she kneaded the muscles in his neck, and the groan that purred from his throat was far more sensual than frustrated. The sexy sound of the rumble from his chest instantly shifted Noelle's thoughts away from crime fighting and to the attractive man sitting beside her.

Despite the serious nature of the work they were undertaking, Noelle had been battling distracting thoughts about Eli all evening. She'd keyed in on how intimate it was to be sitting close to Eli on his couch, where days before they'd given in to the pulsing need that lay just beneath the surface for them both.

The fire in his fireplace and the scent of his aftershave filling her senses only added to the romantic ambience. More than once she'd had to remind herself that they had important work to do and to stop staring at the way his long fingers held his pen as he scribbled notes or the way the muscles in his square jaw bunched as he clenched his teeth in concentration. Her mind kept drifting to the evening they'd tangled limbs on this very couch and might have made love had his brother not stopped by.

Make love to him once and get it out of your system, she'd reasoned that evening. She'd held her feelings for Eli at bay for thirteen years. She'd gotten good at it. With all this practice, surely she could enjoy a night of physical enjoyment without losing her heart. Couldn't she?

She glanced at his mantel clock. It was after midnight. Surely no one from his family would be dropping in to visit at this late hour. If things grew steamy between them now, nothing stood in the way of finishing what they started.

"Noelle? What do you think?"

Her pulse jumped, afraid of what he might have read in her moony-eyed gaze. What had he asked earlier? New angles? "Um, you're right. Maybe we do need to step back and look at this differently."

Noelle quashed the hum of desire that touching him had awakened. Dropping her hands to her lap, she pushed aside the distracting feel of Eli's strong neck and broad shoulders, trying to refocus the random information they had about Scott Montgomery and the string of murders he'd apparently committed. *Apparently* being the key word. They had to find proof.

"I know the fact that he altered the case files is highly incriminating, but what if he's just in league with the person killing the women? He could be getting blackmailed by the real killer and altering the information to avoid being outed for something in his past. Or he could be covering for friend or family member."

Eli's only answer was a dispirited sigh.

Noelle pushed off the sofa and moved to the table where they'd set up her laptop. "This link to your aunt's murder could point to someone that was associated with her killer. A family member of Caroline's stalker wanting revenge? Could someone who worked on the old case have contacted Scott?"

Eli curled his fingers into his hair, growling, "Holy hell, I'm so tired of going in circles on this case! Every time I think we're a step closer, a hundred new questions and possibilities come up."

Noelle gripped his wrist. "Forget my last questions, then. Maybe I'm muddying the water, and we ought to stick with Occam's razor. The simplest and most obvious solution is what we need to focus on."

"Me being the common factor," Eli said darkly.

Without directly answering him, Noelle mulled how to use her analysis software to help with this new twist in the case. "If we factor in everything we know about Scott's contact with your family and add that to the analyses we've already run, maybe something new will pop."

"How do you quantify his contact with my family?" Eli asked. "And how do we reconstruct every family member who has stopped by the office to see me and run into Montgomery?"

"Maybe we can't."

Eli twisted his mouth in thought. "But we can have Parker or Lakin pull records at the family's business to see if Scott used RTA in the past. That's a start."

"Okay," she said, making a note. "We'll do that first thing in the morning."

He dragged both hands over his face as he sighed. "I still feel like this has to be about me somehow. I was the one who went with my dad to my grandparents' house that day twenty-eight years ago and found Caroline's and her stalker's bodies. I work with Scott, and I'm the one who got assigned to solve this case. Now we have reason to believe he's tried to kill me and my partner, and he's gone after you, my ex-girlfriend. But why? I just don't see the reason behind it. What is his grudge?"

He stood up to pace, and Noelle moved to block his path and lay her hands on his chest. "Does he have to have a reason? Can't it just be a matter of something sick and twisted inside him? If he learned about your aunt's murder and already had psychopathic tendencies, he could just be killing these women and getting a thrill that you haven't made the connection to your aunt yet. Maybe now that you've figured it out, he'll stop killing and—"

Eli shook his head. "Serial killers don't stop. They may lie low for a while or move to another state, but the *whatever it is* that drives them to kill doesn't go away. We have to bring him in, sooner rather than later."

Noelle stepped closer and pulled him into a hug. "Okay. Try this on for size. You should put a pin in all this for now and get some sleep. We seem to be going in circles without making any progress at this point."

Eli's expression dimmed. "How am I supposed to sleep knowing Montgomery could be stalking his next victim or *killing her* while we dither around trying to figure out the connection to me?"

"I wouldn't say we're dithering, exactly. And the state and local police have issued an APB for him, right? We'll look at it again in the morning with fresh eyes. Okay?"

He scowled, clearly unconvinced.

Stroking his cheek, she tried a new tact. "Sometimes, when I'm trying to fall asleep..." she took his hand and led him toward his bedroom "...or early in the morning, when I'm not fully awake, my subconscious speaks to me, and I see situations I've been debating in a whole new light."

His eyebrow quirked. "That's happened for me before." He stumbled tiredly in her wake, and his head lolled in concession. "Fine. I'll get some sleep..." he pulled her up short and wrapped her in his embrace again "...if you'll join me. It's late. Come to bed with me."

His voice held a husky rasp, and heat rushed through her. Did he mean his request the way it sounded?

"To sleep?" she asked, her head tipped flirtatiously.

"At some point, probably." He tugged his cheek up, flashing a devilish grin. "But..." he speared his fingers into her hair, combing it back from her face "...anything else that happens is up to you. I won't press you for anything you're not comfortable with."

A sweet mellowness weighted her core. This sort of

kindness and understanding had made her fall in love with Eli in college. Having evidence of that same noble character again was both a potent reminder of what they'd once shared and a warning that, by making love to Eli, she could easily get ensnared in levels of emotion and attachment that were unhealthy for her heart. Yet she wanted just a sip from the cup of passion he offered...

He held her in his blue gaze, his desire and tenderness as clear as the bright Alaskan moon.

Rising on her tiptoes, she pressed a kiss to his lips. "All right. Lead the way. We have unfinished business, you and I."

Chapter 16

Walking backward as he kissed her, Eli drew Noelle into his bedroom. When his legs hit the edge of his bed, he toed off his shoes and pulled her shirt from the waist of her slacks without breaking the contact of their lips. His body was aflame, wound tight with a hunger he'd suppressed for years.

He'd been with other women since Noelle, but none had meant a fraction of what his intimacies with her had meant, and he'd quickly lost interest in pointless sex. When you've had something as rich and powerful as making love to your soulmate, anything else felt empty, even like a betrayal.

To have her in his arms again, to be able to touch her, kiss her, savor the sweet connection that two could share with their bodies and hearts joined was paradise to him. Maybe he could show her physically the truth that his words had not yet been able to convey. She belonged with him. There was no challenge or difference or past heartache they couldn't overcome together.

"I've missed you, missed this, sweetheart," he murmured as he dropped tiny kisses along the curve of her throat. Her breath caught, and the sexy sigh that followed stirred the ache in his core to feverish new heights.

Patience. Savor this. Make it count.

He knew he might not get another chance to set things right with her, and he wanted everything about this night to reawaken the feelings she'd once had for him.

He took his time, nibbling the sensitive spot below her ear, massaging her nape with his thumbs, tracing the shape of her lips with one fingertip. He felt her muscles slowly relax, her body tremble in response to his caresses. He tested all the spots that had once been her favorite places to be kissed, and he grinned when he won gasps of delight and pleasure from her.

She slipped her hands beneath his shirt and dug her fingers into his back, encouraging him by canting her hips and sliding her body against the length of his.

Patience. Savor this, he told himself again, even as his breathing grew rough and choppy, his libido firing and hungry.

One item of clothing followed another, while they stared into each other's eyes. Her shirt, then his. Her slacks, his jeans. Her lacy underwear and bra, a wonder to behold both on her and then off.

When they were both naked, he lifted her, and she wrapped her legs around his hips. Turning, he tumbled them to his bed and quickly wrapped them in the warmth of his blankets.

Burrowed deep in a snug cocoon of blankets, he let his hands roam, his mouth taste and his gaze worship her. As his passion rose, so too did the tender ache in his marrow that could only be called love. "It's only ever been you for me, Noelle. In college, now, forever. Only you."

In the dark of their blanket nest, he heard a hiccupping sob, felt the dampness on her cheeks, and he dried the tears with his kisses. "Only you, Noelle. Only you for me."

* * *

Noelle let Eli's words sink into her soul and nudge aside the pain that had resided deep inside her for so long. Rejection from her birth mother. Rejection from her adoptive family. Rejection from classmates who saw only her differences in her youth.

The scars created when she was young. The longing in her soul for love and acceptance had shaped so many of her choices in life. Perhaps the most difficult choice had been to break up with Eli in order to protect herself from what she'd believed to be inevitable pain in the long term. No one had ever loved her long term. No one had ever kept promises, kept faith, kept her close.

Except Eli.

And she'd pushed him away anyhow.

The stinging truth of that realization, seen afresh some thirteen years later, slashed her with needlelike tines. A sob broke from her throat, and Eli lifted his head from kissing her breast.

"Noelle? What's wrong? Do you want to stop?"

She curled her fingers in his hair and shook her head. "No. I only... I was thinking how much I'd missed this. Missed you."

"Ah, love, me too." Pulling back a corner of the blanket and letting in the dim light from his bedside clock, he continued to stare at her, his eyes intense. "Are you sure that's all that's wrong?"

She gave a wry half laugh. "You know me too well, huh?"

He leaned on one elbow, studying her face while he drew lazy circles on her skin with his finger. "I used to, but I'm not sure I do anymore. Tell me what's bothering you."

"Now? In the middle of—" she waved a hand between them "—and break the mood?"

"We have all night for—" He copied her hand wave between them. "But if something is on your mind, I want to settle it now, before it becomes a problem for us."

"It's not..." She ducked her head to avoid his gaze, and he angled her chin back up again.

"Look at me, Noelle. Talk to me. Let me in."

Taking a breath for courage, she admitted, "I was thinking how I should have fought harder to overcome my concerns about us when I had the chance. You were good to me, and I let worries about the future, clouded by my past, stand in the way."

He lifted an eyebrow. "What about the future?"

Here, she hesitated. After a taut moment of silence, she said, "Your family. Whether they'd accept me as more than a college girlfriend. If my own family couldn't love me, how could I think anyone else's would?"

"Noelle, sweetheart..." He drew her closer, held her firmly in his arms and kissed the top of her head. "My family would love you. Didn't my mom and dad welcome you today? And you've met one of my brothers and my cousin Kansas. Granted, Parker was teasing a bit about having caught us making out, but that was directed at me. Brother stuff."

She shook her head. "It's easy to be polite and kind in the short term, and a whole other matter to welcome someone..." she hesitated, almost said *different*, but went with "...*new* into their ranks. Especially someone like me who hurt you once and who never—"

He stopped her with a kiss. "If that is your concern, then I can ease your mind with conviction." He laced his fingers with hers and kissed her knuckles one at a time as he said, "My. Family. Will. Love. You."

She rested her forehead against his. "Easy enough for you to say. Harder for me to believe considering my experiences with...rejection."

"Fine," he said. "You don't have to take my word for it. The proof is in the pudding, as they say. I deal in facts. Proof. Evidence. So, allow me to show you the truth."

"How?" she asked, narrowing a skeptical look on him.

"My mother's birthday party Sunday. You've been invited by more than one family member. Come with me and meet the family. *All* of the family. I think you'll see why I'm so sure after you've spent time with the whole motley crew for a while. Give them a chance. And if you're convinced, then give *us* a chance."

"I—I want to, but...can you afford to go to a family party with the investigation at this boiling point? With Scott out there—"

"The case takes priority, of course. But if we're not actively following a tip of a sighting or other time-sensitive leads, I can take a few hours off to toast my mother's health with the family. I'm only a phone call away if anything with the case changes. So..." Eli kissed her again, long and deep. "What do you say?"

She let out a sigh, feeling a bit of tension inside her release, as if by making the decision to move forward with getting to know Eli's family, she was taking the weight of a years-long uncertainty off her shoulders. "Okay. You win. I'll go with you Sunday."

"Good." Eli slid a leg up her calf and rolled on top of her. "Now that we've decided that...where were we?" He trailed his lips, his tongue along her throat. "Oh, yeah. I was about to rock you to your core, pretty lady."

He caught her giggle when he took her lips with his. When he moved on to nibble her shoulder, she teased, "Bold talk, Mr. I-deal-in-facts. Where's your proof you can rock anything?"

And for the next several hours, he presented his very convincing case.

The next morning, Noelle woke, sore in places that hadn't been sore in thirteen years, but feeling a hopefulness and happiness she hadn't known in the same length of time. She rolled on her side and watched Eli sleeping in the light that seeped in from the window.

Light from the window? She furrowed her brow. If the sun was up, it had to be almost 9:00 a.m. She hadn't slept this late in months. And she and Eli had work to do on the investigation to find and bring in Scott Montgomery.

She was just debating whether to wake Eli now or let him sleep until she finished her shower, when his cell phone jangled on his nightstand.

Jolted awake, Eli squinted at the daylight and reached for his phone. "Yeah? I mean, Agent Colton. Oh yes. What can I do for you?"

Noelle shivered in the chilly bedroom and pulled the covers up to her chin as she listened to Eli's end of the conversation.

"Oh? Anything helpful? Really? Uh, yeah, that should work. No, it's no problem. Saturday or not, casework comes first. I'll be in shortly." Eli cut a glance to Noelle as he disconnected his call. "That was the lead investigator with the police department. As I asked, he's been working on the evidence recovery at Montgomery's house, and this morning they found a good bit he thinks will be helpful for the Fiancée Killer case. I'm meeting him at my office as soon as I can grab a shower." He shifted to face her and ran a hand down her bare back, sending delicious thrills spiraling inside her. "I hate to leave you by yourself, especially since we believe Scott is gunning for you. You can come with me if you want."

She toyed with a wisp of his hair that curled around his ear. She considered his offer but didn't want to be dependent on him for anything. Including his protection. Dependence led to disappointment and heartbreak. Despite her displeasure over his leaving, she mustered a smile. "I'll be fine. I've thought of a way to run some new analyses that will cross-reference the Fiancée Killer data with your aunt's murder. Do you think I could get access to the old case files from California?"

"Definitely. I'll make a call to the San Diego police and make an official request since Caroline's murder appears to be pertinent to our case. I'll have them copy you with any emails sent." Eli leaned in to give her a deep kiss, then gave her bottom a playful swat. "And now I have to get moving, before your perfect lips and hot little body tempt me to blow off responsibilities today in lieu of a day in bed with you."

A chill found her when he tossed back the covers and crossed the room. The cold had as much to do with the disappointment and the lonely void created when he removed his solid presence, his warmth and the shelter of his arms as it did the nip of the bedroom air. How quickly she'd returned to the place she'd known too briefly in college, where lying with Eli, wrapped in his arms, could make her feel safer and more complete than she'd ever known before.

Climbing from the bed, she found his bathrobe hanging on his closet door and tied it around her. She pushed the empty ache away, reminding herself of the hard work she'd done in the past decade. She'd focused on finding herself, learning to be comfortable in her independence and establishing a balance that wasn't dependent on anyone else's approval or recognition. The process had been slow but steady. In light of all the memories evoked by this trip north, seeing Eli and Aunt Jean and coming to grips with Allison's death, she realized just how far she'd actually come. She refused to let old hurts and ancient memories cause her to backslide.

She inhaled the tantalizing scent of Eli that clung to his bathrobe and let herself relish the intimacies they'd shared last night. Her feminine core tingled at the reminder of his body twined with hers, his hand and lips loving her, arousing her, waking a dormant part of her soul.

Noelle squared her shoulders and set the glow of their lovemaking aside. As enjoyable as the night had been, she had to put those tender feelings back in the box where she kept her treasured memories of Eli and prepare herself for her inevitable return to Seattle. Last night had been about closure for her. She and Eli could part as friends with one last precious memory of the sweetness of their shared passion. But she'd come too far, worked too hard to risk her fragile emotions to a fraught relationship with Eli.

She would help him catch the Fiancée Killer, bury Allison and return to her life in Seattle knowing she could put Alaska securely behind her once and for all.

Eli didn't return from his meeting with the local police investigator until that evening. Noelle had made herself a toasted cheese sandwich and tomato soup from a can in Eli's pantry and was just sitting down to eat when he hustled in from the cold, bringing the mid-November chill with him.

"Sorry I was gone so long. After I finished at the office, I stopped by the hospital to catch Asher up on what I've learned."

"Oh? And how is he?"

"Discharged, it turned out. So then I trekked by his house and found him surrounded by a gaggle of elderly neighbors who were feeding him up on casseroles and homemade sweets. I helped him shoo the well-meaning ladies away so he could rest and gave him the highlights of the new case information. When I left, he was starting an audiobook, grumbling about his doctor restricting his screentime, and enjoying the bounty of baked goods his neighbors had provided." Eli peeled off his coat and draped it over the back of a kitchen chair. "That smells good. I missed lunch, so I'm famished."

He started prowling the kitchen, and she waved him to her chair. "Eat mine. I'll fix more for me while you tell me what the police found in the wreckage of Scott's house. Anything useful for the case?"

Eli looked ready to reject her offered dinner, but hunger clearly won. He picked up half of the gooey cheese sandwich and took a big bite, groaning in satisfaction. "They definitely did."

Noelle tried to ignore how sensual Eli's enjoyment of the sandwich sounded as she dug in his pantry for another can of soup.

"Among the scattered and partially burned papers in Scott's destroyed home office," he said, "they found a file he'd made regarding my aunt's murder."

Noelle spun to face him, a can of minestrone soup in her hand. "Just as we thought. The similarities in the posing of the victims and manner of death weren't a coincidence."

"Seems not." He took another large bite and around the mouthful he said, "That's not all they found. Maps. Photographs of the locations where the bodies have been found. He'd made a plan where to leave his victims, it seems."

"Is there anything we can conclude from those locations?" she asked as she popped the top on the soup and dumped it in the same pan she'd used to heat the tomato soup. "Maybe my software program can predict where he might go next, and we can catch him red-handed."

"If only." He slurped a spoonful of soup, then cut a sharp glance at her. "Wait. Do you think your program *can* do that?" His eyes were bright with hope. "Predict future locations? If so, we can stake out those sites and wait for Montgomery to show up."

Her pulse pattered, and she was flooded by a desire to do anything she could to make Eli happy, to fulfill that look of anticipation and to be the answer to all his wants and desires. She swallowed past the sudden knot in her throat. "I haven't tried it yet, but I will tonight."

He rewarded her with a smile that melted everything feminine inside her. She was warm wax, eager to be molded to his liking, if only to receive that bright look of delight and affection for as long as possible. Or at least until she returned to Seattle.

That thought popped the fragile bubble of joy that had sidetracked her and mercilessly snatched her back to reality. Nothing had fundamentally changed in her situation or Eli's since she'd arrived in Shelby. They'd slept together, sure. And it had been as wonderful and moving as she remembered from college. But she was the same person, with the same difficult history and the same need to avoid further heartbreak. They still had separate lives in different states, and the same challenges of ethnicity and societal bias. She couldn't bear the thought of her relationship with Eli causing any tension or dissension between him and his family.

The sound of Eli scraping the bottom of his soup bowl roused her from her gloomy thoughts, and she pasted on a smile to camouflage her dejection. "I can fix more if you're still hungry."

He wiped his mouth on a napkin and rose to carry the dish to the sink. "Nah. Let's get back to work. I want to show you what the local detective gave me this morning. And I want to see what your software can do about forecasting where Montgomery might be going next."

Chapter 17

Noelle and Eli spent most of the rest of Saturday trying new configurations and trials with her software... and getting nowhere. Eli's frequent calls to the Shelby PD for updates on possible sightings of Scott, any proof he was responsible for the break-in at the hostel and new evidence from the bombed house were equally unfruitful.

Whenever Eli displayed signs of his growing frustration with the case, Noelle did her best to ease the tension in his muscles with neck massages or by coaxing him to use yoga poses and breathing techniques to release his stress. By the time they tumbled into bed that evening, the therapeutic touches and collaborative deep breathing had worked them both into a state of arousal that they satisfied by making love late into the night.

Noelle spent Sunday with a twist of confused emotions in the pit of her stomach. The renewed passion between them had both refueled her affection for Eli and fed the fear that she'd lost control of her feelings. She was certain she'd set herself up for another devastating break from him.

Complicating this tempest inside her was the knowledge that she was going to be thrust into Eli's huge family and closest friends for his mother's party that evening.

She'd toyed with faking a headache or other illness to keep her home, but Eli's eagerness for the family to meet her and vice versa was so palpable and endearing, she quashed her reluctance and mentally braced for the evening's event.

Noelle offered to drive separately in her rental car to the party—the easier to make a quick escape if she needed—but Eli convinced her to ride with him in his Jeep. "There's a forecast for snow to start about the time we leave the party, and I'm betting my Renegade can better handle winter conditions on the roads."

They stopped at a local bakery near Eli's house for their contribution to the family meal, where Noelle bought two loaves of freshly baked bread. Eli shopped next door at a deli, choosing wine and cheeses for his family and Asher's favorite pizza, which they dropped off at his partner's house on their way to the party.

"Give me the latest on the case," Asher asked, clearly bored out of his skull because of the concussion protocol that limited his entertainment options.

"Nothing you need to worry about. Concentrate on following doctor's orders and getting back to work in a couple weeks," Eli said.

Asher grumbled under his breath, especially when he heard they were headed to a Colton family party. "I'd kill to go with you. Colton gatherings are famously awesome, and all I have on my agenda tonight is staring at the old water spot on my ceiling and watching my toenails grow."

Eli clapped him on the shoulder as they headed for the door. "Sorry, pal. Maybe another time. Get well and get back to the office. That's your agenda right now. We need you."

Several minutes later, as Noelle and Eli drove through

the winter-darkened outskirts of Shelby, Eli angled a look at Noelle. He placed a hand on her knee and said, "I do remember that you're an introvert, and I know parties like this are not comfortable for you."

She flashed him a weak smile, grateful for that recognition.

"If it gets too much, tell me, and we'll go." He returned his gaze to the road. "I would like to stay through dinner, though, if that's okay."

She covered his hand with hers, a mellow comfort filling her, knowing he had her back and recognized her personal parameters. "Thanks."

When he turned off the main road onto a narrow private lane, she steeled herself. She could handle a few hours with Eli's family, one way or another. She owed him that much.

Once Eli had parked on the long driveway, already full of vehicles indicating the party was in full swing, Noelle gathered the loaves of bread. Eli carried his sack with several bottles of wine and the selection of cheeses as they climbed from his Renegade.

He held her free hand tightly as they approached the front door of his parents' home. The windows of the large two-story home glowed with golden light in the dark Alaskan evening like welcoming beacons. Eli gave a perfunctory knock on the door but didn't wait for an answer before opening it and ushering her inside.

Just as well he hadn't waited, because the volume inside reminded Noelle of being at a sporting event. Cheerful voices and laughter competed with each other in the crowded living room, and music, ABBA if she wasn't mistaken, played over all the hullabaloo. Noelle smiled, deciding the seventies' musical group fit with the artistic and bohemian vibe she'd gotten from Sasha Colton earlier in the week.

Will Colton spotted them first and drew first Eli, then Noelle into a warm hug of welcome.

"I'm so glad you came with Eli, dear! Can I take your coat and purse? We're just throwing them all in the back bedroom, if you need it before the party breaks up." Will took the wine and cheese from Eli and flagged down a man of approximately his same age. "Ryan, grab that bag from Noelle and take it to the kitchen, will you, bro?"

Noelle could see the resemblance between the older men even before Will addressed the man as *bro*.

Eli shook the man's hand, saying, "How you doing, Uncle Ryan? Good to see you."

Noelle and Ryan exchanged smiles and simple greetings as she handed him the bread. As she shed her coat and handed it over, Eli asked his father, "Is Lakin here yet? I want Noelle to be sure to meet her."

Will twisted his mouth as he thought. "She is. I believe she was in the kitchen with Dove the last time I saw her. They were putting all the food on plates for folks to snack on."

"Thanks." Eli placed a hand at the small of Noelle's back and ushered her past a trio of men who seemed deep in discussion about a recent hockey game.

"Why do you want me to meet Lakin especially?" she asked.

"I want you to meet everyone, but I think we should start with Lakin. Just...trust me."

Before Noelle could say more, he guided her into a busy kitchen where savory aromas filled the air. Several women, including Eli's mother, bustled about and chatted joyfully.

"Eli!" Sasha cried with a wide smile. "My hands are a mess, or I'd hug you!" She held her hands up to demonstrate the dark sticky-looking *something* she was kneading with her hands.

"Happy birthday, Mom," Eli said as he made his way to his mother to kiss her cheek.

Noelle stayed close behind him and added her birthday greetings.

A young dark-haired woman—Inuit, Noelle guessed from her skin tone and beautiful bone structure—tried to squeeze past Eli, saying, "Tuck your butt in, Eli. I need to get by you."

Instead, he turned to block her path more fully and waved a hand from Noelle to the now-frowning woman. "Let me introduce you first. Lakin, this is Noelle Harris. Noelle, my sister Lakin."

Noelle blinked once, her only outward show of surprise. She kept a smile fixed on her face as she nodded to Lakin and offered a hand to shake while in her chest a wild fluttering started. *This* was Eli's sister?

The questions began to roll through her brain like scrolling credits at the end of a movie. She had to intentionally quiet the noise in her head and focus on what Lakin was saying or else embarrass herself with her inattention.

"—so much about you. Please make yourself at home."

"I've heard about you, as well," Noelle returned. That was true, although Eli had never mentioned he had an Inuit sister. A previous marriage for Will or Sasha? Adoption?

Just then Lakin waved her arm, signaling across the room to a light-skinned Black man. The target of Lakin's attention strode in through the back door with Parker, who announced, "The bonfire is ready! BYOM...bring your own marshmallows!"

"Troy, come here," Lakin called. "I want you to meet Eli's date."

Noelle was still processing the moniker of *Eli's date*, when Lakin tucked her arm through the Black man's and lifted a starry-eyed gaze to him. "Noelle, this is my fiancé, Troy Amos. Troy, do you remember Eli talking about his college girlfriend, Noelle?" With her hand, Lakin gestured to Noelle.

Troy's face lit. "I think I do, in fact. Wow, hi! Are you two back together?" He waved his index fingers between Eli and Noelle, his expression hopeful.

While Noelle fumbled, her mind spinning, Eli answered, "That's still to be determined."

Working to keep her smile in place while her mind and her gut spun, Noelle said, "I take it that means you've known Eli and the family for a long time."

"Since I was ten and Troy was eleven." Lakin leaned into Troy, and he hugged her close to his side. "Eli was already in college, but he talked about you so much when he came home for the holidays and summer, I felt like I'd met you. Everyone heard about Noelle!"

An odd buzzing filled Noelle's head. *Everyone heard about her...* But what had he told them?

"Lakin, honey, will you let everyone in the living room know we are ready to serve plates, buffet-style?" Sasha asked.

Lakin touched Noelle's arm as she headed off to do her mother's bidding. "It was great to meet you. I hope we'll get a chance to talk more later."

"I, uh...yes. I'd like that."

Noelle had questions for Lakin. Or Eli. No, it had to be

Lakin. She had to have a firsthand account of what life had been like growing up in this white family, how the Coltons had reacted to her Black boyfriend. Only Lakin could give her the sort of personal insight she needed to weigh the true inclusiveness and acceptance of the Colton family.

And then it clicked. *This* was what Eli meant when he'd said he had to *show* her how he knew his family would love and accept her. Perhaps he knew it wouldn't be enough for him to say they had a racially integrated family. He knew Noelle would want to experience the dynamic, see firsthand how seamlessly Lakin and Troy fit in the Colton dynamic.

A shrill whistle silenced the clamoring crowd that had made its way into the kitchen. Will waved an arm, and in a booming voice, he said, "Before we eat, I just wanted to say a few words about how blessed our family is to have Sasha. She's been more than just my best friend and loving wife for all these many years. She's been a guiding hand, a safe place to fall, a nurturer and encourager, not just to me and our children, but to my brother's family and anyone else that crossed our threshold for our entire marriage. Darling Sasha, I wish you the happiest birthday and many more years of love and happiness. To Sasha!"

"To Sasha!" The family applauded and whistled, and Noelle felt a swell of tenderness in her soul, even though she barely knew the honoree. The affection the family had for their matriarch was clear. Noelle longed for that sort of bond, the sort of maternal relationship she'd never had with her own mother.

Once Will had the group quieted again, he said a prayer over the food and the family, and the serving began.

Sasha put a hand at Noelle's back, gently propelling

her toward the front of the line, "Noelle, please don't hang back. Guests get priority."

Her cheeks heated, awkward with the attention she drew as she was escorted to the front of the line. Eli followed, and Parker called out, "Hey, Eli, save us some!"

"Maybe," Eli teased as he moved up to the line of serving dishes.

After filling her plate with an array of delicious-looking food, Noelle followed Eli to a folding table set up in a corner of the living room.

"We outgrew the dining room table for combined family meals years ago. We just keep adding portable tables and folding chairs as my cousins and siblings add plus-ones to the mix. When the weather's nice, we spill out on the lawn."

"A crowded table is the best kind of problem," a beautiful biracial woman said as she set her plate on the table across from Noelle. Extending her hand, the woman said, "Hi, I'm Hetty Amos, otherwise known as Troy's sister and Spence's better half."

Noelle shook her hand, glanced briefly to Eli. "Spence?"

"My cousin," Eli said, aiming his fork toward the food line. "That's him piling potato salad on his plate."

Eli's equally striking and muscular cousin joined them at the small table, and Noelle goggled. "The Colton family certainly got more than their share of handsome genes."

Hetty grinned. "Right?"

Conversation turned to Hetty's work as a pilot for RTA and Spence's as an adventure guide for the family business.

"Hetty and Spence were the ones who discovered the first victim of the Fiancée Killer," Eli said.

Noelle raised a startled look to the couple. "Oh, my! How horrible."

Hetty nodded. "It was definitely a disturbing discovery on what was a disaster of a trip this spring." She gave a little shudder. "Can we not talk about that while we're eating?"

Spence guided the topic to Noelle's career. While Noelle was sure Spence knew who she was and about her past relationship with Eli, he didn't dwell on it, which Noelle appreciated.

"If you're Troy's sister," Noelle said, mentally making the connections, "then you've known the Colton family for a long time, as well. Is that right?"

Hetty nodded and consulted Spence with a glance. "About fifteen years now, huh?"

"Sounds right." Spence stroked Hetty's cheek. "But it's hard to remember a time when our families weren't close. Troy and Lakin were sweethearts from the start."

Eli snorted. "Which is more than can be said for you two." He turned to Noelle. "These two were about as close as two bulldogs with one bone. Their love language was sniping at each other."

Noelle looked to Hetty for a denial, but the bush pilot shrugged. "It's true. Spence used to irritate the heck outta me." Her expression warmed as she leaned toward her fiancé for a quick kiss. "Then I got to know him better and saw how wonderful he actually was."

Over the next half hour, as the family members finished eating, they moved one by one to either clean up in the kitchen, head outside to the bonfire or move to different tables to chat with someone new.

When Noelle and Eli pushed back from the table, he touched her hand and hitched his head toward the back of the house. "Let's go see the bonfire. They won't serve Sasha's birthday cake until a bit later in the evening. It's a tradition from back when we were kids, and she was trying to teach us about delayed gratification. We couldn't open our Christmas presents until everyone was up and we'd all had a big breakfast together, either." Eli rolled his eyes, silently expressing his opinion of his parents' rule.

Noelle laughed, while privately envying that Eli had had holiday traditions and big family breakfasts. Christmases for her, once Allison grew to age four or so, revolved around watching her sister tear into a pile of presents.

Allison opened toys, candy and extravagances, while Noelle received a fraction as many items—socks and underwear, toiletry items, the occasional used book or hand-me-down puzzle from Allison. The message had been clear. *Your gift is merely being allowed to live with the family and have basic provisions.* To Allison's credit, she had noticed and had shared her less-favorite candy with Noelle. The gesture had meant a lot to Noelle, giving her an indication of some camaraderie with her sister, no matter how small. Those small connections, scattered throughout their childhood and teen years, were why Noelle was in Alaska now. She was compelled to perform one last act of respect and kindness for her sister.

As they passed through the kitchen on the way outside, Noelle spotted Lakin at the sink washing pans and glasses. Noelle changed direction, telling Eli she'd join him after she'd helped with the cleanup.

"You don't have to clean up. You're our guest," he said, motioning again to the backyard where raucous laughter and conversation echoed in the winter night.

Noelle waved him out, grinning her reassurance. "I'll be out soon. I want to help, though. Shoo!"

He leaned in to kiss her cheek—an action that didn't go unnoticed by his mother or sister—then caught his mother's hand and dragged her to the door. "Mom, you should not be on the cleanup team. It's your birthday, for Pete's sake. Come out here and howl at the moon with me."

Once Eli and Sasha had disappeared outside, Noelle took up a position beside Lakin, armed with a towel, and began drying the pans. She worked in silence for a moment, dredging up the nerve to address the topic that had nagged her since meeting Lakin earlier that evening.

Eli had made his point about the diversity in the Colton family and the loving welcome they'd extended the Amos siblings from the earliest days of their acquaintance. But Noelle still had specific doubts and a burning curiosity that only Lakin could resolve. She cast a side glance to Eli's younger sister. "Lakin, can I ask you a question?"

"You mean two questions?" Lakin shot her a teasing grin. "Because you just asked one."

Noelle chuckled. "Two then." She curled her bottom lip in as she dried a pot and mulled how to word her question.

When she didn't ask anything for a full minute, Lakin smiled and said, "Yes, Eli is every bit as nice as he seems. He was a typical big brother, giving me guff at times, but he was protective and funny and good to me, too. He's a great guy."

Noelle blinked at Lakin and frowned. "No. I mean… yes, I agree. And that's all good to hear, but that's not…" She cleared her throat and blurted, "What was it like being adopted by the Coltons? Did you always feel accepted and loved and…like you were really part of the family?"

Lakin's face grew serious, and her brow furrowed. She turned off the water and rested her hands on the edge of the sink as she angled her body to face Noelle more fully, her entire focus on Noelle. "Yes. Absolutely. They adopted me when I was three, and I have never felt anything but loved and safe and included. I am every bit a part of the family in every way. I was never treated as anything but a full member of the Coltons. In fact, Mom and Dad went so far as to tell me I was extra special, because I was the youngest, their only girl, and because they *chose me*." Now her cheek twitched in amusement. "A fact they told me to keep as my special secret so that the boys weren't jealous. But I heard Mom telling the boys reasons why they were extra special when she'd tell them good night, too. Eli was the oldest and most responsible. Mitchell because he knew his own mind and had the courage to follow his own path. Parker because he had a wild energy and passion for the outdoors that made him an asset to the family business." She heaved a contented sigh, her eyes reflecting the same joy as her smile. "They're great parents, and I've never had one doubt they loved me."

Noelle forced a smile to her face for Lakin's sake, but despite her best efforts, tears burned her sinuses. Before she could rein in her tears, one bloomed and seeped through her lower lashes.

Lakin put a sudsy hand on Noelle's arm. "Hey, what's wrong? Oh my gosh. Did I say something I shouldn't have?"

Noelle dried her eyes quickly and took a breath to regain her composure. "It's nothing you said. I'm...so happy to know you were well loved."

Lakin paused. "Wait. Kansas told me tonight that you

are the sister of one of the Fiancée Killer's victims. All the victims have been white."

Noelle pressed her mouth in a taut line and nodded. She hesitated only a moment before confessing, "I was adopted. My mileage, so to speak, with the Harris family varied from yours. After I left for college, I saw no reason to go back to Anchorage. The Harrises were never a real home for me."

Lakin's face crumpled in sympathy. "Oh, Noelle! I'm so sorry. Geez, and here I was gushing about how great the Coltons are to me." She wrinkled her nose in regret. "Forgive me."

Noelle shook her head vehemently. "No, you did nothing wrong. I asked, after all, and I wanted the truth. I'm glad they accepted you. It bodes well for me, if—"

Lakin's face brightened. "If you and Eli get married?"

Noelle gasped so hard she choked. Coughed. Waving a hand and chuckling, she croaked out, "Whoa. Slow down. We're not even dating. I just meant if—" she picked up a glass and started drying it without meeting Lakin's eyes "—*if* we were to get back together."

Lakin threw her arms around Noelle and squealed softly. "Oh yes! I would love that! And I know it would make Eli so happy. He really mourned losing you when you broke up. I don't think he ever stopped loving you."

Noelle returned Lakin's hug before pulling away. "Don't say anything to anyone about that. Not that they aren't all thinking it already, but I still don't know what's going to happen with Eli. We have things to work out, and… I have a life in Seattle. I'm only supposed to be here to handle the final arrangements for Allison."

Lakin's shoulders drooped, and her smile fell. "I promise. But for what it's worth, my vote is for you and Eli to patch things up and let yourselves be happy at last." She pulled a shy grin, adding, "It's been pretty awesome for me and Troy."

Noelle gave Eli's sister a warm smile. "I can tell."

Lakin faced the sink again and handed Noelle the last dish. "I think that's all the dirties until we serve the cake. Let's get outside before all the marshmallows are gone. The guys tend to use them for projectiles rather than dessert, and the puffs disappear rather fast."

Sure enough, when Noelle and Lakin headed out to the bonfire, small white blobs were being hurled around the yard to the amusement of the men. Some were caught in mouths, others caught by hand and lobbed again, a few tossed in the fire to become gooey, blazing kindling.

Sasha tucked Noelle's arm under hers and gave her a withering look. "I apologize for these ludicrous shenanigans, dear. Some things, boys never outgrow."

Noelle watched Eli duck a marshmallow thrown by Parker. In a smooth follow-up motion, Eli returned a puff by underhand toss to Troy, who caught it ably in his mouth and, cheeks stuffed with the sugary treat, grinned broadly.

"No apology needed. I love it." Noelle tugged Eli's mother closer, savoring the maternal connection. "They're having fun. Making happy memories. What could be better than that?"

Eli spotted Noelle then and hurried over, wrapping her in a one-armed hug as they stood beside his mother.

"I'm just happy the predicted storm front held off long enough for us to have a bonfire. The forecast says we're in for possible whiteout conditions and up to a foot of snow later tonight," Sasha said. As if to echo her statement, a stiff breeze crossed the yard, making the flames dance and stretch sideways.

Noelle snuggled closer to Eli and pinched her coat closed at the throat.

After the bag of marshmallows was depleted, the family eased into quiet conversations around the bonfire. Eli arranged two lawn chairs beside Kansas's chair and tugged Noelle over.

"Any news on Scott's whereabouts yet?" Kansas asked Eli quietly as Noelle was settling in her chair.

"Not really. Workin' on it."

"Hey," Will said, snapping his fingers and pointing at Eli and Kansas. "You know the rule at family gatherings. No business talk. Family time is for relaxing."

"Aye, aye, Captain!" Eli called to his father and cast Kansas an amused look and shrugged. "Have you been to see Asher today?"

Kansas looked reluctant to answer but finally gave a quick nod. "What if I did? He's been discharged from the hospital for about thirty-six hours, and *someone* needed to be sure he was following his doctor's orders."

Eli scoffed. "You say that as if I haven't checked on him every day since the accident. I even took him a pizza tonight and shrimp salad from the Cove last night," Eli aimed a finger at Kansas, "which, I have it on good authority, you helped him eat after I left."

"Maybe I did. What of it?" Kansas said with a note of lighthearted challenge.

Noelle listened to the cousins' banter while casting her gaze around the circle of chairs. Only Kansas wasn't paired up with a significant other. The affection between the Colton couples, young and old, snuggling against the cold, made her ache for that kind of forever connection with Eli. The smiles and camaraderie between siblings and cousins tugged at her heart while also raking her soul with claws of longing. Did Eli have any idea how blessed he was to have such a large, loving family?

"You're awfully cozy with Asher considering your ongoing feuds at the office," Eli said, continuing to tease Kansas.

Kansas lifted a casually dismissive hand. "I'm cutting him a break while he's injured. When he's back on the job, being a pain in my backside, I'm sure our relationship will revert to normal."

Before Eli could reply, the jangling of his cell phone interrupted the peaceful evening and murmur of conversation. Noelle jolted, having become so relaxed and at ease, that the strident tones sent a ripple of alarm through her.

"Don't answer it!" someone called, while others groaned.

"No phones!" Will grumbled when Eli pulled out his phone to check the caller ID.

Sasha put a hand on his arm. "It's okay, honey," she said calmly. "Our boy has important work. He has to stay connected."

Eli's screen glowed brightly in the night-darkened yard, and Noelle held her breath, as if sensing the call was bad news. Hadn't most of the calls *she'd* answered lately been something ugly or troublesome?

Pressing the phone to his ear, Eli answered with, "Agent Colton here. What's happened?"

In the light from his phone, Noelle studied Eli's face and saw the swirl of a few fluffy snowflakes beginning to fall. He grunted as he listened, and his brow furrowed. With an angry huff, he lurched to his feet. He paced away from the fire, toward the house, where he could take the call in private.

Noelle and Kansas exchanged worried looks.

"This doesn't bode well," Noelle said quietly.

"Unless it does," Kansas said, a hopeful note in her voice. "Maybe they've caught him. Maybe they've got a confession or located his car or..." She grimaced as if knowing her optimism wasn't likely to pan out.

Noelle gnawed her bottom lip and watched the back door for signs of Eli returning. When he didn't for several minutes, her concern grew.

Kansas, too, seemed restless, and finally Eli's cousin stood and signaled to Noelle. "Come on. Let's go see what's up. I'm sure it's not nearly as bad as we're imagining."

The women hustled inside and found Eli at the kitchen table, his head bowed and his phone set on speaker as he talked to a male caller. While Eli took notes on a scratch pad, the man on the line said, "We've alerted teams in all the nearby districts to keep an eye out. They have full descriptions of all the principals and for the car."

"Good. Send some uniforms to the area and have every business in a one-mile perimeter pull up their CCTV recordings for the time around the sighting—no, make that the last twenty-four hours." Eli paused and frowned. "Damn it, go back as much as five days on every camera in the area since that's when he disappeared. He may have been casing the region and targeting this woman."

Targeting this woman?

Noelle heard Kansas muffle a gasp, and her own stomach dropped. Bile filled her throat. Had another woman been killed? The grave expression on Eli's face said that was likely the case.

He angled a glance to find them standing at the end of the table and rubbed the back of his neck with his free hand. "Look, I should go. I need to get to my office and dig into the matter from there, watch the footage for myself."

"I should tell you," the man on the phone said, "we're keeping an eye on this storm front that's moving in. It's ugly and getting here faster than predicted. Towns to our west are already reporting high winds and heavy snow. Our search capabilities will be severely limited within hours."

Eli sighed and scrubbed his face with his palm. "Understood. Keep me posted. All right? Anything and everything you learn, no matter how trivial it seems."

"You got it." The man disconnected.

Sighing deeply, Eli raised a dark gaze to Kansas and Noelle. "That was Bobby Reynolds." Eli's eyes shifted to Noelle's as he added, "He's a senior officer at the Shelby PD."

Holding her breath, Noelle nodded for him to continue.

"Witnesses reported what appears to be a kidnapping in a key shopping district downtown about two hours ago. A man grabbed a woman off the street and shoved her in his car before racing away. They're gathering CCTV footage from cameras in the area, but the description of the man and the car the two witnesses gave fit Scott Montgomery."

"Which if we're right about him," Kansas said, her voice hoarse, "means he could be about to kill again. Another victim of the Fiancée Killer."

Eli's jaw hardened, and his blue eyes grew flinty. "Not on my watch. Not if I can stop him." He gathered up his scribbled notes and shoved his phone in his back pocket. "Kansas, will you let the family know that the bad weather is ahead of schedule and roads will start getting bad soon?"

His cousin nodded.

"And see that Noelle makes it home safely? I have to go in to headquarters."

Noelle raised a hand to halt Kansas's response. "Forget that. You made me a consultant on the case. I'm coming with you."

Kansas edged toward the door to the backyard. "I want to help, too. I'm sure the SAR team will be put on standby any minute. As soon as I let the family know the weather update and tell Will and Sasha we're leaving, I'll be right behind you."

Chapter 18

Because of the distance the senior Coltons' home was from town and the first wave of snow sticking to the roads, Eli, Noelle and Kansas didn't arrive at the ABI offices until forty-five minutes later. When they reached Eli's office, the light was already on, and they heard the low muttering of a male voice.

Eli raised an arm, stopping the women from proceeding until he poked his head around the doorframe.

Asher sat at his desk, on the phone with someone, and looked up when Eli stepped into the room. Asher held up a finger, asking Eli to wait a minute.

When he didn't signal any danger to the women, Kansas and Noelle crowded forward to peer past him into the room. Kansas gave a discontented grunt when she spied Asher.

"What are you doing here?" she fussed the instant he disconnected his phone call.

"Last time I checked, I worked here," Asher said, narrowing his eyes. "Why are *you* here?"

"Why shouldn't I be? Within a few hours, I can bet my team will be called out for a search and rescue for the woman that was taken."

Asher shifted his gaze to Eli. "So you heard about the abduction then?"

Eli nodded. "I'll handle it. You should be home recovering. Until we know more about who the woman was and where the guy took her, it's all office work. I can manage that, especially with Noelle as my sounding board."

Asher's eyes widened. "She's a sounding board now, too?"

Eli huffed his pique. "She's been through the files as meticulously as we have at this point. She's smart, logical, good with analysis, and her software could prove valuable again." He squared his shoulders. "You got a problem with me including her?"

Asher raised both hands. "Not if you think she can help. I'm ready to nail this bastard once and for all."

"So…" Kansas strode over to Asher's desk and pinned a narrow-eyed look on him. "Since Eli has Noelle's help, you can go home and rest. The doctor told you to take it easy for at least a week before you returned to work."

"You're not my nurse, my mother or my conscience," Asher replied, his own tone firm and somewhat irritated. "I can help here, and I feel fine. I'm staying."

Eli chuckled. "It's good to see your relationship back in form. I got nervous when you two were all friendly and concerned for each other's well-being."

Both Asher and Kansas sent Eli churlish glares.

Noelle made a T with her hands, signaling a time-out, and cleared her throat. "Um, folks, we have a kidnapped woman to find before she's murdered. Can we focus on that now?"

Instantly the mood in the room shifted. Sobered.

"Of course," Eli said, settling behind his desk and waking his desktop. "Who were you on the phone with when we came in? Is there any new information?"

"Not much. Reynolds at SPD says they have the footage of a couple security cameras from nearby businesses in their possession with more in the works. They're sending it via encrypted email as we speak. Check your inbox."

Noelle pulled the guest chair in front of Eli's desk around beside him for a better view of his monitor. Kansas did the same at Asher's desk.

The subject of Asher's recuperation, Eli noted, had been tabled apparently. He was privately glad to have his partner's help in light of the new turn the case had taken.

When his new emails loaded, the message from the Shelby police department had arrived, and Eli clicked through to open the attached video. Holding his breath, he watched the low-quality images play out.

When the man in the video hit the woman in the head and her body went limp, he heard Noelle suck in a sharp breath. His reaction mirrored Noelle's. His gut tensed as they watched the man, whose jacket hood was up and obscuring most of his face, shove the woman in the passenger side of a blue sedan.

Leaning back in his chair, Eli ground his molars together before casting a glance to his partner. "Correct me if I'm wrong, but doesn't Scott own a blue Hyundai Sonata?"

Asher's returned glare was dark and angry. "He does."

"Well, that's what we expected, isn't it?" Noelle asked. "That the kidnapper was Scott?"

"Doesn't make it any easier to accept that a guy you worked with and trusted could have betrayed you, the office and the public he works for," Asher hissed in disgust.

"And he could be responsible for such heinous crimes." He slammed a hand on his desk. "Damn him!"

Kansas gave an exaggerated shudder. "Ugh! The guy *flirted* with me! Thank God I had the sense not to date a coworker."

A ripple of ill ease spun through Eli. He recognized the feeling as the same whisper when he was on the verge of a breakthrough. This edgy feeling had haunted him for several days, telling him he had all but one piece of an important puzzle. When he fit it all together, he knew he wouldn't like the picture he discovered.

He growled his frustration and impatience under his breath. Yet another woman had been taken. The kidnapped woman's life was in danger, and he had to think harder, destroy any stumbling blocks that might have him shy away from the truth.

"Do we know the woman's identity yet?" Noelle asked.

Kansas pulled out her phone and tapped at the screen. "I'll check with my team and see if we have any new missing person reports."

"No name yet," Asher said, still studying and replaying the video of the abduction. "Witnesses describe the woman as Caucasian, medium height, long dark hair, slim and attractive."

Eli hit Replay on the security footage, leaning close again to see what details he could have missed. "Well, the video confirms the witnesses' description anyway. But it's not much to go on." When Noelle mumbled something under her breath that Eli missed, he cut a side look toward her. "What's that?"

She twisted her mouth, hesitating. "I said, 'I bet we can guess her eye color.'"

A chill raced through Eli, and he fisted his hands as he realized the truth of her assumption.

"How's that?" Asher asked, a frown denting his brow.

Eli scrubbed a hand over his face and met his partner's gaze. "It's something Noelle and I realized a couple days ago when analyzing the information in the case files about the victims. They all have blue eyes. Dark hair and blue eyes."

"Which is a somewhat rare combination, statistically speaking," Noelle added.

Kansas jerked upright. "Wait. All of us Coltons have dark hair and blue eyes. Well, except Lakin."

"Who was adopted," Eli reminded her. "And you're right. Every other Colton has blue eyes and dark hair." He paused and sighed. "Including our Aunt Caroline."

Asher's frown deepened. "The one who was murdered when you were a kid?"

Eli nodded. "Exactly."

Kansas threw up a hand. "Hold on. The guy that killed Aunt Caroline and our grandparents also killed himself at the scene. That case has been closed for decades."

"True. But Scott is a forensic specialist. And evidence from his house proves he had accessed the case files from Aunt Caroline's death. The Fiancée Killer is copying elements of the crime."

The color in Kansas's face drained away, and Asher divided a look between Eli and his cousin. "What elements is he copying? What exactly happened to your aunt? And why didn't you tell me about this link earlier?"

"Because you were—are—on medical leave. You're supposed to be resting, not working," Eli said. "Besides, when we first made the connection, I wasn't sure it would bear fruit." He groaned. "Or maybe I was praying it wouldn't."

Asher scowled darkly, and Kansas leaned toward Eli. "So tell us now. It's clearly important."

Over the next several minutes, Eli and Kansas filled Asher in on the thirty-year-old murder and how the family had tried to put it behind them, not speak of it and move on when they relocated to Alaska.

"So the engagement ring, the pose, the victims' similar physical description, the manner of death... Scott's copying your aunt's murder. But why?" Asher asked.

"Because he's sick," Kansas said with a sneer.

"True. But the last couple of days, Noelle and I have been working a theory that these murders, everything Scott is doing—" Eli hesitated, knowing how it egotistical his idea would sound "—comes back to *me* somehow. He's mocking me or getting revenge or something."

Asher sat straighter, then winced, and rubbed his temple. "You? How? Why?"

Eli elaborated on the details of being at the scene when Caroline was found, the very specific physical description and pose of the new victims, and his position in charge of the investigation.

"But... Uncle Will was with you when you found Caroline," Kansas said. "Could your father be the focus of all this?"

Eli twisted his mouth and shook his head. "More recently, Noelle's brake line was slashed, and she wrecked her rental car on the highway just outside of town. Noelle—who I dated in college and have been spending lots of time with in the past two weeks. Scott knows I care about her. What better way to strike at me?"

Noelle added, "My hostel was ransacked while I was

out on Friday, as well, and the hard copies of the Fiancée Killer case files were stolen. We don't have proof yet, because the thief was careful to stay out of view of security cameras, but Eli and I are working on the assumption it was Scott."

"So..." Eli spread his hands, palms up. "Because I find it hard to believe any of this is coincidence, the facts seem to point to me."

Noelle cleared her throat. "Again, people, we're on the clock. A woman's life is at risk, and we have a storm closing in. Unless there's something about your aunt's murder that will help us track Scott, we need to change direction here. We have to find this woman..." she pointed to Eli's monitor "...before she becomes victim six."

Chapter 19

Eli pushed his chair back and stood up. "She's right. Let's move to the conference room where we have the maps that lay out where the other bodies were found. We'll compare that with what we know about Scott and look for a pattern, see what we can figure out."

Asher nodded, then winced again as he tried to rise from his chair. Kansas gave him an I-told-you-so glare before offering a stabilizing arm to help him limp across the hall.

"I'm fine," Asher repeated through gritted teeth.

The foursome gathered around the conference table where Eli spread the map that he, Asher and the rest of the investigative team had marked and labeled over the past months. A second three-dimensional map reflecting the topography of the region and the few existing roads and trails hung on the wall.

"Okay, what do we know about Scott? Does he have any properties where he could be staying now that his house is kindling? Are his parents alive? Any siblings?" Eli asked, a sense of urgency pumping through his veins.

"He never talked about family that I remember," Asher said. "But he isn't someone I shared personal stories with." He glanced at Kansas. "You were friendly with him. What can you tell us?"

Kansas scowled at Asher. "I was polite to him, but I didn't encourage him, if that's what you're implying."

"I wasn't implying anything," Asher tossed back. "Why so touchy?"

Kansas folded her arms over her chest. "Oh, I don't know. Maybe because you're suggesting I had a relationship with our coworker, who has kidnapped a woman and appears to be a serial killer?"

Asher raised his hands. "I only—"

Eli loosed a shrill whistle to stop the tense exchange. "This isn't getting us anywhere. Save the lovers' quarrel for when we're off the clock, huh?"

Asher and Kansas both jerked offended looks at Eli, which he dismissed as he leaned over the map again. Kansas turned her back to the table and stalked over to the wall map with a huff, while Asher drummed his fingers on the armrest of his chair.

Noelle stepped closer to Eli and pointed to the last spot where a body had been recovered. "Consider this—the last two bodies were both found close to Shelby. One here at the Two Bears River hiking trail and more recently one here in the lot behind Shelby Fish Cannery."

Kansas turned to look over her shoulder with an odd expression creasing her face, then returned her attention to the wall map, studying it more closely.

The niggling voice in Eli's head was shouting now. What was he missing?

"It stands to reason Scott will pick a place near Shelby again," Noelle said, "especially since he knows we're onto him and the roads upstate could be getting treacherous. Statistically speaking, the crime scenes are—" Noelle fell silent, her brow furrowing as she leaned closer to the map, her gaze and her finger moving from one marked crime scene to another, muttering, "Lake Chahoogee... Muskee Glacier Pass..."

Eli's heart beat a double-time rhythm. "Noelle? What is it?"

Noelle spun around to face Kansas, who was still gaping at the topographical map. "Kansas, at the hospital earlier this week, you said you conducted rescues at Lake Chahoogee and Muskee Glacier Pass, didn't you?"

Eli pivoted his chair to study his cousin as his gut churned. Kansas nodded slowly, her attention still locked on the wall map, her complexion gone pale. She raised a shaking finger. "And Two Bears River and the lot behind the cannery."

Like a gong sounding, the message his brain had been whispering now shouted to him. He bit out a curse and plowed both hands through his hair.

"What?" Asher asked, then, his face blanching, he muttered the same curse word.

Kansas slumped against the wall, looking like she might collapse any second. She sent her troubled blue gaze from Eli to Asher and back again. "Please tell me this is just a very freaky and disturbing coincidence."

Noelle sat heavily in the nearest chair. "What is it you just said, Eli? There are no coincidences?"

"Yeah. That," Eli said hoarsely and lifted a troubled look to Noelle. "Remember the other day when I explained that a law enforcement investigator's job wasn't to build a case but to gather information and follow where the evidence leads?"

She nodded, her expression glum.

"I broke that rule, despite my best intentions. I got sidetracked, blinded by thinking this was about me. But..." Eli shifted his gaze to his cousin "...it looks like *you're* the link, Kansas. He's copying your aunt's murder and leaving the victims, all women who match your general description, at places you've been on rescues in recent months."

"But...why?" Kansas asked, her voice cracking. "Wh-why me?"

No one said anything for a moment, but finally Noelle answered quietly, "You said yourself he's flirted with you, and you've rebuffed his advances. Maybe his interest in you grew into an obsession. If he was already unstable and had within him the ability to murder without compunction, maybe he thought killing the women would snag your attention."

Kansas gaped at Noelle, then Asher...then clapped her hand to her mouth and raced from the conference room.

Asher started to rise, but Noelle lifted a hand. "Let me."

Once Noelle left the room, seeking Kansas, Eli pinned a hard glare on Asher. "If we're right about this, if Montgomery is doing this because of an obsession with Kansas, he could come after her next."

Asher's jaw clenched, and his eyes darkened with fury. "Over my dead body."

"And mine." Eli took a calming breath. He needed to weed out his own turbulent emotions and think clearly. "He could be hoping this latest kidnapping will trigger a search and rescue that will lead Kansas to him. Hell, now that he knows we're onto him, he could have been planning to snatch Kansas tonight. Thank God she's been with our family all day prepping for my mother's party."

"So we're agreed she needs twenty-four-hour protection until Montgomery is brought in?" Asher said, his jaw rigid.

Eli exhaled. "Good luck convincing her of that. She might be freaked out over this turn of events, but she's strong-willed and independent."

Asher only grunted.

Eli cast a glance to the map again. "Okay, so we have a better idea of Montgomery's motive and possible future target, but we still have to find the woman he took tonight—before it's too late."

Chapter 20

Knowing Kansas was likely the driving obsession behind Montgomery's heinous crimes, Eli attacked the investigation with renewed vigor. The perspective that the women's bodies had been left at sites where Kansas had participated in rescues gave them more geographic focus.

With Kansas's help, they began reconstructing a map of all her rescue work over the past three years. The possibilities were mind-boggling. Kansas went on dozens of rescues every year, both close to Shelby and far out into the hinterlands of the Alaskan wilderness.

"How on earth do we pin down where he's going?" Noelle moaned, the frustration in her tone matching the tension and urgency pulsing through Eli.

He stroked a hand over his mouth as he studied the well-marked map. "Will you enter all these sites and run cross-references and the like with your analytics software?"

"I will, but it's going to take some time to get it all entered, and my laptop is still at your place," she said.

From the corner of his eye, he caught the curious look Noelle's last comment roused from Asher. He didn't have time to address his partner's speculations about his relationship with Noelle.

"I can't help but wonder, though..." Noelle said. She paused, biting her fingernail while her brow dipped in thought.

"Go on," Eli said. "All brainstorms are valid."

"Now that he knows we're onto him, he might have guessed we put together the reason behind the previous crime scenes, the link to Kansas's search sites. And if he doesn't want to be caught, then wouldn't he break that pattern? Are we wasting time with the SAR locations?"

"You may be right on that point. If so, that would bring the possible locations Montgomery could have gone back to...anywhere in the world," Asher said, waving his arm at the map, his tone dark with frustration.

The foursome exchanged tired looks. It was already late, and their general lack of progress clearly ate at them all.

After an extended silence, during which Noelle's gaze remained fixed on the map, she suddenly blinked and jerked her head up. "Oh my gosh. I've been doing it, too— making assumptions based on small bits of information."

Eli cocked his head. "Explain."

"We've...well, I've been assuming he's traveling by car because of the kidnapping footage. But look at this map! This state! So few roads. So many lakes." She divided a look between Asher and Eli. "Does Scott have a pilot's license?"

Eli frowned but immediately rocked his chair forward, his mind picking up her train of thought. "Asher, can you send out notices to every bush pilot and plane-for-hire operation in a hundred-mile radius? If he was going anywhere too far afield, he'd have needed help getting there. Meanwhile, I'll contact the FAA and state licensing board to see if Scott has a pilot's license or owns a plane we didn't know about." Eli glanced at Noelle. "I'll take you back to my place, so you can start entering this new information and cross-referencing."

"What should I do?" Kansas asked.

Eli exchanged a look with Asher, then back to his cousin. "You need to stay safe. Don't go anywhere alone. If you think of anything Montgomery may have said to you about his favorite places to visit or a vacation home or a relative's house he inherited, let me know right away."

Kansas frowned. "That's not what I meant!"

But Eli didn't stick around to hear his cousin's complaint about wanting to be more involved in the investigation. He grabbed Noelle's hand and led her to the elevator and out to his car.

A heavier snow had begun to fall, and Eli bemoaned the fact that as the snow accumulation grew, it would affect road and flying conditions enough to hamper any pursuit of Montgomery. In his head, the countdown clock to find the latest kidnap victim clicked faster. *Please, Lord, don't let them be too late!*

As he drove through the night-darkened streets of Shelby, Noelle looked up the phone number for the Federal Aviation Administration's closest office and dialed the number. When she reached their after-hours emergency operator, she put Eli on speaker. Within a few minutes of giving his credentials and explaining the situation, Eli had reached the right person to look for any records regarding Scott Montgomery of Shelby, Alaska. The agent promised to do the required research and call him back.

They'd been at Eli's house for thirty minutes, beginning the process of Noelle's analysis of the SAR sites, when they had a return call from the FAA source.

Scott did, in fact, have a pilot's license and had registered a floatplane with the FAA five years ago. Since floatplanes typically fly under eighteen thousand feet and in low-traffic areas, flight plans weren't required, meaning Eli had no way of knowing if, when or where Scott might have flown tonight. Eli thanked the FAA official and disconnected, his thoughts splintering in new directions.

"If he has a plane at his disposal, where does he keep it?" Noelle asked. "The plane would have to be kept on a lake or river, right? While there are any number of places he could moor a plane here in Shelby, that water would have to be near a road, even if just a dirt track or logging road, in order to get the kidnapped woman to the plane without anyone seeing him. Once he gets wherever he's going, he'd need a body of water to land the plane, too." Frowning, she pinched her nose. "Which really doesn't help much. There are lakes and rivers all over Alaska and Western Canada."

Eli nodded, squeezing his eyes closed, replaying everything he could possibly remember ever discussing with Scott Montgomery. Had they talked about the activities and sport challenges that Rough Terrain Adventures took customers on? Had they ever talked about vacation rentals or family holidays or travel or—

Eli's heart tripped as a shadowy memory of a conversation long ago wafted through his brain like smoke from a distant fire. Hobbies. Fishing. A lake. Barely there, but...

"What if we—"

He held up a hand, signaling for Noelle to hold her thought. "Just a second, I'm trying to remember the name of a place..." He snapped his fingers repeatedly as he dragged his memory for the name of the lake that was alluding him. "Run a search for a lake... Starts with a G or G-R."

Noelle turned to her laptop, her hand poised over the keyboard as she waited for him to give her more information to narrow the search.

"Graybill? Grandiose? Grundy?" Eli said, trying out names and discarding them. "Montgomery told me once he liked to fish at a cabin. The cabin was on private property by a lake called..." Eli groaned and tapped his fist against his forehead. "Think, Colton!"

Using what little information she had, Noelle began searching databases and Alaskan maps. "Grouse Lake? Grant? Grayling?"

The name danced just beyond his grasp, and he waved Noelle silent again.

Gr—.Gr—.Gofer? Gross—

"Grossford!" He swung to face Noelle. "Look up Grossford Lake. See if anyone named Montgomery owns a property anywhere near there." Eli went to the duplicate map he had on his dining room table and searched for Grossford Lake.

He found the small remote lake roughly one hundred miles north-northwest of Shelby and tapped it with his finger just as Noelle announced, "Bingo. Public records show that a Harold J. Montgomery bought a fishing cabin there in 1986. Could that be his father? Grandfather?"

"Don't know," Eli said, his jaw tightening. "But I'm sure as hell going to find out."

Eli stared out his living room window in dismay as the snow streamed down harder by the minute. The panes rattled as gusts kicked higher, and the storm quickly worsened to whiteout conditions.

Moving up beside him, Noelle sent him a worried glance. "How are we supposed to mount a search in this weather? Assuming we can find a pilot willing to fly us to Grossford Lake, will the FAA even let us take off in this storm?"

"Unlikely. We can only hope the weather has stalled Montgomery's progress as well. But bad roads and unfriendly skies or not, the woman with him is in peril." He bit down on his back teeth, grinding out, "This waiting is unconscionable when we know her life is at risk."

"I agree, but what can we do? Heading out in this mess by land or air is far too dangerous. We're just as likely to get stranded as not. We aren't any help to the woman if we get our car stuck in a snowdrift or get ourselves and a pilot killed in a crash in the process of chasing Scott down."

"I know. It just sucks!" Eli grimaced, and Noelle wrapped a comforting arm around his waist.

After another moment of staring at the swirling blizzard, Noelle asked, "Didn't your cousin's girlfriend, Hetty, say she was a pilot for your family's adventures business?"

Eli gave her a side look. "She is. Why?"

"Any chance you could convince her to take us to Grossford Lake?"

He shrugged. "I'm sure she would, but she's grounded during this mess same as official state trooper pilots."

"But state troopers could be tied up with weather-related rescues, medical emergencies and the like long after the storm breaks. But if we're watching the weather maps, and she's ready to go the minute the weather is clear enough to get airborne…"

"She flies a seaplane. We'd be constrained by the

amount of ice on the lakes, both here and at Grossford. If the lakes are frozen—"

Noelle groaned. "Right. Of course."

"But she's licensed for helicopters, too, and RTA has a contract with a local helicopter rental company. Question is, would they sign off on her taking up one of their birds under these conditions, even if most of the bad weather has passed."

"So we continue to sit here and *wait*?" Noelle's tone mirrored the impatience and anxiety that wrenched his insides in knots.

"I'm afraid so. We can keep watching the weather maps and getting reports from the state troopers on road conditions, but even if we can drive north and get closer to Grossford Lake, we'll still need a floatplane to get to the cabin."

Eli turned back to his coffee table where the large paper map had been unrolled, the curling corners anchored with books. He stabbed the map with a finger. "This doesn't show any private roads or logging trails around Grossford, and it's the most up-to-date GPS-verified map the Alaska State Troopers have."

Noelle used a hair band from her wrist to tie her hair back in a ponytail. "I'll make coffee." She paused and faced him again. "Unless you think conditions won't change before sunrise, and we should try to get some sleep now? Be rested and ready for what may be a long difficult day tomorrow?"

She'd posed it as a question, down to the rising inflection of her voice, but he knew her well enough to know it hadn't been an inquiry. She was right, as she so often was. Nothing could be done tonight, while snow piled up and the winds howled.

And when he looked at her, her face free of makeup, her hair back and her eyes bright, waiting for his response, Eli couldn't think of anything he wanted more than to hold Noelle in his arms.

Whether they slept or not... Well, that was another matter entirely.

Chapter 21

The howl of the wind and shaking shutters outside Eli's bedroom window kept Noelle awake long after Eli finally dropped off to sleep. With his arms around her, his slow steady breaths against her cheek, she cuddled close to him under layers of bedding.

Some undetermined time later, she roused to the nuzzle of lips on her ear, toes stoking her calf.

Not a bad way to be woken, she decided with a jaw-cracking yawn. She rolled closer to his solid warmth and muttered, "What time is it?"

"Don't know. Don't care. Still dark." Eli's voice was thick with sleep and...lust.

His hand slid down her back to cup her bottom and tug her closer to him. In response, she hooked a leg over his hip and raised her chin so he could drop kisses on her lips.

Like a match to kindling, one kiss set them both aflame. He opened his mouth to hers and their tongues clashed and parried. Her hands found the draw string of Eli's sleep pants and untied it, roamed inside and earned a moan of satisfaction and contentedness.

Her limbs tangling in the sheets and blankets, she wrapped herself around him, taking pleasure in his every touch, until—

Eli's cell phone rang.

The sound sliced through their heat and doused cold water on their passion, a reminder of the outside world and the serial killer still on the run. When Eli hesitated for a heartbeat, giving every indication he might ignore the call and finish what he'd started, Noelle pushed him away. "That's bound to be important. Answer it."

Resignation and agreement filled his face, and he snatched his cell phone from the bedside table. "Colton. What's happened?"

The response came through loud enough for Noelle to hear a male voice say, "We have an ID on the woman kidnapped last night from Shelby. Her name is Grace Galloway, and she works at Rise 'N Shine, a bakery downtown near where she was taken."

Noelle stilled, her chest clenching. Rise 'N Shine was the bakery where she and Eli bought the bread they'd taken to Sasha's party. She remembered a pretty young woman with dark hair and gray-green eyes working behind the counter. Not bright blue like the Coltons, but apparently close enough for Scott when targeting the rare coloring in the small town.

"Her roommate called the police worried about her when she didn't come home on time and the storm broke," the voice on Eli's cell continued. "When they showed the roommate the security footage of the abduction, she made a positive ID."

Noelle's stomach flipped, knowing they were among the last people to have seen Grace Galloway before the kidnapping. Could Scott have been following them? Could the bakery clerk have been victimized because she and Eli chose to shop there? Was the kidnapping a sick way for the serial killer to taunt them? Her gut soured. She squeezed handfuls of bedcovers in her fists.

Her ears buzzed so loudly with the surge of adrenaline in her blood that she missed part of Eli's call.

Eli rolled from the bed, throwing back his bedroom curtains, despite his dishabille. "How are the roads? What's the latest on the storm? The radar show more coming?" He pelted the man on the phone with questions without giving the caller a chance to answer. "Have there been any new sightings? A ransom call?"

Knowing she'd not be getting anymore sleep—or sex—this morning and that a long day of hunting Scott Montgomery and hoping to rescue Grace Galloway had begun, Noelle crawled from the bed and headed for the shower.

She was done bathing by the time Eli stumbled into the bathroom, dropped a kiss on her lips and took over the shower stall. "Grab some breakfast and put some warm clothes on. I need to be at RTA in thirty minutes."

Rather than question him about the call, she got busy dressing, drying her hair and finding food in his kitchen with enough protein to stick to their ribs for several hours. Who knew when they'd get a chance to eat again?

Twenty-one minutes later, they were headed down the freshly plowed highway in Eli's Jeep, headed to the main office of his family's outdoor adventure company, Rough Terrain Adventures. Eli ate a protein granola bar as he drove. Noelle had stashed extras in her coat pockets for later. Based on what Eli had told her of his update from the state troopers, today could be a long, tense day…

The storm had quieted, leaving significant accumulation across the southernmost part of the state. Snowplows were busy clearing roads and landing strips, and lakes needed for seaplanes were being assessed for ice.

"No sign of Scott or Grace since the surveillance video," Eli said, giving her a rundown of his call, "but his car was found abandoned at a marina where both seaplanes and fishing boats are moored. We're working on the assumption that he got out ahead of the worst of the storm and could be almost anywhere upstate. State troopers are working a number of angles and sending searchers to several remote lakes, moving the search outward in an increasingly larger radius of Shelby."

"And you?" she asked, watching him stuff half of a snack bar in his mouth at once.

He chewed, swallowed. "I've arranged with Hetty to take me to Grossford Lake."

Dread slithered down her back. "Alone? What about backup?"

He cut a glance to her. "This storm has left law enforcement rather shorthanded and overstretched. And Asher can't—"

"Then take me."

Eli frowned and did a double take. "What! No. Hell no!"

Noelle grunted her affront. "Excuse me?"

His lips compressed for a moment as he exhaled heavily, his nostrils flaring. "Pardon my language, but I can't allow that."

Noelle angled her body toward him, tugging at her seat belt when it cut into her neck. "Why not? Hetty will be with the plane, and it only makes sense that you'll need someone to watch your back, be an extra set of hands, help with—"

"I don't want you in harm's way, okay?"

"But you're putting Hetty in harm's way. How is that

different?" She folded her arms over her chest, challenging him with a hard stare.

"Because she..." Eli fumbled. He scowled and started again. "You're not trained for this sort of thing. Can you even shoot a gun?"

Noelle huffed a humorless laugh. "I'm not saying I have to play cop and charge in with guns firing. I just don't want to be sidelined. I can be an extra set of eyes and hands in case they're needed."

The discussion continued until they reached RTA and found Hetty waiting.

Overhearing the ongoing disagreement, Hetty cleared her throat. "I know you didn't ask for my opinion, but I'm going to give it anyway. I, for one, would feel better having Noelle go with us. You may remember, I was in a bad position not long ago when extra help would have been welcome. You can't over plan going into an unknown situation like this, and I'd feel more comfortable if I weren't your only plan B."

Eli's mouth opened and closed as if trying to form a counterargument and falling short. He scrubbed a hand through his hair and divided a disgruntled look between the women. "Look, we don't have time to stand here and debate this any longer. We're already a day behind Scott, thanks to the storm." He pinned a stern look on Noelle. "You can go, *but...*" he aimed a warning finger at her "... you stay with Hetty in the plane. No heroics or putting yourself in the mix. I don't want you—"

Noelle took hold of the finger pointed at her and pushed it down. "Fine. No heroics. Can we go now?"

Hetty muffled a chuckle as she shrugged into her coat and marched toward the door. "Shall we ride together in your Jeep to the dock?"

* * *

Thanks to a combination of high winds churning up the lake, a stint of warmer weather earlier in the week and overnight temperatures that stayed close to the freezing point, little ice had formed on the lake where Hetty moored the RTA seaplane. The lucky break meant they had little trouble with takeoff, but Hetty warned them conditions might not be as good at Grossford Lake. "No guarantees whether I'll be able to land."

Eli didn't like the news, but he knew Hetty was right. He sat in the copilot's seat, a headset allowing him to talk to Hetty and Noelle over the seaplane's engine. He gave Hetty a grim nod and peered through the windshield at the snowy landscape below them. "How long will it take to get to Grossford Lake?"

Hetty twisted her lips as she consulted her flight equipment. "Maybe an hour?"

Eli bounced his heel restlessly and nodded. "Okay."

As they traveled north, Hetty kept him updated on her reading of the conditions below. "So far so good. There is some ice at the edge of the lakes, but the sun is catching ripples, indicating movement on the water." She turned to look at him. "But also surface wind."

"Can we land?" he asked, cutting to the chase.

She hesitated but finally nodded. "I'll do my best. Grossford Lake is just up there." Hetty pointed out an area just to their left, beyond a low mountain.

As the blue-gray waters of the small lake came into view, Eli reached a hand behind him, casting Noelle a satisfied glance. "I see a floatplane tied up at a dock on the east shore. I think we've found him."

Chapter 22

Noelle took Eli's hand and squeezed it, knowing that finding Scott was only the beginning. They had to bring him in...and pray he hadn't already murdered Grace Galloway.

"Hang on," Hetty said through the headset. "The winds are tricky. I'll do my best to set us down gently, but be ready for bumps and swoops."

Noelle swallowed hard and clutched Eli's fingers with one hand while her other grabbed the edge of the seat. She kept her gaze on the small dock until a cabin came into view, nestled in a copse of winter-bare trees and lodgepole pines. A thin line of smoke rose from the stone chimney, testifying to an inhabitant. When she pointed out this detail to Eli, he nodded, his mouth in a grim line.

"Remember, I want you to stay in the plane with Hetty. I don't want you anywhere near Montgomery."

Noelle lifted her chin. "Well, I don't want *you* anywhere near him, either, but here we are. I won't take unnecessary risks, but neither will I sit on my hands if a situation arises where you need help."

Eli frowned. "Our deal was you stay with the plane. Period."

"I agreed to no heroics, not staying on the plane."

Eli opened his mouth to argue, just as the plane dipped and lurched to the right. He braced a hand against the side door and cast a glance out the windshield, as did Noelle. They were hovering above the water, and Hetty was working hard to level the wings as they touched down on the glassy lake.

Once they were on the water, Hetty made a careful turn and pulled up to the dock opposite the floatplane that was already tied up.

Noelle ducked her head to better view the cabin, watching for further signs of life.

In the confines of the copilot's seat, Eli withdrew his sidearm and readied it. When he lifted his eyes to Noelle again, his gaze was hard and unrelenting. "Stay. Here." Turning to Hetty, he said, "Can you keep the engine on, ready to take off again quickly?"

She checked her fuel gauge. "I think so."

"And radio back to base for support. I need *armed* backup—" he gave Noelle a pointed look "—from whatever law enforcement agency can get here fastest."

Hetty nodded and put a hand on his arm. "Be careful. Your family will never forgive me for bringing you here if you get hurt."

Eli flashed a lopsided but clearly uneasy grin. "Careful is always the plan."

Noelle gritted her back teeth, choking back tears of fear and frustration. She did not like being told what to do, even if she knew why Eli had ordered her to stay with Hetty and the plane. But the directive chafed. She wanted to be useful, wanted to play a more active role in having Eli's back and wanted to decide for herself what level of risk she took to help bring Scott in.

"Eli!" she called, whipping off her headset as he climbed out of the plane and made the leap to the dock.

He turned back, pressing a finger to his mouth to signal for quiet.

Hetty chuckled as she opened her door, saying softly, "As if he didn't already hear us fly in and pull up here."

Noelle had been thinking the same thing, that Scott had to have been alerted and was now watching Eli from the cabin, but she said nothing. Eli had to be aware of as much himself.

Hetty climbed out, staying low as she looped ropes and straps to the dock that would keep the plane from drifting.

Noelle divided her attention, half of the time scanning the cabin for movement and the rest following Eli's progress. He moved quickly, his weapon raised as he hustled down the dock and onto shore. Shoulders hunched, he darted to the nearest tree—and barely reached the hardwood's cover before the first shot blasted from the cabin.

Noelle clamped a hand to her mouth to silence her scream.

Hetty scrambled back inside the plane, hissing, "Get down!"

She slumped lower, but Noelle kept her head high enough to keep Eli in her sights. If anything changed the current dynamic in Scott's favor, Noelle intended to race to Eli's aid, his directive be damned.

Bark splintered from an old-growth tree as Eli flung himself behind the wide trunk. His adrenaline pumping, he took a beat to catch his breath before he carefully turned toward the cabin without allowing any part of his body to protrude.

How many weapons did Montgomery have in the cabin?

And how good of a shot was the forensic scientist? Eli had taken top honors at the academy firing range, but Scott had the advantages of better protection and clearer line of sight.

After a moment, Eli pulled a small mirror from his coat pocket, the one he kept handy for signaling rescuers if he ever got stranded in a remote area. He angled the mirror to check the cabin windows. One of the windows nearest him was cracked open, and he spotted the dark shadow of a body standing just to the left side. The weak sun that leaked through the cloud cover glinted off the metal of a rifle barrel in the narrow window gap.

"It's over, Scott!" he shouted, knowing Montgomery could hear him through the window. "Lay down the rifle and come out unarmed, hands up. I don't want any more bloodshed." When he got no reply, he added, "If you surrender without resisting, it will go easier for you at trial. We've got you dead to rights, and this can only end one of two ways for you. Prison or the cemetery. Your choice."

"I'll take option C, thanks," Scott shouted back. "I kill *you* and walk out of here to live another day."

Eli gritted his teeth, remembering how his colleague, a man he had trusted, had rigged a bomb for him and Asher. "You already tried that once, and it didn't work." He considered what else he should say, how best to win Montgomery's cooperation. Antagonizing him would put Scott's back up, but the man was a scientist. Would logic work?

"Scott, listen…it may just be me here now, but a whole SWAT team is on its way." At least he prayed they were, storm conditions and workload notwithstanding. "You'll soon be outnumbered."

"Maybe soon, but not yet," Montgomery called back. "Right now, it's just you and me. I like those odds, and I'm playing to win."

***

Noelle peered over the edge of the back seat, Eli still in her view. The shooting had stopped, and Eli was in a verbal exchange with Scott.

"What are they saying?" she asked Hetty.

"I don't know. My focus has been on trying to raise someone on the radio and call in some backup. Nobody's responding."

Noelle's heart scampered at the notion that any assistance Hetty might alert could arrive too late to help. Knowing she could do nothing to help Hetty with the radio, Noelle retrained her focus on Eli and Scott. A compelling need to know what was transpiring, what direction the standoff was going swamped her. How could she be of any use to Eli if she stayed huddled in the back seat of Hetty's plane like a lump of useless cargo?

While Hetty continued to appeal for backup, changing the radio frequency and repeating her handle and location, Noelle sucked in a lungful of courage and cracked the passenger door open. Climbing awkwardly from the back seat and earning a panicked frown and vigorous head shake from Hetty, she wiggled her way out to crouch on the dock beside the seaplane.

Noelle peered under the belly of the aircraft and decided she'd get a better view from nearer the nose and propeller. Staying as hidden as she could behind the landing gear and fuselage, she perked her ears over the hum of the engine to hear what was transpiring on shore.

"We can end this now, without further bloodshed, yours, mine or Grace's," Eli shouted. He paused, and in the lull, Noelle strained to listen for a reply. After a few seconds, Eli continued, "Yes, we know you have another woman in there with you. We know her name, and we want her released unharmed. Let's start with that as a goodwill gesture."

"Counteroffer," Scott shouted. "I trade you this woman for Kansas."

Noelle's gut roiled. So they'd been right about what, or rather who, was at the heart of Scott's crime spree. Poor Kansas. Noelle could only imagine how she'd feel if a sociopath had killed innocent women because of an obsession with *her*.

She thought back to the night at the ABI offices when they'd realized the connection. Noelle had tried to comfort and support Kansas in the ladies' room after Eli's cousin had fled the conference room in horror. Kansas had been pale and shaking, emptying her stomach in one of the ladies' room stalls. And though her disgust and dismay over the twist in the case remained as shadows in her eyes, Kansas had regained her composure in short order. Kansas, who faced difficult circumstances, rough terrain and occasionally gruesome discoveries on the job, was a model of strength and courage to Noelle.

Mustering some of that same bravery for herself, Noelle mentally searched for a way to gain Eli the upper hand. Could she create a distraction? Find him access to the cabin from another direction? Provide him valuable time for the support teams to get here?

She saw movement from Eli's post behind the large tree and peeked between the propeller blades to see what was happening. His gaze was on her, his mouth scowling darkly as he waved a hand, signaling for her to get back inside the floatplane.

Before Noelle could either signal back a refusal or follow his direction, Scott fired a shot from the cabin. The bullet carved a hole in the dock a few feet from where Noelle stood.

Then another even closer.

Eli returned fire, and Noelle plastered herself closer to the plane, adrenaline making her head spin.

"Noelle!" Hetty shouted, jolting her from her shock. "Get away from the propellers! I have to get the plane out of range!"

Noelle gaped, scuttling closer to Hetty. "You're leaving!"

"I have to! This plane will be of no use to us if he shoots the engine or punctures a float and sinks it!" Even as she shouted her reply to Noelle, Hetty revved the engine and restarted the propellers. She tossed a flare gun out onto the dock. "Use this to signal when it's safe to return. Now, untie me!"

"But—"

"Untie me! I have to protect the plane. I can't risk him hitting the gas tank or other parts critical to getting us out of here. I'll be back when I get the all clear."

Another shot hit the slushy water at the edge of the lake, sending up a spray of ice and pebbles. Noelle had no time to debate with Hetty. She had to trust that the pilot knew what she was doing. Staying crouched low, Noelle pulled up the ropes securing the aircraft, and immediately Hetty had the plane in reverse, backing into the open water.

Noelle scooped up the flare gun and stuck it in her coat pocket, then darted to the far side of the dock, next to Scott's plane as Hetty left. Her stomach rolled as she reassessed her situation. The cold that washed through her had nothing to do with the weather and everything to do with how exposed she felt, how drastically the situation had changed and how furious she knew Eli would be with her for disregarding his directions. But then a new thought occurred to her.

Parts critical to getting us out of here...

If she could disable Scott's plane in some way, keep him from escaping, she could buy the time Eli needed for backup to arrive. Huddling close to Scott's floatplane, she dug into her limited knowledge of aeronautics and the physics of airplane design. Jamming the propeller or rudder? Puncturing his gas tank? She looked about for something heavy and sharp enough to pierce the gas tank. A rock? Scrap metal? A tool? What if—

Behind her, she heard a shout, then a woman's panicked cries. She spun to find Scott coming out of the cabin with a dark-haired woman in front of him and a handgun to his hostage's temple.

Eli's attempt to stay calm and focus wavered when Scott started firing near the plane, where Hetty and Noelle were waiting. He'd believed Hetty's plane was the safest place for them, but now—

His composure dipped further when Hetty pulled the seaplane away from the dock and disappeared from the cove. He gnashed his teeth and let his shoulders drop in frustration. He'd wanted her standing by, ready to fly them off in an instant if needed. Yet when he considered Hetty's actions more practically, he realized she'd made the right move, protecting herself, Noelle and the plane.

Then he noticed a figure scurrying next to Montgomery's aircraft. *Noelle.* His heart added a beat, and he muttered a foul word. She hadn't gotten back in the plane before Hetty left? Why hadn't she stayed safe like he'd asked her, *told her* to?

But when had Noelle ever been one to follow someone else's wishes when she believed she had a better plan for her life? Certainly not when he'd wanted to continue their relationship after college. He set aside the pang of disappointment tinged with bitterness. Now was not the time to dwell on past hurts.

As if to prove Eli's last thought true, Montgomery shoved through the front door of the cabin with his hostage in front of him, a human shield. The woman's eyes were wide with fear, and Scott had a gun pointed at her head.

"Scott, damn it, man! Don't do this! Do you really think killing Grace or anyone else is going to win Kansas's heart?" Eli shouted.

Scott hesitated, glaring in his direction. "Maybe winning her affection is no longer my goal. We'll just see what happens once I have Kansas to myself, without any interference from you or Asher!"

"Let Grace go," Eli returned. "Any negotiation concerning Kansas starts with you letting your hostage go. She's an innocent in this. Can't you see clear to release her to me?"

Scott jerked Grace closer, making the woman whimper her fear. "No deal."

Eli growled his frustration. Where was his backup? Surely Hetty had reached *someone* before she moved the plane out of danger. He turned his attention briefly to the dock where he'd last seen Noelle.

She'd moved off the dock to the edge of the lake where she was scrounging around on the ground...for a rock? Did she plan to defend herself with a stone?

Eli took a breath to restore his control over his emotions. He had to stay focused. Not act rashly... "Scott, do the right thing," he said, mentally searching for an argument or tactic that would change the mind of a man who'd already acted without compunction in murdering five women.

Instead of complying, Scott dragged Grace across the snowy yard toward the lake. Toward his plane. Toward Noelle.

Eli pursued, knowing he couldn't fire on Scott without risking Grace's life. Or hitting Noelle. Damn it! Where was Hetty? How did he signal her to return?

He needed a plan. And fast. Or Scott would get away.

Noelle found a rock the size of her hand with a narrow end she thought might work to puncture the gas tank or a pontoon on Scott's plane. Glancing back to shore, she saw Scott and his hostage, her hands bound behind her, staggering through the snow, coming closer. Her heart beat triple time as she hurried back to the moored plane and smashed her rock on the pontoon as hard as she could. The reverberation of the strike sent painful judders through her freezing hand and up her arm. She swung again and made a dent.

"Hey!" Scott's angry voice rang across the frozen landscape. "Get the hell away from my plane!"

She angled her gaze to see him shift the aim of his weapon from Grace to her. She realized she was exposed, and her chest tightened.

A shot rang through the winter stillness, and she heard the ping of the bullet hitting the plane.

Scott clearly heard it, too, and realized his mistake. He cursed a blue streak and moved faster, all but carrying Grace as he hustled to the dock to rescue his getaway vehicle from Noelle's tampering.

She darted around to the far side of the aircraft, banking on the idea that Scott wouldn't shoot at her if it risked damaging his plane. Tucked behind the plane, she continued smashing the rock against the hull, anywhere she thought she could inflict enough damage to hinder its ability to get airborne.

When she felt the vibrations of heavy footfalls on the dock, she didn't have to look to know her time was up. Scott was almost upon her. Soon he'd be able to kill her at point-blank range. Her gut swooped, and she choked back a moan of fear.

She'd drawn Scott's attention away from Eli, but now what did she do?

Eli set off, retracing his steps in the snow as he raced after Montgomery. He weighed his options rapid-fire, needing to choose a plan of action. If he could catch up to Scott, could he tackle his opponent and free Grace? Or would that move cost Grace her life? The one thing he knew for certain was that he couldn't stand by and let Scott and his hostage escape. He had to find a way to subdue Scott, while prioritizing the safety of Grace and Noelle.

And the nearer the serial killer got to Noelle and the floatplane, the more both of those goals dimmed. Fueled by adrenaline, Eli pushed his legs to run faster.

As Scott drew closer, Noelle backed toward the far end of the dock. She had nowhere to hide…except in the icy water under the dock. But could she do it? Could she make herself climb into the freezing lake? It wasn't a perfect solution, but it was better than staying here, waiting for Scott to shoot her.

Hearing a loud cry, Noelle shifted her attention to Grace Galloway. The woman had fallen, and Scott was struggling to haul her back to her feet.

"Get up!" Scott shouted cruelly to Grace, yanking her arm.

But the woman, whose hands were bound behind her, wobbled, her legs not supporting her.

Raising his gaze, Scott clearly spotted Eli's rapid approach and made a decision. In the next instant, Scott planted a foot in his struggling hostage's backside and shoved her into the icy water.

Hands tied, Grace sank under the surface, and Noelle gasped her horror. Without her hands free, how did Grace swim or tread water? How did the woman get out before her body shut down from the dangerous cold?

Where earlier Noelle had hesitated to go into the icy water to save herself, now her choice was clear. She charged to the edge of the dock, pausing only long enough to take her shoes off and pull the flare gun from her pocket. She fired one flare in the air, and seeing Scott glance her way, she fired the second in his general direction. While he dodged the sizzling rocket, she leaped into the water.

When Grace fell, Eli gained ground on Scott. He was nearly on his prey when Scott dumped Grace into the lake. Eli sucked in a sharp breath, as if he were the one dunked in the icy drink.

He veered toward the side of the dock where Grace had sunk beneath the surface, mentally bracing to go in after the woman, when he heard the crack and sizzle of a flare firing. He jumped out of the way as one of the flares zipped close to him. Montgomery, too, had to scuttle out of the way, but he quickly recovered and, jerking free the straps securing his aircraft, he dashed toward the cockpit of his plane.

When Noelle jumped in the water near Grace, Eli's heart stopped for a moment. A strong tug pulled him toward the lake, demanding he go in after both women. But Scott was getting away.

Noelle's head broke the surface, and she swam closer to the drowning woman.

"Noelle!" Eli shouted, toeing off his boot, readying to dive in.

"Go! S-stop him!" Noelle shouted back, sputtering from the icy lake water.

With one boot on, Eli raced toward the seaplane. He fired at the cockpit, then dropped to his stomach when Scott returned fire through the open cockpit door. From his prone position, Eli squeezed off two more shots as the propeller of the small plane started turning. The engine revved, and the plane moved slowly away from the dock.

Gritting his teeth, Eli sprang to his feet. He aimed for the gas tank and fired again. A small stream of fuel started leaking from the bullet hole. But that wasn't enough to stop Scott or the floatplane's departure.

Without stopping to debate his choice, Eli ran to the edge of the dock and leaped onto the closest pontoon, grabbing a stabilizing bar connected to the wing.

Montgomery, obviously having felt the jolt as Eli landed on the plane, aimed another shot in Eli's direction.

Eli ducked, dropping to a crouch and losing his grip on his gun as he fought for his grip on the slippery bar. The floatplane bobbed and waggled as Montgomery accelerated across the lake, preparing to take off.

Eli's unbooted foot slipped, and again, he struggled to

cling to the plane and stay on the float. How fast would the fuel tank empty? How far could Scott get before he ran out of gas?

And how the hell did he get inside the passenger door without Montgomery shooting him? Eli grimaced as icy cold spray, kicked up by the pontoon, hit his face. The changing sounds of the engine told Eli Scott was nearly ready to lift off.

Eli tightened his grip. But as the aircraft lifted from the lake, Scott dipped his passenger-side wing once, then again, clearly trying to shake Eli off. The third time he dipped the wing, Eli's foot slipped again, and he came perilously close to sliding off the pontoon.

Eli had a choice to make. Cling on and risk his life in one reckless attempt to get in the plane with Scott and stop him...or jump off before their elevation made such a feat a fatal drop.

With a sinking sensation in his gut, Eli knew his only real choice was to let Montgomery get away and save his own life in order to fight another day. Shouting a blistering word of frustration, Eli leaped from the float.

His arms windmilled, and he arched his back, trying not to pitch forward. He lifted his arms over his head as he reached the lake, making his body as pencillike as possible as he pierced the surface.

The icy cold hit him like a sledgehammer, and he mentally shifted into survival mode. He had to swim to shore, get out of this frigid water before hypothermia claimed him.

Chapter 23

Noelle gasped for air as the icy lake stole her breath. A thousand needles pricked her as she kicked her legs, struggling with the weight of her saturated coat and clothes. She forced herself not to think about how painful the cold water was or what was happening with Eli and Scott. She had to focus instead on reaching Grace. The sooner she got Grace out of the lake, the sooner they could both get warm and dry.

Forcibly shutting out the drone of the seaplane's engine, she goggled at how hard it was to move in the freezing water. Her limbs were leaden. She seemed to be swimming through sludge. With numb fingers, she tugged at her zipper and peeled off her coat. Once free of the encumbering weight, she kicked her feet and stroked her arms as best she could to reach Grace. The panicked woman's eyes found Noelle's as Grace sank under the surface again.

Noelle slid her arm under Grace's and kicked harder, struggling under the burden of Grace's weight dragging them both down.

Noelle was finding it harder and harder to breathe, the icy chill sapping her energy. *Just get her to shore...*

Turning her head toward land, Noelle estimated the distance to be no more than fifty feet. As she swam, increasingly more of a flail than a productive stroke, she began to realize the distance might as well have been a mile. She wasn't making fast enough progress, and both she and Grace were becoming still and stiff as the cold lake chilled their cores.

Fight. She heard Eli's voice in her head as if he were standing on shore shouting to her. *Don't quit. Survive. Live for me.*

The pain that wrenched inside her now came from a longing for a future with Eli. Here, splashing helplessly in this freezing Alaskan lake, the yearning crystalized for her. She'd wasted years on foolish fears. Eli was nothing like her mother and father. Sasha's party had demonstrated that Eli's family was the complete opposite of the one that had rejected her. Pushing him away had been the biggest mistake of her life and had caused her more pain than it had spared her.

Regret and frustration churned inside her. But rather than draining her, her new understanding mobilized her. She clenched her teeth, determined not to fail Eli again. Not to fail Grace, or herself, in this moment. No matter the pain in her arms and legs, no matter the effort, she *would* get out of that water and bring Grace with her.

Grunting with the strain, she hauled Grace up until the other woman's head was above water and shouted, "Kick, Grace! With everything you have, kick!"

The woman's feeble effort was enough to keep Grace's head up as Noelle rolled to her side and did the best sidestroke she could under the circumstances. But they were moving, drifting closer to shore. Slowly, inch by inch.

Eli was far from shore, and every kick as he tried to swim to shore told him he'd wrenched his ankle when he hit the water. The numbing cold stung so fiercely he found it hard to draw air in his lungs, but he kept moving, kept stroking his arms toward land.

When a droning sound reached his ears, he checked the sky for Scott's plane. Had the bastard circled around to come back and shoot him? Instead, the low rumble was at ground level.

Eli blinked as he attempted to wipe icy water from his eyes. *Hetty! Thank heavens!*

Hetty pulled alongside him and tossed him a line to grab. With her help, he climbed from the water onto the floatplane, then moved stiffly onto the copilot's seat.

"Kinda cold today for swimming, isn't it, Eli?" Hetty quipped.

"Much, much too c-cold," he replied, his teeth starting to chatter.

"I saw the flare and was on my way back to pick you up when I saw your acrobatics...or whatever you call that derring-do you just performed." Hetty sent him a worried look as she drove the plane back toward the cabin.

Eli squeezed his eyes shut and shook his head. "I call it a failure. Montgomery got away."

He heard Hetty grunt. "You're lucky to be alive! I call that a success. I've radioed local authorities and given our location—Montgomery's location and aircraft ID number—to the ABI. At last report, a team from Fairbanks is thirty minutes out."

"Good." He returned his gaze out the window, his body shivering and his nerves strung tight as he strained to see ahead of them. "Can we go any faster?"

He'd left Noelle in the water to rescue Grace by herself. But as he learned himself moments ago, the frigid lake could hamper normal capabilities surprisingly fast.

When they finally reached the dock by Scott's cabin, he found Noelle and Grace mostly back on shore but still lying in shallow, ice-crusted water.

He stumbled out of the floatplane as soon as it was near enough the dock for him to make the leap. When his foot landed, a sharp pain in his ankle reminded him he'd not survived his drop into the lake unscathed. But an ankle ache was not going to stop him from getting Noelle and Grace inside the cabin to warm up.

Once Hetty secured her plane, she was right behind him, racing down the dock to wade into the shallows.

Noelle raised her beautiful brown eyes to him as he approached, and, her chin quivering with cold, she stuttered, "S-Scott-t-t?"

He squatted beside her, shaking his head. "He got away." He hooked his arms under hers. "Can you stand?"

"T-t-try."

Working together, Eli and Hetty dragged, supported and carried the women into Scott's cabin.

A fire still smoldered in the grate, and though his hands were shaking from his own hypothermia, Eli fed the embers and stoked a blaze. Glancing at Hetty, who was helping the women strip out of their wet clothes, he called, "See if you can find anything hot for them to drink."

He shucked his own wet coat and shirt as he turned up the cabin thermostat and went in search of blankets, towels and dry clothes. He found enough of the first two, but no clothes. Scott hadn't prepared for his trip north, clearly. But the cabin had a washer and dryer, and while Eli, Noelle and Grace wrapped themselves in blankets, Hetty started a load of wet clothes in the drier.

As they huddled by the fireplace, catching their breath and towel drying their hair, Grace burst into tears.

Hetty, the most mobile of the group, hurried to put an arm around the frightened woman. "Hey, you're safe now. You're going to be okay."

"H-he said h-he was going to k-kill me. He was w-waiting for someone named K-Kansas." Grace swiped her face with a cold-reddened hand. "Someone h-has to warn h-her! K-Kansas..."

Hetty sent Eli a wide-eyed look of horror.

Eli gave the trembling woman a nod. "We know. Kansas knows." He paused as a shudder raced through him. "That rat bastard won't get anywhere near her if I have anything to say about it."

"How d-do we find him now?" Noelle asked, her voice thin as she shivered. "It seems un-l-likely he'll come back h-here now that he knows w-we know about it."

"His fuel tank was leaking fuel. He'll have to land somewhere soon." Eli looked to Hetty. "Any guesses how far he could make it?"

Hetty gave him a withering frown. "Hardly. Too many unknown factors. How much fuel did he have to start with? How fast is the fuel leaking? What sort of tailwinds or headwinds will he encounter? Did he—?"

"Okay," Eli said lifting a hand. "I get it." He scrubbed a hand over his head, mussing his hair. "Damn it! We were so close to bringing him in!"

Noelle ducked her head. "It's m-my fault he got away. Isn't it?"

Eli's pulse jolted, and he cut a sharp look toward her. "What?"

"No!" Hetty said. "Don't you dare take this on yourself."

"If I had stayed in the plane like Eli wanted—"

"You wouldn't have been there to save Grace from the lake," Eli finished for her.

Grace nodded, her movements still stiff and choppy as she sniffled. "You s-saved my life. You *all* did. Th-thank you so m-m—" The young woman dissolved in sobs again, and Hetty rubbed her back.

Noelle wouldn't meet his eyes, and Eli said, "Hey. Noelle, look at me."

She angled a dubious look at him. "I thought I could do more to help. I wanted to stall him...or distract him...or—"

Eli moved to squat right in front of her, his ankle protesting. But Noelle mattered more than the throb in his ankle. In a low voice meant only for her, he said, "Listen to me. If you'd stayed in the plane, Scott would still have used Grace as a human shield. I still wouldn't have had a clear shot of him. He would still have gotten to his plane. He might have still pushed Grace in the water, or he might have taken her with him. We don't know. But what you did, tampering with his plane, distracted him enough that I got close enough to at least make an effort to stop him." He pressed his lips in a frown of frustration at the reminder of Montgomery's escape. "If you'd been at the other end of the lake with Hetty, though, you couldn't have gone in after Grace."

"But you would have," she said, correctly. "You'd already started to."

He sighed, scowling as he acknowledged a hard truth. "And either way, Scott still escapes. So you—"

"I was still too stubborn," she said, her voice stronger now as she cut him off. Tears bloomed in her eyes. "I was too determined to do things my way, thinking I somehow knew better. But I was wrong. Again. Like I was in college. I should have listened to you. I—I should have trusted you more!"

Eli flinched. "In college? What are you saying?"

She drew a long, slow breath and cupped his face with hands that were at the same time freezing cold and a balm to his heart. "I'm saying I made a mistake. I should never have left you. Should never have shut you out."

Eli furrowed his brow, startled by her change of topic. His pulse pounded so loud in his ears, he could barely hear his own voice asking, "A mistake?"

When the women's heads all lifted, their gazes darting toward the cabin door, Eli realized the thrum in his ears had drowned out another noise. Someone was outside the cabin.

Chapter 24

Noelle heaved a huge sigh of relief when the men outside the cabin identified themselves as from the state trooper detachment from the Fairbanks office. A medic with the responders checked her, Grace and Eli, and though they all would need further treatment and checks once they arrived at the hospital in Fairbanks, they were all doing remarkably well under the circumstances.

Grace was showing signs of shock. Eli had a sprained ankle. And Noelle had a huge case of guilt, despite Eli's attempts to assuage her regrets. She needed time to process her feelings and talk to Eli alone, and neither looked likely to happen soon.

Eli stayed behind, returning to Grossford Lake to take charge of the state troopers as they continued the search for Scott. Noelle, having signed a waiver refusing further medical treatment once she'd gotten warm and dry, accompanied Hetty back to Shelby.

Having gotten snippets of information about what had transpired at Grossford Lake, a large representation of Coltons, plus Asher, awaited Noelle and Hetty at the RTA offices.

Kansas was among the first to rush to Noelle and wrap her in a hug. "Good grief, Noelle! You don't do things by half measures, do you? I'm not sure how you translated 'case consultant' to mean 'risk your life saving a hostage,' but kudos to you for your bravery!"

Noelle flashed a sheepish grin. "I'm not sure how you translated 'foolish stubbornness' to mean 'bravery.' But, no, I'm not known for holding back. I'm headstrong to a fault, and…" she choked as a bubble of emotion rose in her throat "…and Eli has paid the price of that stubbornness and fear for too long."

Kansas took her by the arm to pull her away from the clamoring family. "Hey, are you okay? What does 'Eli's paid the price' mean?"

"I saw it so clearly today, everything I'd been trying to hide from, but I'd only been hurting myself and Eli instead." She sucked in a deep breath, not wanting to cry in front of Kansas and the other Coltons.

"Noelle?" Sasha said, stepping over from where she'd been clustered with Troy and Lakin, listening to Hetty recount their day. "I promise I wasn't intentionally eavesdropping, but did you say Eli was hurt? Is that why he's not with you?"

Noelle mustered a smile to calm Eli's mother. "He's fine. Well, mostly. A twisted ankle." She summarized how Eli had stayed with the phalanx of state troopers and local searchers to hunt Scott, and Sasha shook her head.

"Lord, protect my young man," Eli's mother said under her breath before meeting Noelle's gaze squarely. "And you… Noelle, dear, you look worn out. Can I get you anything? Food? Coffee? A quiet room with a pillow and blanket?"

Noelle chuckled, even as moisture filled her eyes. "All of the above. And…the last thirteen years back to do over again the right way?"

Sasha squared her shoulders and took hold of Noelle's hands. "Oh, my dearest. I wish I could do that for you. But the important thing is, whatever you wish you could change about the past can still be a lesson for today. Go forward living the way you want the next thirteen years to unfold, whatever that involves. Forgive whoever needs forgiving. Love whoever needs loving. Change whatever needs changing."

Noelle, her throat too tight with unshed tears to speak, nodded hard. She flung herself into Sasha's arms and clung to the woman who'd been a better mother to her in a few days than her birth and adoptive mothers had been her whole life. And in the woman's comforting arms, she felt optimistic about the future for the first time in far, far too long.

Noelle didn't hear from Eli that night or for most of the next two days. She rattled around his empty house, feeling like an intruder. She began to worry that something had gone awry with the hunt for Montgomery—or her relationship with Eli—that the Coltons were keeping from her.

She'd checked in with Kansas, Sasha and Asher on a regular basis over the last fifty-six hours and was assured Eli was fine, just busy upstate with the search. Noelle wasn't convinced that was all there was behind his ghosting her. Was he staying away, knowing she was in his house?

She thought about the grim expression he'd worn in Scott's cabin as they'd warmed themselves by the fire. Hetty had tried to absolve Noelle of any fault for the way things had unfolded. But she couldn't help but feel a dark, angry vibe from Eli.

She was sure he blamed her for Scott's escape, no matter how he'd dismissed her explanations. The dour slash of his mouth as he contemplated Scott's getaway hadn't eased for a moment. Even her admission of wrong regarding their past had yielded a heavily lined brow and a querulous expression.

Was she too late in recognizing the error of her ways? The notion sat heavily on her chest. Not even Sasha's and Kansas's reassurances could lift her from the funk that hung over her, waiting for Eli's return to Shelby and time alone with him to make amends.

During the same two-plus dreary days, however, she *did* hear from both the interim coroner appointed to take Scott's place and the funeral home director. Both men reported to her that Allison's body had finally been released for burial. The funeral could be held in the next day or two. Afterward, Noelle would have no excuse not to go home to Seattle.

Though she'd finally have closure on that front, she longed for the chance to talk with Eli and set things right with him.

When she still hadn't heard from Eli by the evening of the second full day back in Shelby, she packed her few belongings and moved to a small motel room near her former hostel. Noelle had heard from Sasha that Eli had returned to Shelby just hours after she'd vacated his house, but he'd continued his radio silence. Telling, Noelle decided.

The next day, the day of the funeral, she donned the dress she'd packed more than two weeks earlier, thinking she'd only be in Shelby for a couple of days, and prepared her suitcase to leave. As she checked out of the motel, she put her bag in the rental car, ready to drive to the Anchorage airport that afternoon after the funeral. She'd booked a seat for the red-eye back to Seattle for that evening.

Holding her head high and bracing for the likelihood of another confrontation with Aunt Jean and Uncle Clyde, Noelle drove to the small church where she'd arranged the funeral service. When she arrived, she was stunned to see a large number of vehicles in the church parking lot. She dismissed her surprise, reminding herself Allison likely had many friends, and the funeral home had printed the funeral announcement in the Anchorage paper.

Taking a deep breath and smoothing her skirt, she made her way into the church's chapel, where her second surprise of the day awaited her.

The crowd assembled for Allison's funeral was overwhelmingly comprised of Coltons. She blinked as her gaze drifted from face to face—Lakin, Troy, Mitchell, Dove, Kansas, Parker, Sasha and Will—and on and on. Row after row. A show of family support unlike anything she could have ever imagined. Even Asher had come. Her eyes filled with tears, and a bittersweet stab of longing pierced her chest. Because the one face missing was Eli's.

In the front row, Kansas waved to her, indicating the empty seat she'd saved for Noelle. Walking numbly to the pew, she glanced at the coffin, draped with a simple but lovely flower arrangement. *Oh, Allison! I'm so sorry for what you suffered because of Scott.*

Noelle sat beside Eli's cousin and dabbed at her damp cheeks and runny nose with her gloved hand.

Kansas pulled several tissues from a box printed with the funeral home's logo and handed them to her. "We wanted you to know you're not alone today. We care about you."

"Thank you. You can't possibly know what this means to me." Noelle forced a tremulous smile, belatedly realizing how difficult it must be for Kansas to be there, knowing Scott had killed his victims due to his twisted obsession with her. One more reason to respect and admire Kansas.

As they settled in for the service, Kansas put a reassuring arm around Noelle and gave her shoulder a squeeze. The warbly music of a small electric organ played, signaling the start of the service, and the minister walked out from a door beside the choir loft.

"Dearly beloved, thank you all for joining us today as we remember Allison—"

The door at the back of the chapel thunked as a late arrival entered. Noelle was blowing her nose and gathering her composure when the latecomer settled into the seat beside her. She glanced up, and her heart jolted.

Eli.

The minister continued, but Noelle only half heard the words spoken as she studied the man sitting beside her. He gave her a tepid smile, before facing the pulpit, more evidence of his pique with her, and she worked to hide her disappointment.

He smelled good. Of pine and ocean and frosty air, as if the very essence of Alaska had been bottled just for him. His cheeks showed raw spots where he'd clearly just shaved and nicked himself, and his hair was still damp from a shower. He wore a well-tailored dark blue suit that fit him perfectly and emphasized his broad shoulders and lean physique.

But for all his fine features, she saw signs of fatigue and worry and wear. His eyes were shot with red, as if he hadn't slept. Tiny lines radiated from the corners of his mouth and smudges of blue-black shadowed beneath his eyes. His lips were chapped and peeling, and his cheeks and nose bore witness to time in the winter sun and bracing wind. Most telling to her was the sag of his posture. He seemed beaten down. Worn out. Defeated. And her heart ached for him.

Turning her attention back to the service, Noelle restlessly twisted the clean tissue in her hands...until Eli's hand covered hers. He laced his fingers with hers. Squeezed. Noelle cut a quick look to him, and with his face inscrutable, he gave her a small nod.

She held tight to his hand, her heart breaking, as the minister said a prayer, eulogized Allison and led the congregation in a closing hymn. When the funeral director motioned for Noelle to follow the casket out as it was wheeled to the waiting hearse, she refused to let go of Eli's hand. Instead she tugged him from his seat. Snagging both his coat and hers from the pew, he fell in step next to her.

Once outside, while the casket was loaded for the drive to the cemetery, Eli helped her into her coat, then wrapped Noelle in his embrace.

"Can we talk later, after the burial?" he whispered and kissed the top of her head.

"I—I don't know."

He backed out of the hug and gave her a puzzled look.

She dropped her gaze to the ground. "I'm leaving town right after the burial. I fly out of Anchorage at six."

"You're leaving...*today*?" He took a step back as if punched in the gut. "But..."

"I thought it was best if I—"

"Best for who?" he said bitterly, his volume loud enough to attract the attention of the funeral home staff. "I thought we'd gotten past this...this delusion of yours that you were somehow better off alone! Do my wishes not count for anything?"

She looked up at him, her brow pinched. "Of course they do! That's why I made a reservation to go home! To get out of your way!"

He huffed loudly and tugged her by her arm to stand away from the crowd of mourners emerging from the church. Melting snow crunched under their feet as they crossed the churchyard. When he stopped and faced her, irritation and—was it panic? desperation?—lit his bright blue eyes. "Tell me, please, what I have done or said that makes you think for *one second* that I don't want you here?"

She lifted her chin, battling back the sting of tears and flurry of self-doubt. "It's not what you said so much as what you haven't. For the last three days! I've been worried sick about you, and if not for reports from your family, I'd have gone nuts thinking you could be hurt or… or d-dead! Why haven't you answered any of my texts or calls?"

He groaned and chuckled without mirth. "Oh, Noelle. You have been gone from here a long time, haven't you?" He cupped her chin and stared deep into her eyes. "One, this is Alaska, not Seattle."

"Meaning?"

"Cell reception is sketchy at the best of times, and in the part of the state where I've been the past three days, it's nonexistent."

Her mouth tightened. "But you talked to your family."

"I reached Kansas through the SAR and ABI satellite phones and shortwave radios, and she relayed messages to my mother and the others as I asked."

Noelle blinked, lowered her gaze, though his palm still gripped her chin. "Oh."

"Oh," he repeated. "Second, I've been *a little* busy tracking Scott the last few days." He arched an eyebrow to highlight his understatement. "I've had *maybe* seven hours of sleep in the last sixty, and the only reason I'm here in Shelby instead of up north still looking for Montgomery is I was determined to be here for you when you buried Allison."

Eli's face blurred as tears puddled in her eyes. She tried to choke down the tears, but the constriction in her throat made swallowing difficult and talking impossible.

"So, let's try this again. Why are you leaving?"

She opened her mouth, struggling to make some sound, but before she could, he added, "And don't go with the easy answer. Don't tell me you have a job and a house in Seattle. I want the truth. The real truth. Why are you *really* leaving?"

Pain slashed deep to her core, because she knew the answer. Fear. She'd thought she'd moved past feeling scared about giving Eli her whole heart and trust. Yet the minute he didn't—couldn't—answer her texts, she let the doubts creep back in.

Love and trust have to be unconditional.

Sasha's words from last week sounded in her head like a gong. What was she doing? She couldn't run away again, couldn't shut Eli out of her life and hide like she had thirteen years ago. If the past weeks had showed her anything, they'd proven her fears had been unwarranted. Eli's love had remained true. His family had proven warm, accepting and supportive. Hadn't they all showed up for her today to love her through her grief?

"Ms. Harris, we're ready to go when you are," the funeral director called to her.

Eli's eyes narrowed on her. She hadn't given him an answer yet. But he deserved more than an answer. He deserved a demonstration of her love and full commitment.

She did a quick mental calculation, then turned to the funeral director. "Please go ahead. I'll meet you at the cemetery in a little while."

The man gave a nod and turned to go.

Eli was frowning when she faced him again. "Come with me. Please." She started back across the churchyard, but Eli didn't. She turned back and found him scowling, clearly unhappy with her lack of response. "Please," she repeated, and he trudged toward her, then followed her back to the church steps.

Eli's family was filing out of the church and heading to their respective cars. Feeling a confidence and rightness that kicked up her pulse, she waved her hands over her head and shouted, "Excuse me! Can I ask that you all reassemble inside for a moment?"

Turning back to Eli, she said, "I'll be with you shortly. Have everyone take a seat again."

"Noelle, what's going on? What about the burial?"

"We'll go. Soon. I just need a moment..." She waved him inside, then hurried to the edge of the parking lot where she pulled out her phone and checked for a signal.

Eli gritted his back teeth as he moved back into the church and sat in the front pew where he'd been for the funeral. What was Noelle's plan? Why couldn't she just give him a straight answer? If she was leaving him again, this time he *would* have the truth from her. *If* she was leaving him? He snorted and balled his hands in his lap. Hadn't she just confirmed that she was flying out of Anchorage tonight? Once again, he'd let himself fall for her only to have the rug jerked out from under him.

He could only blame himself this time. How did the saying go? *Fool me once...*

"Do you know what this is about?" Parker asked as he settled in the pew next to Eli.

"No," he answered tightly, not bothering to hide his frustration or disappointment in his tone.

The church door thumped shut, and his family fell silent as Noelle marched to the front and stood before them with her shoulders back and her chin high. Despite her body language, Eli read anxiety in her gaze as she cast her eyes toward him.

"Thank you for staying just a few moments longer. I need to be going soon to the cemetery, but first... I wanted you all here to be witnesses... I mean, I wanted you all to share..." She buzzed her lips in exasperation. "I'm already blowing this. Eli, will you come up here?"

He glanced to Parker, looking for confirmation he'd heard Noelle correctly. His brother waved a hand, motioning he should go.

Fatigue and achy muscles dragged at him as he joined Noelle at the chancel railing.

She took a deep breath and said in full voice, "As I look around this little church, full of family and friends and flowers, I can't help but think it would be a nice place to have a wedding."

A murmur rippled from the pews. Eli tipped his head and fixed a curious look on Noelle. Had he heard her correctly? Suddenly blood was pumping through him so hard and fast he could barely hear her over the whoosh in his ears.

"Eli, I have no excuse for the heartache I've caused you these last many years. Nothing I can do will erase that hurt. The choices I made after graduation are my biggest regret."

He opened his mouth to reply, to tell her she was forgiven, but she placed her fingers over his mouth, adding, "But... I'm not finished."

A few chuckles from his family twittered in the sanctuary.

"I'm asking you for the opportunity to go forward with a clean slate." Noelle swallowed hard. "I'm asking you for a second chance, and...and I don't take my request lightly or without offering you long overdue assurances. Today, in front of your family, I'm pledging you my full, unconditional love and trust." Noelle cut a quick glance to the pews, and Eli followed her gaze to his mother, who beamed and nodded.

Noelle cleared her throat. "I want to spend the rest of my life making it up to you and showing you how deeply I love you."

Eli's body grew still, and he dared not breathe for fear he was dreaming.

She took both of his hands in hers and got on one knee. "Eli Colton, I want to come back to this church in a few months and marry you. Will you be my husband?"

He sucked in a gasp—or maybe the sharp sound of an inhale came from his family. He couldn't be sure, because he was numb. Dreaming. So damn tired he was hallucinating.

Except Noelle was down on one knee. Looking up at him with wet eyes and a hopeful expression.

After some awkward amount of time, Parker stepped

up beside him and poked him in the ribs. "This is the part where you say yes."

Eli exhaled and pulled Noelle to her feet. He felt the prick of tears sting his eyes as he framed her face with his hands and kissed her soundly. "Hell yes, sweetheart. Absolutely, yes."

Epilogue

One week later
Thanksgiving

Eli sat back in his chair and put his hands on his stomach with a happy groan. "My compliments to the cooks, one and all. Everything was delicious!"

"Hear, hear!" Troy said, lifting a glass and leaning over to give Lakin a kiss on her cheek.

Noelle chuckled and said, "This is the first Thanksgiving I've celebrated in about four years, since my friend Emma moved out of state, and I think I made up for it in one sitting."

"Not so fast! We still have pies," Eli's Aunt Abby said, rising from her chair across the room at another table and waving Spence and Parker back to their chairs.

"What if we save the pies for later and have them with coffee this evening once we've...well, digested for a while?" Will asked.

"Yeah," Eli replied, "what Dad said."

A round of voices in agreement lifted from one end of Will and Sasha's home to the other. The scrape of chairs followed as people began to depart the tables for other activities.

Aunt Abby stood at her place and called to the family. "Hey, hey, hey! Where are you going? We may be saving pie for later, but after the past year we've had, both the good and the bad, I feel it is more incumbent upon us than ever today, this Thanksgiving, to give our thanks for our blessings."

Sasha stood as well. "I agree."

The Colton siblings and cousin exchanged glances. Nobody seemed prepared to defy the matriarchs on what, in past years, had seemed a somewhat cheesy tradition. This year, Eli and his siblings, cousins and significant others shared glances and nods that affirmed they were eager to share their gratitude with the group. One by one, the younger Coltons and their partners sat back down.

"I'll start," Mitchell said, his posture and booming voice reflecting his comfort speaking to a courtroom. He stood and beamed at Dove, who was at the table beside him. "First and foremost, I'm thankful for Dove and the life we have together."

The family clinked their forks and applauded in support and agreement.

"And I'm thankful for you, love," Dove replied.

Troy shot to his feet. "I'm grateful that Lakin is officially my girl and that we're planning our wedding."

More cheers erupted, but Troy held up a hand. "And… I'm thankful the renovations on Suite Home are back on track after the delays the snowstorm caused."

"Ditto!" Lakin said with gusto as she stood and lifted her glass. "And of course for you." She gave Troy a kiss and sat again.

Across the table from Noelle and Eli, Kansas stood, and she took a deep breath as she glanced from one face to another. "I'm grateful for my family, every last wild and wonderful one of you. And I'm grateful that Eli is back safely from looking for Scott Montgomery and that Grace Galloway is alive and well." Her voice cracked, and Eli saw the strain Kansas had been under these last few weeks in the creases around her eyes.

As Kansas sat back down, the family clapped and voiced their agreement in a more subdued manner. Abby placed a hand on her daughter's shoulder and spoke softly to her. Kansas offered her mother a wan smile.

Spence rose to offer his gratitude, but the discussion faded to background noise as Eli leaned across the table to say quietly to Kansas, "Thanks for that."

"I meant it," Kansas replied. "I don't know what I'd do if I lost you or A—" She cut her words short and frowned. "I feel bad enough that Scott is doing all of this because of me."

"No." Eli reached across the table to take his cousin's hand. "*None* of this is because of you. One hundred percent of the blame is on Scott's head. Do you hear me?"

Kansas sighed but finally nodded. "I hear you."

"And hear this, too," he said, squeezing her fingers before letting go. "I promise you, if it is the last thing I do, I will see that Scott Montgomery is caught and that he pays for his crimes." He glanced to Noelle, who was listening to the exchange. "I promise you both. This isn't over. Asher and I will get that bastard, and he will pay."

When Noelle winced, Eli tipped his head. "What?"

"I only just got you back. When Scott was shooting at us, I was more scared of losing you than getting hurt myself. I just...don't want you in the line of fire again."

Eli stroked a hand down Noelle's face and pressed his forehead against hers. "I'll be careful. I swear."

"Eli? If we can drag you away from your lovely lady

for a minute," Parker called across the room, "I think it's your turn."

Eli leaned back, moved his napkin from his lap to his plate and pushed his chair back.

Before he could stand, Noelle rose to her feet. "I'd like to go next if you don't mind. Because I have to tell you all how much I appreciate—no, that's not a strong enough word—how much I treasure all of you. You have welcomed me to this family in such a warm and loving way. I've never had this. Family support. Inclusion. Acceptance. Love. And…to gain a family like yours in addition to finally being with the man who stole my heart years ago—" Noelle paused and chuckled. "I've won the love lottery. That's how it feels. So thank you all, so much for letting me be part of your big, incredible family."

A boisterous cheer rang from the ceiling and walls, but before she took her seat, Noelle added, "And I am most thankful this year for Eli and for second chances." She bent to give him a deep kiss on the lips, whispering, "I love you so much."

"The feeling is mutual, sweetheart. You are worth the wait."

Scott Montgomery lay on his lumpy air mattress, his flashlight his only illumination in the Alaskan wilderness. He shone the beam on the only picture of Kansas he'd salvaged before he'd blown up his house. It was his favorite shot, one he'd taken with a high-power lens on his camera. She was completely at ease in her home, unaware that he was watching from a few blocks away. He'd had to cut down a couple bushes and some branches to have a clear line of sight, but it had been worth it.

He'd seen so many candid moments of Kansas's life

through the years through that window. Mornings in her nightgown, evenings when she ate dinner alone, weekends as she practiced yoga, even times she clearly thought no one could see her as she danced and sang with music he couldn't hear. Her uninhibited moments, when she was most vulnerable, were the ones that stoked the fire in him. Catching a glimpse of unguarded moments...

Planting a microphone in her house should be next on his agenda. First, he had to lie low for a few more days, allow his trail to go cold, before he resumed his observations of Kansas and found a new way to get her alone. Once he had her alone, under his power, in his control, he could win her over.

He clicked off the flashlight and allowed his senses to focus on the sounds and scents just outside his makeshift shelter. This would be his last night shivering in the cold, he promised himself.

One week ago, he'd watched from a vantage point on the next mountain ridge the moment the state troopers had found his abandoned plane. They'd swarmed over it like ants on dropped bread crusts at a picnic, Eli among them. After that, Scott had hidden in the frozen hinterland, staying one step ahead of search teams for long, miserable hours.

But tomorrow, he'd steal a car or a floatplane and go somewhere well outside Eli Colton's and Asher Rafferty's purview. His beard had filled in, changing his appearance at least a little. He hadn't maintained his anonymity as the Fiancée Killer for three years without having some skill for staying hidden up his proverbial sleeve. Then, in a week or so, he would shift his plans into the final stage of execution.

But not yet. He'd give the authorities a little time to

realize he'd truly gotten away, let them relax their vigilance...

Then he'd step up his plans to bring Kansas to heel. Enough of her baseless rejection. They belonged together. He'd lied for her. Waited for her. Killed for her. The time had almost come. Soon Kansas would be his.

Very soon.

* * * * *

Get up to 4 Free Books!

We'll send you 2 free books from each series you try PLUS a free Mystery Gift.

FREE Value Over **$25**

Both the **Harlequin Intrigue®** and **Harlequin® Romantic Suspense** series feature compelling novels filled with heart-racing action-packed romance that will keep you on the edge of your seat.

YES! Please send me 2 FREE novels from the Harlequin Intrigue or Harlequin Romantic Suspense series and my FREE gift (gift is worth about $10 retail). After receiving them, if I don't wish to receive any more books, I can return the shipping statement marked "cancel." If I don't cancel, I will receive 6 brand-new Harlequin Intrigue Larger-Print books every month and be billed just $7.19 each in the U.S. or $7.99 each in Canada, or 4 brand-new Harlequin Romantic Suspense books every month and be billed just $6.39 each in the U.S. or $7.19 each in Canada, a savings of 20% off the cover price. It's quite a bargain! Shipping and handling is just 50¢ per book in the U.S. and $1.25 per book in Canada.* I understand that accepting the 2 free books and gift places me under no obligation to buy anything. I can always return a shipment and cancel at any time by calling the number below. The free books and gift are mine to keep no matter what I decide.

Choose one:
- ☐ **Harlequin Intrigue Larger-Print** (199/399 BPA G36Y)
- ☐ **Harlequin Romantic Suspense** (240/340 BPA G36Y)
- ☐ **Or Try Both!** (199/399 & 240/340 BPA G36Z)

Name (please print)

Address   Apt. #

City   State/Province   Zip/Postal Code

Email: Please check this box ☐ if you would like to receive newsletters and promotional emails from Harlequin Enterprises ULC and its affiliates. You can unsubscribe anytime.

> Mail to the **Harlequin Reader Service:**
> **IN U.S.A.:** P.O. Box 1341, Buffalo, NY 14240-8531
> **IN CANADA:** P.O. Box 603, Fort Erie, Ontario L2A 5X3

Want to explore our other series or interested in ebooks? Visit **www.ReaderService.com** or call **1-800-873-8635**.

---

*Terms and prices subject to change without notice. Prices do not include sales taxes, which will be charged (if applicable) based on your state or country of residence. Canadian residents will be charged applicable taxes. Offer not valid in Quebec. This offer is limited to one order per household. Books received may not be as shown. Not valid for current subscribers to the Harlequin Intrigue or Harlequin Romantic Suspense series. All orders subject to approval. Credit or debit balances in a customer's account(s) may be offset by any other outstanding balance owed by or to the customer. Please allow 4 to 6 weeks for delivery. Offer available while quantities last.

Your Privacy—Your information is being collected by Harlequin Enterprises ULC, operating as Harlequin Reader Service. For a complete summary of the information we collect, how we use this information and to whom it is disclosed, please visit our privacy notice located at https://corporate.harlequin.com/privacy-notice. Notice to California Residents – Under California law, you have specific rights to control and access your data. For more information on these rights and how to exercise them, visit https://corporate.harlequin.com/california-privacy. For additional information for residents of other U.S. states that provide their residents with certain rights with respect to personal data, visit https://corporate.harlequin.com/other-state-residents-privacy-rights/.

HIHRS25